# LOVE/AGGRESSION

# Love/Aggression

a novel
by June Martin

a tRaum Book

A tRaum Book.
Munich, 2024.

For all of us that have to live together.

www.ingramcontent.com/pod-product-compliance
Lightning Source LLC
La Vergne TN
LVHW040026240125
802047LV00038B/1815
*9783949666292*

Every week, the black grandfather clock that cost Zoe too much money would chime. The sound reverberated out of the living room, into the kitchen with its pile of unwashed dishes, where each phrase got bogged down in pools of cloudy water and never again breached the surface. Up the staircase that still bore scuff marks from the move-in four years ago, into Lily's sparse bedroom—decorated with a framed picture of her and Zoe on the wall (Zoe's idea) and other pictures leaned against the baseboards, trapped in the purgatory of indecision. Down the hallway where artwork made by Lily and Zoe's friends hung interspersed with pictures and film stills of Zoe herself, and into Zoe's bedroom where the clock's sound lost its strength amid the canopy bed, the open closet packed full of clothes, the enormous mirror ringed by soft white lights that never turned off while Zoe was near.

"Zoe, get down here. It's time," Lily said from the kitchen and folded the bag of chips she'd been eating under itself. It crinkled right back open, but Lily could not concern herself with staleness at this moment. It was time. Five minutes passed before Zoe's feet slapped down the stairs.

Zoe asked "It's time?" faux-incredulously over and

over as Lily walked into the bathroom and opened the medicine cabinet. Between all of Zoe's skin care goops and oils and Lily's half-consumed jar of drugstore moisturizer lay two vials. Both estrogen. She used injectable valerate, and Zoe used cypionate—the same as the cis ladies got. Zoe's cost a lot more, worked a little better. She grabbed the two bottles by their tops and swung them into her palm, then retrieved two syringes from beneath the sink, still clothed in paper and plastic.

"It's time? It is time? Right now? This?" Zoe was still asking and gesticulating to a world disinclined to provide an answer as Lily entered the living room.

"It's time. Get your pants off."

"Uh, hm. I don't know. Is it my turn?" Zoe finally held herself still, photo-ready as the overhead light caught her high cheekbones and delicate but sharp jaw, and pooled in the huge, piercing eyes she pointed at the ceiling. As if the answer would waft down from heaven and settle with barely a ripple amongst the white reflection and green irises. "I feel like I didn't go first last time. I think it was you, wasn't it? You first."

"It was me last week." Lily perched on the edge of the couch; it was a beige suede sectional which had suddenly—just two days after Zoe's first big paycheck from the web series she starred in—replaced an old pleather loveseat that the two of them had found on the street right after they'd moved in. Lily set the two vials gingerly on the table, rotating them so each label pointed the exact same direction, and arranged the syringes symmetrically on each side.

Zoe disrupted this little tableau to their shared condition by snatching up Lily's bottle. She performed the various preparatory motions with practiced grace until the solution was drawn down to the .5 ml line, and a drop at the tip of the needle glistened, ready. It was too late to protest, and who went first didn't really matter enough for Lily to fight about it. She pulled up the hem of her ratty old T-shirt. It was a remnant of the post-hardcore band she'd been in eight years ago, Neat Regrets. They'd broken up because no matter what songs they had played, people had gotten into fights at every single one of their shows, and Lily hadn't had the stomach for blood back then. By now the black fabric had faded into patchy medium gray and bore the miles of its experience like a tire. Cold welcomed her torso to exposure. She cringed as Zoe grabbed ahold of some of the fat on her stomach. Always better not to look. Nothing beneath her gaze would be as she liked it.

"Come on Lil, deep breath. Nice and easy." Zoe jabbed the needle in, and Lily winced. She'd liked the pills better, which dissolved sweetly under her tongue, and occasionally stained her bedsheets blue whenever she fell asleep with one in her mouth. But now the needle was out, the blood wiped, the bandage applied, and it was like Zoe had said when she had convinced Lily to get on injections: a few seconds, and nothing more to think about until next week.

"Your turn. Pants off."

"These aren't pants, they're designer workout leggings. I'm on my way to the gym. Relentlessly." She pulled them down in one smooth motion. Zoe had a scene on *Drama Dolls* where her character needed to do this, and muscles remember even after the director yells cut.

"Good thing, too. Unhealthy girls take weeks to recover from an injury like this." Lily smiled as she broke the protective wrapping around the syringe and removed the cap, exposing the two-inch-long needle.

Zoe flopped onto the couch and entrusted her legs to Lily. "I hear some girls pop like balloons, you know. Only the fake ones, though."

Lily withdrew .25 ml from the vial, sure as ever to get it exactly on the line—unlike Zoe, who always delivered Lily's dose just accurately enough that it wasn't worth complaining about. "Good thing you're never acting when you get your shot."

"I'm defying the odds." Zoe slammed her hands over her eyes as Lily held up the needle. "Don't tell me it's about to happen. Just do it."

Lily spread a hand on Zoe's thigh and seized some flesh, holding it tight enough that Zoe wouldn't feel the needle much.

"Fuck," Zoe said as Lily gently plunged the estrogen into her body. "Tell me when it's over. Is it over? Tell me. Tell me it's over already."

Lily withdrew the needle, released her grip, and a little semi-sphere of blood emerged from the wound. Rather than travel down Zoe's thigh in either direction, it was content to wait until Lily wiped it away with a tissue. Over the years, she'd had no choice but to get used to blood.

Zoe said, "Why haven't you told me it's over yet? It has to be over."

"It's over, the needle's out."

"God, why didn't you tell me? There should be a shot you get once a year." The tension had evaporated from her voice, but her body had never shown the fear in the first place. Zoe's soft thigh had been relaxed the whole time, and her posture had been like someone relaxing at the beach. An actress down to her bones.

"You would be fully insane with that much estrogen in your blood."

"Maybe. But maybe I'd finally be able to get pregnant." Zoe scowled. "Ugh. Not like my career needs that. Make room."

Lily scooted into the corner, amid the numerous throw pillows that had accrued over their years living together, and kicked her feet onto the coffee table. "The spell is complete. We're going to stay girls for another week."

"They've gotta be working on the one big shot." Zoe rested her feet on the cushion behind Lily's head. Whenever Zoe wanted, she took up as much of the couch as possible. And she wanted often. "Put on something trashy."

"Sorry, I went first and I choose anime."

"At least make it a trashy anime."

"I can do that. But first..." She lit a cigarette and exhaled a joyful cloud of smoke. Blood clots were supposedly a risk with smoking and estrogen, but Lily had never heard of anyone actually getting one. Maybe her blood would gradually thicken over the years into cords of armor wired through her arms and body. Every blow would glance off her, rendered harmless by her perfect blood. Or maybe a blood clot would pop up into her brain and obliterate her in an instant. But that could only happen if it was a little one, so if she smoked a lot more, she had a better chance of getting her blood armor.

Zoe coughed, but not a sincere one. It was her acting cough. Her real one rumbled deep from her throat, like it was trying to shake stone from the earth. The one she did instead was a high-pitched whine with just enough scratchiness to sell it. Totally without function, except to flatter the cougher's femininity. That's why Zoe favored it. Not like she'd ever admit that she needed to move phlegm around.

"What's wrong?"

"It smells like shit," Zoe said.

"The cost of looking cool."

"Bitch, everyone hates smokers. You're the worst. They're going to hate me on set." Zoe stared at Lily, daring her to object again. Lily declined and blew out a little more smoke. "They're going to think I'm a smoker, that I'm not dedicated to keeping myself pristine as I age, and then I'm not going to get considered for long-running series roles. Because they'll think I'm going to look like a goblin by the time season five rolls around." She half-heartedly raised her lip and squinted her eyes, which didn't evoke a goblin nearly enough for Lily's taste.

"Oh, wait. Snarl your face like you were."

"Like this?" Zoe bared her teeth a bit in a grimace.

"No, no." Lily held her cigarette between two tight-pressed lips, and with her hands pushed one corner of Zoe's mouth down and another up, molding it to her vision. "Like that. Can you hold it?"

"Mm-hm."

"Okay. See, you already look like a goblin."

"Fuck off." Zoe snatched the cigarette from Lily's mouth and rushed over to the sink. "I'm throwing it in the water." Zoe could be heard in any room of the house while speaking in any other room of the house. Not that she was always loud. Sometimes Zoe would whisper and, way up in her bedroom, Lily would hear her as clear as day.

Usually Zoe was bluffing. She didn't want to hear the whining from Lily about how cigarettes were expensive—as if she had no choice but to smoke them—but this time the smell felt oppressive, like it was holding her down and demanding she breathe it.

Lily heard the difference and ran to the kitchen, already complaining about how she couldn't afford to waste one. The window creaked shut. Zoe had thrown it outside already. The cleanup would come for them, same as it ever did, once it rained and the tobacco, dampened and dried a hundred times, oozed down the cement walkway. Or—Lily walked out the back door, along the yet-un-oozed cement and picked up the cigarette from the ground. A few granules of dirt poked at her lips when she inhaled. Half-hearted attempts to blow them off didn't work, so she licked her lips and swallowed them. By the time she re-entered, Zoe was already pouting on the couch.

"It's my voice, too. It's my skin, but also it's my voice. My voice is my tool. I can become anyone, but not if it gets raspy from your smoke. If that happens, I'm so limited."

"So lie. Isn't that what acting is?"

"No. You bitch. I know you're trying to get under my skin. I know it."

And she was.

Nothing on Lily's phone caught her interest during the intervening silence. She half typed out a tweet claiming to know the one true gender of god, but erased it. Not worth five likes and an hour of fidgeting in terror that someone online would be mad at her.

"Okay, fine. Fine. Acting isn't lying. It's teasing out and embodying the deeper truth within all of us through performance. And you know that very well because we have been over this."

"I always forget that." Lily turned her head and shoulders to blow a plume of smoke away from Zoe. "I'm going to work anyway. It'll smell normal in like fifteen minutes and then you can blow that disgusting grapefruit vape everywhere. Worse than just the weed smell, if you ask me. You should get a different flavor."

"It's perfect the way it is."

"See you later." Lily cracked the front window as she got up. By the time she had her old leather jacket on and stuffed her keys into the pockets and got out the door, the smell of grapefruit was wafting out onto the porch. Everything was in its usual order.

# LILY

The walls were Lily's favorite thing about the tattoo parlor. Thin cracks of paint the same color as classic red lipstick peeked out from between the dense arrangement of frames and posters and signs and mirrors, drawings of sailors and naked women riding dragons and backs covered in sweeping lines. The history of tattooing wrapped close around her, welcoming her to its lineage despite her recent entry. She'd only been at it for a year, but she'd managed to learn under the best tattoo artist in Pittsburgh: Sveta Kosolov. For as long as Lily had been in the city, she'd seen people show off intricate sleeves covered in foliage, or knives, or abstract shapes that made their arms look like the future. New limbs, faces with subtly enhanced features or transformed into perfect cubes, bodies full of bloodless holes that, when the wind blew through them, whistled one of Ke$ha's minor works. All of it led back to Sveta. And one day, while Lily had been getting a tattoo of a chain link fence on her thigh, she had looked up at those walls and at Sveta and asked if she was taking on apprentices. After a short but intense stare into Lily's eyes, Sveta had hired her.

In the subsequent year, Lily had come to appreciate more than just the walls. She loved the tables designed to adjust to a hundred different bodily configurations, the cabinets full of bandages and towels, and especially the tattoo guns. Before her apprenticeship, she'd been a stick-and-poke specialist. A hundred Bart Simpsons saying "Shit" had flowed from her fingers to the skin of friends and lovers, the last fifty perfectly on model. There had been an intimacy in tattooing that way, but the gun felt special in her hands. A thick barrel gripped in her fingers, shooting delicacy into a client's skin, demanding of her only that she guide its power along the correct path.

Most of those paths were very simple: a little star on a girl's wrist, a circle on a shoulder, a simple penis on the back of a guy's calf, while the guy kept asking, "Bet you've never done a tattoo like this, right?" Lily didn't have the heart to tell him he was the second guy who had come in for a calf dick just that week. She wanted to use the gun to impose her vision on the world, bold lines etched in permanence. Ugly new buildings morphing with a wave of her gun, the wire coiling into the distance behind her. A different set of lines could turn the ugly patchwork textures into a tasteful brick wall. But she wasn't even allowed to use it to change her customer's face or fingers or knees or anything. Just lines on skin.

Several of the pictures on the wall were of her boss, but all of them merited display: one of her suspended by hooks, another of her submerged in ink so that she was invisible except for her bright green eyes, another one of her body sliced into thin segments and displayed all around the room. Lily didn't know if that one was real, but the magazine said "Sveta Kosolov, Spread Thin" and when Lily leaned in close, she could see tiny horizontal lines running across Sveta's face and body where the slices would have been. The tattoo parlor itself felt like Sveta had cut from her body and extended herself across the walls. Every decoration, every shelf, every chair felt like it had emerged whole from Sveta. Maybe it all did, by way of the special tattoo gun that buzzed in her left hand.

Between customers, Lily looked over Sveta's shoulder while she worked on someone's face. Sveta kept her wrist and elbow as rigid as if they were in a cast and guided her arm with her shoulder. The gun pulled the client's nose into a sharp point, then spun a section of their forehead into a green ribbon fluttering infinitely far back into the distance. With each flourish, another section of their face flattened and spiraled, until there was nothing above their neck but a rainbow whirl that flared in its endless colors that could not be contained by space. Colors that were all well-contained within the parlor's four solid walls, and wound together into a white tip so bright it looked like a star. As they paid Sveta, the various ribbons of color moved and twirled. The door opened and Lily's eyes couldn't quite register the tangle of colors and folding space which allowed them to exit, but when it closed, the parlor was empty again. Sveta tucked the money into her back pocket. "They tipped two hundred, that's sweet. See that, Lily? It's what you get when you see what someone wants more clearly than they do." An accent gently touched Sveta's vowels. A small spin on each one, though they still got to their destination precisely.

The two of them spent a little time discussing technical questions about how Sveta had gotten the point on the front of the customer's face so sharp. As they talked and Sveta drew a diagram, Lily noticed light scars and gnarled muscle on the back of Sveta's hand. The subtle bumps, which might have once been slices, interrupted the elegant line of her wrist and arm leading up to her body, a brutality where grace should be. With one stroke of that tattoo gun, it could have been fixed. Once, Lily had asked why Sveta hadn't bothered to do so. Sveta had held up her hand and softly dragged her fingers over the little ridges with wistfulness in her eyes. She had said, "You're here to learn how, not why," and that had been the end of it.

That afternoon, Sveta gave her an exercise: to tattoo a grapefruit. The goal was to turn it into an apple, then a pear, then a handful of strawberries, and finally into orange juice. Lily turned on the gun. She held her breath and kept still, the only motion in her body the reverberations from the gun's reality-bending power. Careful,

careful. Start with a straight line down the middle of the grapefruit, to warp its shape. But as soon as she moved the needle, juice splattered on her face and she flinched, tossing the gun aside. Its vibration stopped when her thumb fled the button. What had gone wrong?

The sting in her eyes affirmed that it was still grapefruit juice. As she cried the acid out of her eyes, Lily discovered two halves of a human heart, coated in rind. One half was still, while the other flinched and pumped weak spurts of grapefruit juice onto the table. Lily couldn't contain her revulsion and crawled across the floor to puke into the nearest trash can. As nausea heaved her body, Sveta's delicate laugh rang out.

"Ah, you pulled too hard. It hooks the flesh and then, boom, a nightmare. Remember, the gun understands your mind as it beholds the potential of the object." The buzzing sounded again. "So keep your mind empty. Want an apple? Feel its potential to be an apple. No other thoughts."

Lily's body continued to retch, far beyond her control. Sveta crouched beside her. They both waited a few minutes until the image of the heart lost its immediacy and Lily could retreat from the trash can. Sveta handed her the grapefruit. "Your schedule is clear. This afternoon, meditate. Hold this grapefruit. Empty thoughts, except for breath, and except for grapefruit."

Lily wouldn't get any more of Sveta's patience that day; as much as sitting quiet in a corner was a useful exercise, it was also a way to make sure Lily didn't cause a distraction. Sveta would forgive her error once Lily progressed. Nothing flatters the teacher like learning a lesson. Until then, meditation. She rolled the grapefruit around in her palms. Tough rind against soft skin, but the rind felt wet, and her hand too dry. Had Sveta returned it to a normal grapefruit? Or did it contain a secret for her to discover? Lily pushed her thumbs into the rind and the sensation of gouging out someone's eyes burst to the forefront of her mind. She dropped the grapefruit. It was eyes. Of course it was eyes. Some juice dribbled from the cracked rind. A normal grapefruit returned the eyes to Lily's imagination, but peace and focus would have to wait until tomorrow.

For the rest of her shift, Lily pretended to meditate, nestling the grapefruit's crack in her palm. At five, she hustled out the door, hoping to conceal her failure. With the grapefruit safely thrown away, she could breathe again. Had it been a trick? Sveta wasn't one for tests or obscure lessons. There would be more grapefruits, more lessons, and for another day, Lily would try to climb the sheer wall to mastery.

# ZOE

When Zoe was cast in *Somnolences*, she couldn't believe her luck. After a stint on the web series *Drama Dolls*, itself dramatic, she was so excited to work on a real production. Not only that, but with a director whose name she'd heard before: Sage Almstead. This was their first movie since they had shaved their head and had taken on a new name, in keeping with the non-binary ceremonial tradition. Zoe found it all to be a bit much. When she came out, she just did an Instagram post. Easy enough. Still, Sage's insistence on an all-trans cast for *Somnolences* came just as Zoe's hype peaked, and at the audition, she had nodded along while Sage blabbered about "re-situating heterosexuality in a context unblemished by heteronormativity." Zoe couldn't wait to get to work with professionals who would recognize the enormity of her talent.

That day, months later, they were on the tenth take. Retakes were inevitable. Mistakes were made, risks were taken, and sometimes, the director just needed options. But nine times she had delivered perfection. Each slightly different, as the truth she plucked from shapelessness never presented itself the same way twice. And nine times, her co-star had given her the same muddled garbage.

This time, Zoe summoned an audible little breath. Exasperation. Not hers, but her character's. The repeated takes were an opportunity to dial into the truth of that emotion. "When is it going to change, Aidan?"

"Everything's always changing," her co-star Tevin responded with a tired mumble. Again. His character was supposed to be fixated on the systematic destruction of his own life. That solidity was supposed to contrast with Zoe's flexibility, constantly shifting and contorting to reach Aidan before he went over the edge. But if he was going to play it soft, she'd supply the contrast. Zoe stepped into Tevin's space. Fuck the blocking.

"I'm not." That line was supposed to be dramatic irony. A loss for the viewers. They wouldn't even know they should blame someone. "I'm what you need."

"CUT." Sage's voice boomed through their megaphone. "The line is, 'I'll be whatever you need.' Not to mention the rest of that. What the fuck was that, Zoe?" They hopped down from their chair. Sage, a five-foot-tall androgynous pixie, could only assert their authority over Zoe with the fetters of cinematic production. Otherwise, a child-sized person could never hope to command an Amazon.

"I wanted to give you an option that actually worked. I had to change the line to make that happen."

"Oh, okay. And where was the scene going to go after that? After you changed the whole thing?" Sage thumbed through the script. As though Zoe hadn't memorized all of the lines.

"Ask him. He wants to change the vibe of the scene. He's the one who's supposed to lead here. I'm reacting. And my reaction is: I want this scene to make sense."

"You worry about you. Do your lines the way you're supposed to do them. Are you the director?"

"No."

"Okay. I'm the director, then?"

"Yes."

"Great! I'm the director. Great news, everyone. I made it. So Zoe, let me worry about Tevin's performance. I just need you to do what I fucking say."

"Hold on there. No. You do not talk to her like that." Nate—Zoe's agent, who was already sweating in a thick alpaca sweater—jogged down to the set and stuck two fingers in the director's face. "That's not how you treat a star." He flipped through a stack of papers on a clipboard, not even looking down to pretend he had read any of them. "I have her contract right here, and it says she has full discretion over her performance choices."

"None of our contracts say that. Hers is standard."

"Oh yes it does. I have it right here." He smacked his hand against the clipboard for emphasis. "Your job is not to tell her how to do her art. Your job is to create an environment where she can flourish. Does she look like she's flourishing to you?" Nate gestured to Zoe's face, her cue to let the tears flow and ruin her eye makeup. "We'll be in her dressing room until you're ready to work with her appropriately."

"Have her back in makeup in thirty minutes. Then we'll go again." Sage sneered at Nate and climbed back into their rickety wood-and-fabric throne.

On the way back to her dressing room, Nate defended her from any encroachment. There, he leaned all one hundred and forty pounds of his body against the door to bar any intruders who could overcome the lock. No matter how long it took for Zoe to gather her thoughts, he would be there for her. Sometimes Zoe fantasized about Nate and his husband adopting her, somehow. But Nate's husband had a thick neck and weird ideas about real estate, and Zoe couldn't be around that all the time. She might start thinking about it too, and she couldn't have fortune distracting her from fame.

"I don't know what's wrong with them," Nate said. "You're the best actor they've ever worked with. By far."

Zoe nodded as she dragged her middle finger along her lower eyelid, smudging the charcoal gray eyeliner—not black, in accordance with her contract. Soon the gray cloud expanded to her cheekbones.

"I mean. I've seen their other movies. C-tier talents, start to finish. Then an A drops in their lap and they squander it. They're squandering you."

"There's a higher tier than A, you know."

"No, it's like grades. A-tier, tippy-top, then B, C, D, F."

"People put things in an S-tier. Above A. Am I not S-tier to you?"

"I'm sorry. I'm so sorry. Fire me. Crush me beneath your heel." Nate abandoned his post and fell to his knees, then scooted towards her with his pleading hands clasped. In a life where Zoe was destined for less, she could've been a dominatrix. Though Nate's supplication didn't please her sexually, it satisfied her in harder-to-name regions. He went on. "Have me arrested. Say I sexually assaulted you. I won't dispute it. You are on a tier all your own, such that your word is indisputable fact, even if you use it to condemn me on a whim."

"Oh, I would never. I need you here. I'm ready to go back out. Tell Sage I'm not redoing my makeup because I like it this way." Zoe rubbed some of her mascara off, so that little flakes of dark brown situated among the eyeliner. But the message never made it past Sage, and Zoe couldn't fend off the makeup artist, and soon she was back in front of the lights, performing on someone else's terms.

# LILY

A single mile separated the tattoo shop from Lily's home, so she always walked. Sometimes she took the route along Penn Ave., a two-lane road always full of cars. Always full of people walking along the cracked sidewalks, so that Lily got to feel plenty of the little moments of tension when two people were about to collide and had to coordinate and avoid each other, and so prevent themselves from being caught up in each other's lives. Exclusion is a social act, after all. We can't all know each other, or else the burden of observation would lie upon our bodies like chains. Such was the curse of the small town. Better to be a flicker of a person, a brief gesture drawing of interiority that fades as soon as the two ships pass and paths diverge.

That evening, Lily decided to cut through the cemetery. It was a longer route, which took her downhill in equal measure to the hill she had to travel up at the end of her walk, but the crumbling asphalt pathways amid the steadfast granite tombstones called to her. Not least for the memento mori, the cemetery was the premiere gay first-date spot in the city, as well as a frequent workout path for everyone in the neighborhood. As she ambled down the winding roads, she saw a tiny woman in yoga pants stretching her hamstring by using a small tombstone as a footrest. All around Lily, the dead seethed. Trapped beneath stone and dirt and mortality, they could do nothing but hate this woman. Would they hate Lily too for witnessing it and doing nothing? She tried to object, but her voice caught in her throat, and it took a little cough to dislodge it, and once that moment passed, the woman had jogged far away from Lily's chance to speak. With any luck, the attempt would be enough. She could jog away from the dead too, though the soles of her boots were worn thin enough for her to feel every step.

A squirrel wandered down from a tree, perched itself on a nearby tombstone and stared at Lily. She stopped and returned the favor. Their mutual incomprehension felt like an easy peace, and as she crept nearer to the squirrel, it didn't move. Between its little hands, it grasped a fun-size Snickers—judging by the lurid vein on top—which must have been left by some child visiting the grave of a dead relative. Misfortune begat fortune. The squirrel didn't flee as Lily drew close enough to see its face clearly. So enthralled it must have been by the candy bar that it no longer believed in fear. It ate, looked up at Lily, ate, and so on. Lily left the squirrel to its feast and continued on her path through the geese which lived around the pond, the deer that watched her from behind the trees, and the centuries of dead who had nothing to say nor hear from her.

As she emerged, she decided to stop at her favorite coffee shop, though it hadn't been part of the decision to walk through the cemetery. Indisputably Coffee sat at the exact halfway point between her job and home—and everyone else's—no matter which route she took. Today that meant it separated two halves of a house just a block away from the cemetery gates, the walls shimmering at the breaking point. Hopefully it would come together seamlessly once the coffee shop left. Had anyone ever been caught at the midpoint? Would they just linger half-and-half until the shop left? Or would they still be able to move? Lily got up on her tiptoes for new viewing angles, trying to spot a dangling arm or split face, but all she saw was a woman shitting in her bathroom, aggravated at the sudden exposure to the fresh air. Elena, who worked at the shop, once told her that people often tried to sue Indisputably Coffee for these architectural interruptions. But anyone carrying legal papers was, by definition, at work, rather than on the way to or from, and so the coffee shop wouldn't appear to them.

A bell jingled to announce Lily's entrance.

The inside of the coffee shop was packed with people, all similarly at the halfway point to or from work. Men in suits intermingled with punks who smelled like cooking grease and tech workers who brought their one-wheel electronic skateboards in with them, for fear of losing their two thousand dollar toys to theft. Large murals lined the walls, without any thought paid to cohesion: impressionism, expressionism, abstraction, caricature, all clashing wherever one employee's fancy met another's. If you worked, you got wall space. Simple as that. Lily's favorites were the giant skeletons painted in stark perspective, bones shrinking and curving and growing so that the skeletons existed in impossible dimensions. But then, their artist was also her favorite.

That same artist extended her muscular arm out above the crowd, nail polish glittering in the light. She kneeled and looked down, smacking her hand against the counter to make her own noise above the clamor. "Todd!" she shouted. A man wearing a tie with little bicycles on it clapped his hands like a seal, and she dropped the latte into his hands. The crowd around him cheered and slapped him on the back, congratulating him like a victorious athlete. Then another barista called another name and Todd walked out of the restaurant and disappeared back into his route home.

"Elena!" Lily said, vaulting on some nerd's shoulders to prop herself above the crowd.

"Get up here, Lil!" Elena dropped a rope ladder. Other customers tried to climb up, but Elena had a long pole to prod them in the face until they let go voluntarily or fell off. Only Lily was allowed to finish the ascent, and once she'd perched herself twenty feet above the crowd, the ladder retracted. She drew her thighs close together, no free shows for the crowd, but let her feet dangle off the counter.

Elena slipped a ceramic mug into Lily's hands, her fingers lingering on Lily's for a second.

"Here. You've earned it."

Spinning around, Lily faced the tea vat. Thousands of tea bags floated on top, lazily swirling in the circular current. She waited, passing up a handful of green tea bags and one jasmine. She was after something a little more fun. The yellow and orange tag! Ginger. Lily scooped a mugful of tea out along with the bag and held it beneath her nose. The steam wafted into her nostrils, pleasant and warm. Ginger tea, steeped to the perfect concentration. She took a sip, heat prickling her tongue and throat. With an exaggerated exhale, she set the cup down. The crowd below cheered for her, then forgot her as another lucky person got their to-go cup dropped into their hands. It was their moment now. It suited Lily just fine. She had no desire to put on a show.

"I'm on break! Don't bother me," Elena said to the other baristas. Someone new snagged the aiming visor, which dangled crosshairs in front of the wearer's left eye and took over dropping duty. Free of the demands of the masses, Elena scooted in close next to Lily, touching thigh to thigh. "How was work?"

"Oh, I fucked up a grapefruit today."

"Me too. Not business, though. Strictly personal." She pumped her fist into her palm a few times, and grapefruit juice bled down her knuckles.

"A grapefruit, cut in half and ready to be served for breakfast says: you should see the other guy."

"You should see the (she/her) other guy."

The exchange took place with Lily's hand grasped around Elena's forearm, the two of them dancing for position, lunging forward and pulling back, personal space in perpetual flux but never ceded, never merged. Eventually, Lily had to remove her hand before sweat complicated the situation. She said, "What have you been up to?"

"Hmmm. Oh, ugh. Remember the shattered glass art piece?"

"Yeah! That sounded really cool."

"My roommate thought they were being helpful and melted it all back together. I walk in and it's just sitting on the floor, like a regular pane of glass. Pristine. So now I've gotta re-crack the whole thing."

"Same way?" Lily didn't think there was much intentionality in breaking glass, but wanted to give Elena an opportunity to explain something to her. "I don't know much about glass."

"It's kinda random. Obviously I decide where the hammer hits. No one's taking that away from me. But what happens after that?" Elena shrugged.

"I'd just hit in the correct spots."

"That easy?"

"Yep. Just line it up..." Lily closed one eye and stuck her tongue out of the side of her mouth. "And pow. Right in the good spot."

"I'll try that this time. If it goes bad, I'll send you the results. Be careful when you open the envelope." The two of them kicked their feet off the ledge. While the crowd had cheered for Lily, as is their way, many of them looked up at Elena like she was a goddess. And wasn't she, in a meaningful sense? They asked her for relief, and she dropped it down to them. Eventually, if they didn't displease her.

"What are you doing after your shift?"

The crowd murmured below. "She's asking out the barista." "You're not allowed to do that." "Forbidden, dangerous."

A man in a suit jumped onto the shoulders of the woman in front of him, who bore the weight despite her tiny frame. "Forget her, barista! I will take you on the finest date of your life. Gourmet food, artisanal lubes, your wildest dreams, realized." The crowd tore him down, and he vanished beneath their hands.

Lily waved away their gloomy stares. "We already know each other."

Elena's giggle tinkled over the chaos around them.

"I'd love to hang out but I've got plans tonight. I'm closing on the new house tomorrow and I need to make sure my shit's together. But they don't need to know that." Elena kissed Lily on the cheek, leaving an immaculate purple lip-print. The two said their goodbyes, and Lily rappelled down from the counter.

The lipstick shone on her face, encasing her in a bubble of light that even the most irate customer couldn't pierce. Once she walked out the door, the coffee shop was gone: the house's halves were reunited and whoever lived inside was probably done shitting. Lily had gotten some respite on her way home. Indisputably Coffee offered no more than that.

# ZOE

Zoe couldn't stand being hemmed in by so many unremarkable people. All of them were shorter than her except for that one guy who was like 6'8" and stood at the front of the crowd at every local show and concert. But Lily had told her that the headliner, The Dainties, was incredible, and assured her that it wasn't a moshing-and-fighting kind of band. God forbid some beanie-clad rando break her nose with a wild elbow and force her to watch all of her beauty pour out between her fingers.

When the opening band came on stage, Zoe wanted to leave. Four guys in ill-fitting T-shirts scattering fifty guitar pedals along the stage. But she couldn't go until Lily showed up. At best, hanging out with Lily would make this more fun. At worst, Zoe could explain why inviting her to hear a post-rock band play was unacceptable. Some of those guitar pedals were going to light up. Hell awaited. As the opener's aimless melodies began, Zoe felt some eyes on her. Not unusual; she stuck out from the crowd in every conceivable way. But the attention felt like some pressure to react to the music in front of her: it would be part of however this watcher evaluated her. Though they might have also recognized her from one of her roles. It had only been a five-minute short film, but her last project had caused a brief sensation online for the subtlety of her performance as well as for the emotional accuracy of the scene where her character discovered that her pet snakes had tried eating each other and had become a dual ouroboros. Unlikely that anyone here had seen her in *Drama Dolls*. That one had a narrow audience, passionate though they were.

Zoe would give the crowd what they wanted. As the

music began, she bopped her head around, despite the lifelessness of the guitar melody that vibrated through her. Too much enjoyment would seem sincere. Despite all the discourse—t-girls love everything post: post-hardcore, post-rock, post-op, post online and you get ten thousand desperate girls vying for your attention—Zoe didn't care for it. This wasn't music for screaming and dancing to; in fact, it was made by and for a crowd too insecure to do either. Instead, the goal was detached appreciation, a music that made you think and deign to bop your head as a note to the performer that you were enjoying what you heard. None of these half-bearded losers had the confidence to lose themselves to the music, to dance and holler and let themselves be wild. So they pretended it was beneath them, even as it was the very thing that dangled above: that when you stripped away all pretension, their inadequacy would be laid bare.

Her greatest fears came to life when the lead guitarist stamped his foot on the pedal board, and a sea of LEDs lit. Zoe could take no more and pushed her way to the exit. After parting a sea of wispy men, she emerged into the cool night air. By the door, Lily smoked a cigarette.

Zoe said, "There you are."

"Here I am."

"Why didn't you come in?"

Lily peered in. "It seemed like smoking was a better use of my time." She whistled. "Oh, that board is lit up. Hot damn."

"Ugh, whatever." Zoe leaned against the wall. Now she was the cool girl outside the show. Boys could file past, each of them fantasizing about ending up pressed against her in the crowded venue. First shoulder to shoulder, then flank to flank, and finally their eyes might meet and from there, anything else could touch. Not that any of them had a chance with her. The crop of guys at this show was particularly unappealing. Far too many warm-weather beanies. But Zoe was generous, willing to lend out the image of herself for them to use in whatever fantasies they pleased. All of them might desire to possess her, to keep her as proof of their social status. Only the king of the beanie boys could have a woman like her, oozing sex appeal into the air around her until it became muddy and soft. She'd done the same thing once: stared at the hot girl at the show and hoped to wrap the girl around her pitiful boy body and scream that she was a success. That she was not only a viable boy, but the greatest of them.

It was a dream for fools. To desire and be fulfilled was nothing compared to being desired. To dream a waste compared to the thrill of being dreamed of. If satisfaction could be won from being attained, then reason dictated that the satisfaction existed inside her at all times. Within, the source of a thousand running rivers which would never reach the ocean.

A boy approached them. A thin coat of facial hair which swelled to full coverage only near the jaw. A lip ring to feign being at battle with mainstream culture, but some finger tattoos which made it real. Zoe prepared to spurn him. Would she do it with a flip of her hair? A sneer? A little smile which made it clear she'd been approached by oh so many boys and he didn't have a chance of making the cut? But Lily said, "Oh my god, Tyler," and hugged him with just a single hand across his back. An embrace too shallow to be romantic in nature, but his inclusion in their circle bolstered his reputation no matter the facts of their entanglement. People saw Tyler next to Zoe and he would benefit, leeching off of her image without her permission—he even posed a little bit whenever someone's phone rose up in their hands, though it never resolved into snapping a picture of the two of them. And she couldn't do anything about it because Lily wanted him there.

"Zoe, have you ever met Tyler?"

"Nope. Nice to meet you." A perfunctory smile and light eye contact, and then she turned her eyes on the crowd. He'd gotten enough. This was all demeaning, but it was a sacrifice that she could make for Lily.

"He used to DJ down at Remedy. You know, the place that always has porn projected on the walls during dance parties?" Lily laughed. "Zoe can never remember the names of any bars she's been to."

"Can too! Like last night we were at the, uh." Humiliation loomed in the shadows behind her. What was the bar's name? It had a sort of poetic name to it, a little touch of irony that had made her feel at ease the first time she had read it. Here was a bar owner who understood that there was an art to this, a sociality created by the designation of space. But time was out and she had to remember now in order to have any hope of maintaining her dominant position in the conversation. "The Rictus Room!"

Lily cackled. "The Rictus Room! Oh my god, Zoe."

"What? That's it, isn't it?"

"It's the Recovery Room!" Lily laughed, high-pitched little screeches she probably picked up from some YouTube voice trainer, who mostly taught viewers how to shred their vocal cords in four months or less. Tyler picked up the laugh a second after Lily started. She'd set Zoe up to take the fall and raise her own standing in this random dude's eyes. Who was he, anyway? Not important enough for Lily to mention, yet she was willing to tease Zoe for prestige. If he were a secret lover, they'd have been more clandestine in their greeting: a meaningful glance across the room, a subtle brush of their hands in the crowd before the stage. No, there was nothing substantial between the two of them. Though a peek down Lily's shirt from Tyler did clarify his interest, Lily didn't notice it or didn't care. Only spite could explain Lily's actions. This was the danger of competition; two cool girls at the show diluted the effect. The value of being the sole object of desire was immense, and being one of two was far less than half of it.

Zoe ignored Tyler for the next few minutes, and eventually he joined the crowd and was gone from her sight.

"How was the tattoo shop today? You get that grapefruit turned into fruit salad yet?"

"You ever wonder if you don't have any imagination?"

Lily smiled. She had little dimples in her cheeks, which drove Zoe crazy. If she had those dimples, she'd have booked a mid-budget historical romance by now. At least.

"Not really."

Eventually they wandered into the room and nestled themselves into the crowd, fighting their way toward the front. While Zoe stood above most of the boys, Lily's two-inch disadvantage was enough to plunge her into the depths of the audience. The headlining band came out to cheers—they began to tune their instruments. At the lead microphone, Tyler. That was why Lily had been so cruel to her. All to impress the singer of a cut-rate touring band. Under no circumstances could this stand.

Twinkly emo bullshit sounded from their guitars. Uninspired. Unoriginal. A hack job where art should go. At least the opening band's post-rock had been sincere. This was a crime, and Zoe couldn't let it go unrecognized. She cupped her hands around her mouth. "Is this song about the government?"

They continued, undeterred by her jeer. Lily tugged on her sleeve, and shot a glance into her eyes. Lily wanted to discourage Zoe, bind her with decorum. She didn't understand why Zoe had to do this, but as someone who had dedicated her life to the arts, Zoe had to defend art from the mediocre. At every moment, hands were trying to grasp the muse's arms and legs and pin her down and keep her from the diaphanous form which she thrived in, and in which form they could not take advantage of her.

Once the song was done, Tyler leaned into the mic with an unearned pretty-boy smile.

"Hey there, Pittsburgh, it's good to be back. We're The Strongest Arms. I'm honored to be here on our way from Seattle to New York, not just because your city lets us get there in a couple days. It's wild. It's so damn wild."

"You're a low-rent Menzingers!" Zoe yelled.

"Excuse me?"

"You're a dogshit Los Campesinos, faggot!"

The room gasped. A rush of carbon dioxide flooded the crowded space. If there were any mercy in the world, everyone would pass out from a lack of oxygen and bring an end to the show early. But reality was cruel and the night went on.

"Zoe, what the fuck?"

"I am allowed to say that." She spun around, making eye contact with as many betas as she could endure. "Don't any of you dare tell a trans woman that she can't say 'faggot'."

"That's not the problem, Zoe. You're being rude."

Tyler leaned close enough into the microphone for the speakers to broadcast his weak beard's scratch. "I do actually have a problem with her calling me a faggot in the middle of my show.

Zoe shouted back, "Woah, hey, how much dick have you sucked, dude?"

The crowd worked up into overlapping shouts, a hundred flapping mouths all beneath Zoe's eyeline. All she had to do was look a bit up, and their complaints were invisible. All that remained were Tyler's uninterested annoyance and Lily's focused glare.

"I think you should go. Obviously you don't want to be here." Lily pointed a glitter-black nail toward the door. Even burdened by anger, her wrist was dainty in its femininity.

"You're right. I don't." Zoe nudged her way through a crowd that refused to part for her. Obstacles all, refusing her the place that belonged to her even if it was only to pass through for a moment. That was what Lily wanted, wasn't it? To exclude Zoe and take her unworthy place at the center of the crowd, where all eyes stole glances at her, and every action was tied to her with invisible gossamer. She could have it now and be a queen at a ruined show.

# LILY

After Lily got home from the show, she approached Zoe's door to try and figure out why Zoe had blown up, but an audio recording of Zoe saying "Don't bother me" was playing too loud for her gentle knocks to overcome. The next morning, Lily got up early and it wasn't on anymore, but even so, waking Zoe up would have been a mistake. Except for days she had to be on set, Zoe slept until noon, and as much as Lily hoped that this morning would be an exception, the time came to leave so she could help Elena move. For the entire walk over to meet up with Elena, Lily played the previous night's events over in her mind. Had Tyler done something rude to Zoe without Lily noticing? Or had she done something to upset Zoe? With any luck, they'd have a chance to talk it out that evening and realize it was all a misunderstanding.

After the laborious process of moving out of Elena's old apartment, the two of them arrived at the new house. Elena's cat, Lewis, perked up from his spot in Lily's lap, leaving behind a scattering of elegant white hair. The metal door on the U-Haul slid open in one motion. Elena flexed in the opening, the whole of their worldly possessions jammed into the back half the truck, then grabbed Lily's hand and yanked her up onto the truck, only afterward releasing the ramp that made walking up and down a simple task. A trace of Elena's sweat lingered on Lily's arm, and she didn't bother to wipe it off. Lewis peeked his head into the truck. Lily yelped and approached Lewis slowly, trying to lure him into her grasp, but Elena waved her off. "Don't worry about him, he does his own thing." On cue, his ears perked up and he stared off toward Elena's new house for a moment, focus so perfect that neither Lily nor Elena existed to him anymore.

And like he was launched from a spring, Lewis chased whatever it was. Elena laughed, and if she wasn't worried for the cat, Lily didn't see any reason why she should be. Though she still was. Just a bit.

Each of them picked up a box and traveled down the ramp, which creaked at the indignity of supporting their weight. Ivy slithered across the exterior of the house, but only covered half of it at any given time. In its wake, the ivy revealed bricks painted blue like the sky that Pittsburgh constantly hid from them with clouds. Standing before them felt like resting in a patch of sunlight, and the bricks were warm to the touch. But Lily couldn't keep her hand on the wall for more than a second before the ivy rustled over her hand. Beneath the prickling branches, the ivy stole the heat away from her and left her fingers frigid and numb.

"Isn't it cool?" Elena said as she ascended the cement steps, avoiding the delicate blades of grass and shoots that squeezed through the cracks.

Lily nodded and stared up at the ivy. What stopped it from pouring into the house, wrapping itself around a childhood bed where a little girl had once had the best dreams and worst nightmares of her childhood, creeping over the table where a man asked his husband for a divorce, consuming the dog's favorite spot on the floor where the heat from the radiator was most potent? Perhaps the interior was just less appealing. Cracked paint, crumbling plaster, holes everywhere. Hardwood so scratched it looked like someone had wandered around wearing ice skates for years.

Lily's nose twitched. She smelled the absence of an odor. How such a destroyed room could be perfectly scentless confused her; she walked up to the wall and sniffed, but still nothing. Was it a sterile environment somehow? Could the various holes and scuffs create an airflow that eradicated all life and threatened her if she stood still for too long? It would keep the ivy out, but Elena would've noticed that.

The kitchen was, like the living room, in disrepair. Lily set the box gingerly on the kitchen counter. Beneath the dry and scuffed boots that Lily often wore, there were more cracked tiles than whole. A leaf of wallpaper dangled from the wall. So easily, she could pull, and pull, and maybe reveal a whole section of blank wall that it had protected from the ravages of time. Kept pure. But she didn't. She was a guest, and for all she knew, Elena would want to keep the wallpaper just this way.

Elena slouched against the countertop, all of her weight on her elbows. Star tattoos radiated out from their points. "So, I know what you're thinking."

"Do you?"

"Yeah. You're thinking this is a shithole and I'm crazy for buying it. Right?"

"Not exactly."

"Yeah, you are. And you're right. This house is terrible. Look at it. But it's only terrible right now. Wait until you see what I do with it."

A scorch mark ran from the light fixture to the wall. "I think there's something beautiful about it now," Lily said.

"Goth girl sees a corpse and thinks it's art." Elena left the kitchen, heading back to the truck.

"I'm not a goth girl!" Lily tagged behind her. "I'm a regular girl with just a few goth tendencies."

"What's that necklace about, then?" Elena asked, heaving a box into Lily's arms.

The old razor blade dangling from Lily's neck was the last she had ever shaved with, before electrolysis had burnt the last few hairs squatting on her face and freed her forever. Everything could be changed, and no obligations had to last. It was a matter of dedication and effort, but Lily didn't want to reveal all this to Elena, so she said, "...It looks cool."

"Goth. Girl." Elena snapped her fingers after each word. "Anyway, my non-goth perspective on this house is that it's a skeleton."

"That sounds a lot like a goth perspective."

"Not as an aesthetic. I can clear away all the decaying flesh and create something new with the bones."

Lily pushed her glasses up her nose. "Actually, the house is called 'Elena's monster.' 'Elena' is the doctor."

"Actually, actually, Frankenstein's monster is the name of his twelve-inch cock. If you're going to tease me, do it while moving boxes." Elena pushed Lily toward the mouth of the truck.

Elena carried two boxes to Lily's one. They bounced as they walked, so much more vital than anyone Lily had ever known. Just like the ivy, they never stopped moving.

When Lily caught up to Elena, setting her box down in the putative living room, Elena said, "Imagine, this room could be anything I want it to be. Any color, any texture, anything. Maybe I'll dangle shards of mirror from the ceiling. That would be cool, right?"

Lily arched an eyebrow.

"Bitch, that is not goth. It's artsy; this house is going to be art. It's going to be beautiful."

Elena strolled around the room. They wore femininity like a flimsy veil stretched taught by powerful muscles, calling attention both to beauty and to the false nature of decoration. If Lily tried to do that, there would be nothing beneath the facade. A dramaturge's mask slipping to reveal an abyss.

"What do you want it to be?"

"Not sure. I'll figure out what I want while I do it."

Lily didn't know what to say to that, so the two of them caught their breath until the remaining boxes called to them. But a lanky person in a ripped tank top, with pink hair, black lipstick, and two days' stubble on their round face stood between them and the truck.

Their eyes always darted off to the side, as if trying to catch someone looking at them.

Elena smiled. "Oh, hi—"

"Wait right there." They held their hands up. "I'm going by the name Dicks now."

"Dicks?" Lily asked.

"It's a thing I'm doing, don't worry too much about it. But also only call me Dicks." They scratched at their chest hair, a sparse meadow in the valley of their cleavage. "Sorry I'm late, I really wanted to help with those boxes. But I guess you're all done by now, right?"

"Oh, no, we have plenty left. Lily and I stopped for a while to chat, you know how it is." Elena put a hand on their shoulder and guided them toward the truck, her grip strong enough to pull Dicks's tank top tense.

Lily said, "Thank god you got here when you did. I think there's a desk still in there." Lily was sure that there wasn't any furniture left in the truck beyond the box spring, but that wasn't going to stop her from having a little fun. "I was afraid that I was going to have to carry it. Now I can just relax."

"You know. I've got a rare back disease."

"If that was true, Dicks, you probably wouldn't have volunteered to come help me move, right?" Elena dropped a box into their hands, driving them down into a squat.

"Oh my god, what's in this?"

"Turn it around so I can read it." Dicks complied, their breathing becoming heavier as Lily read the box. "It says 'supplies.'"

"Guess it's full of supplies, then. Thanks, love." Elena cackled as she disappeared back into the truck and her laugh echoed into a cacophony.

Lily followed Dicks up the walkway as they waddled to compensate for the heavy weight in their arms. They hadn't noticed that Lily wasn't carrying anything and probably wouldn't. During the first year or so of her transition—and sometimes even now, years later—she was the most visible person in a crowd, the most memorable face and body in any interaction, so she appreciated the spotlight Dicks cast on themself, which allowed her to disappear in the glare.

Dust fled from the box's impact on the ground. "That's my duty done. Let's see what the hell 'supplies' are." Dicks knelt and pulled open the flaps of the box.

"Wait, this is Elena's stuff. You can't just dig through it."

"It can't be that serious. They risked me dropping it and everything."

Elena wouldn't care. Lily knew that, and also knew that there was nothing she could say to convince Dicks to alter their course. And her listlessness was rewarded when a box full of books revealed itself. Twelve copies of *Eragon*, stacked in a flat layer on top. Dicks pulled up a few from the first layer, frantically tossing them aside as if they could dispel an illusion. Beneath, another layer. *Eragon, Eragon, Eragon*, all the way down. "What the fuck."

Elena walked in the door holding a lamp like a spear. Lewis chased after her feet, swatting her boots, retreating, and then advancing again to try and slay his invincible enemy. Elena said, "Oh, you started unpacking them? That can wait until I get a nice big display table in here. Until then, I don't know where to put them."

Struggling to find the words she needed, paralyzed between curiosity and politeness, Lily just made a soft sound when she opened her mouth. But Dicks was able to find their voice without much delay. "This is way too many *Eragon*s. Why are there so many *Eragon*s?"

"Look inside them, dummy."

Elena snorted and went upstairs. Lewis stayed behind and peered into the box, found nothing of interest and slunk into the kitchen. These books were already mundane to the two of them.

Lily and Dicks each picked up an *Eragon*. Lily opened hers and found a rough sketch of a woman with long hair flowing down the page, with their face buried between the legs of another person whose hair wafted up from their head and consumed a quarter of the page in dark rings and waves. She flipped to the next page, a drawing of a half-erect penis. The next, a drawing of a topless woman, with a thicket of scratches instead of a face. Grasping the theme, she looked over to Dicks's copy, but didn't see any drawings.

"What's going on in yours?"

"I don't know, it just looks like the regular book."

Lily scanned the page, but couldn't find any drawings or other alterations, until partway through a sentence, she found the word "dragon."

"Oh my god. Oh my god."

"What? What is it?"

Lily was laughing too hard to say anything, so she jabbed her finger at the page over and over while Dicks interrogated her more loudly about its meaning until they stopped, realization dawning.

They slammed the book back down on the pile and yelled toward the staircase, "When did you even have the time?"

"I can't handle this." Still giggling, Lily left to sit on the shallow concrete stoop and pulled her cigarettes out of her purse. She lit one and inhaled deeply, then laughed out a few puffs. The first pull was always the best. The rest would range from fine to miserable, depending on how the smoke hit her. What she exhaled disappeared into the gray clouds swirling in a spiral above, calling the smoke to join them. She raised her face to the warmth radiating from the walls with the cigarette dangling from her lips like the sword of Damocles above her yet-unruined tights. Not quite sunlight, but.

Some muttering off to the side interrupted her peace. The neighbors were glancing at her, talking amongst themselves. Maybe it was just her outfit. The boots, the tights, the razor-blade necklace, all of it was quite noticeable. Convincing a case as it was, Lily couldn't make herself believe it. So she tried to ignore them and stared up at the sky. It was fine, it wasn't fine, let them talk.

Dicks sat down next to her, blocking the neighbors' eyeline. "Can I get a smoke?" Lily wordlessly opened her pack toward them. They took one, but instead of grabbing the lighter, turned their attention to the neighbors. "Are they staring at us? Are they staring at me?"

"Yeah, who cares though?"

"Oh, I care."

Dicks tucked the cigarette behind their ear and turned to face the neighbors, but Lily held onto their tank top. The two of them were frozen in a moment: Lily silently pleading with Dicks not to go, the fight wasn't worth it, leave it leave it leave it. But they escaped Lily and, with each step towards the neighbors, a fury built up around them. "Hey fuckers! What are you looking at?"

Either the neighbors were going to fold and run inside or they were going to yell back, and Lily couldn't make things any better in either case, but she could make them worse. And Elena might blame her for it. So she would cut off that possibility at once.

She called up the stairs, "Dicks is getting into it with your neighbors."

"Shit, already? Every time, that one. Come up here, nothing to be done about it now."

Each step creaked beneath Lily except the last one. It was sturdier than any ground she'd ever walked on, as if the entire house could crumble and this one step would be floating above the wreckage. Immovable, unchangeable. Elena was sitting on the floor, her back against the faded blue wall with deep cracks running through it. Lily, not seeing any chairs or other furniture, sat next to her. The window in the room was broken, and some of the ivy had managed to creep inside, but only a few tendrils which didn't have the strength to do more than twirl their leaves. Their grasp was not as large nor as strong as Lily had hoped it might be.

"C'mere. What's Dicks worked up about?"

"Gawking, whispering. Taking in the spectacle of Dicks, in a bad way." Better to omit her own presence and feelings about the situation. The last thing Lily wanted to be was an object of Elena's pity. So Lily shrugged as if she didn't know what it was like to be stared at, and Elena laughed and wrapped her arms around Lily and drove her head into the crook of Lily's neck.

"It's just so stupid. Like, I love Dicks. I do. But it's always like this."

"I don't know." Elena's fingers interlocked around her shoulder. Short with black polish chipped to only a small island sitting in the center of each nail. Hands from which creation spilled with every touch. Hands that subordinated themselves to a wild and piercing eye. "Like, I respect that they're willing to fight when they need to."

"And when they don't."

"Sure. But who knows when it's time to fight?"

A ceiling fan dangled from the ceiling, one blade missing and surely inoperable. "My fault for inviting them. I knew what the deal was." One of Elena's hands left Lily's shoulder and traced a circle in the air, enacting the vision of a working fan. "Do you think I made a mistake buying this house?"

"Are you second-guessing yourself?"

"No. I know what I think. I just don't know what you do."

Lily followed Elena's finger up to the ceiling fan,

to the holes in the ceiling around it, the visible boards along the walls where the plaster had been destroyed, down to the broken window and the warped, rotten wood that lined it. Shreds of carpet still clung to nails poking up from the floor here and there, but otherwise, it was board after board of dull gray-brown, a hopeless house that time and everyone had forgotten, except for Elena. She'd noticed something in this. Lily knew her own fears—that this house was a nightmare, that Elena would lose years and all her money to its hunger—but she also knew what Elena wanted to hear and couldn't help but give it to her. "I think you are going to turn this house into something wonderful. If it were in anyone else's hands, it'd be a disaster. But you? You'll get this all done in like two weeks."

Elena laughed. "Stop. Really, what do you think?"

"Fine, four weeks. I was being nice, you caught me." Lily settled her head against Elena's part-soft-part-hard chest, a pattern they'd acted out a hundred times before. A dance that led nowhere, but a thrilling one nonetheless. The sound of Dicks yelling outside filtered through the window. The neighbors must have pushed back, and now Dicks was at war. Lily found herself picturing the finished house, the one which she believed would never arrive, often during the next few weeks. An older Elena, a little wrinkled but still sturdy and vital, stood at the center of her imagination. Much too old for only a few years' worth of work, if Elena actually stuck to it. But that was the Elena that Lily saw, smile lines jumping from her eyes as she invited guests into a completely mirrored foyer, which led into a sensory room and so on and so forth as each room offered new art and new excitement. And she pictured herself there, not kissing or holding hands with Elena, but simply sharing a knowing glance across the party. Only those who were there at the beginning of the endless project can know the significance of its completion.

# ZOE

There were people in Zoe's kitchen. Not admirers, or dates, or even anyone she'd invited. How was she supposed to prepare chips and guacamole with a full-blown tableau in the middle of the room? Lily and her friend Steph—Zoe's least favorite of all of Lily's friends, and not just because she was in a cult—were nude and intertwined in some kind of balletic pose, while Elena painted them. Zoe stomped through the room and got her chips, but forgot the guacamole, her concentration ruined by the spectacle. On the way back, she circled behind the canvas.

"Why are you doing this in here? The light's terrible."

"It's fine," Elena said, dabbing a bit of paint to create a highlight on Lily's ribs.

Zoe sneered. What did she know about lighting anyway? Every mediocre painter thinks they're a genius about light because they can put some shine on an apple. Actresses, they lived and died by light. Specific colors and qualities of light made Zoe look like a goddess, but others made her look like a troll. One time she'd been on set, and when she saw a light hoisted overhead, she'd walked off. And sure enough, in the hard lighting coming from the side window, Lily's brow ridge was just a little too visible. A shame that Elena didn't feel like listening. She'd regret it.

"It's my kitchen too," Zoe said.

Lily offered a fake, closed-lip smile. She was pretending to the others that she was being nice, but wanted Zoe to know that she wasn't. Lily said, "No one said you had to leave."

"I know." She crunched her chips as loud as she could.

Without moving her head away from its position nuzzled into Lily's chest, Steph said, "How's it going, Zo? You still doing those commercials?"

"I haven't done commercials in years. And—" That's when she caught a tiny smirk on Steph's face. She was making fun of Zoe. Caught too late, but Steph probably expected her not to notice it at all. One little expression; a secret between you and yourself. But only an idiot could hope to pull that off in front of Zoe, who had conquered every human emotion and could pull them from her breast at a moment's notice. "How's the cult? Daddy save the world yet?"

"Zoe, what the fuck?" Elena gestured at Zoe with her brush, as if it was an extension of her hand. Such was the nature of being an artist; one's tools became as familiar as hands or feet. "Not cool."

"It's my kitchen." The moment called for taking a big bite out of a juicy apple. A dramatic way to flaunt her nonchalance. She crunched one of her chips as hard as she could, but it didn't achieve anything.

Steph said, "No worries. We don't call it a cult, but we know how some people see us. Jesus had a cult at first too." Steph embraced Lily a little tighter, who stiffened her posture in response. Subtle movements, maybe unconscious. Either way, Lily looked uncomfortable. Only Zoe could follow the lines of Lily's body right to her mind, her heart, her soul. Like looking at the map of a city you've lived in all your life. Steph continued. "And it's all going according to schedule. The Divine Plan happens right on time, and before long, Daddy's left hand will burn with righteous fire and the Clenched Fist of God will scorch a path from coast to coast."

"When you say Daddy, do you mean your dad or Jesus or God?" Lily asked.

"This time I mean my dad. But I do mean all kinds of people sometimes." Steph stuck her tongue out at Lily.

Playful flirtation, and this time, Lily smiled. A certain amount of comfort with each other was a prerequisite for the way their bodies coiled around each other, flesh upon flesh.

"Stay still. Keep your head up." Elena brushed some darker paint beneath Lily's chin.

"That'll give her man chin. Don't do that. She doesn't have one." Zoe couldn't help herself. Annoyed as she was, misrepresenting Lily's delicate, feminine features—which she'd gotten without surgery, the bitch—felt like a travesty to Zoe.

"It'll look great when I'm done."

Zoe imagined this conversation would hardly be different if the two of them had fucked once. A night of perfect sex that led to resentment and yearning tangled up into a burning animosity stretched taut between them in every interaction. Zoe imagined what it was like to fuck everyone she met. Not only out of curiosity. Everyone who met her imagined the same, so imagining it in return was a defensive maneuver. That way they remained on equal ground, with mirrored speculations echoing in their minds.

Elena.

The two of them would sloppily make out in the bathroom of a coffee shop, their bold red and purple lipsticks melding into a magenta smear all over their faces. Elena, using her stout legs and low center of gravity, would easily hoist Zoe up onto the bathroom sink. As Elena tugged Zoe's jeans down, Zoe would glance in the mirror: her eyeliner wing would be perfectly sharp and her two-toned eyeshadow would be blended into a smooth gradient. In the heat of the moment, Elena wouldn't think about hygiene and would toss Zoe's jeans on the floor instead of hanging them on the hook. Zoe's objection to that treatment of her designer jeans would lose its way as Elena lowered her mouth between Zoe's legs. The two of them would stop abruptly when someone banged on the door. Elena would smile sheepishly at the three people waiting in line, while Zoe would focus on swinging her hips even more than usual. No matter how impatient those people were, they'd suddenly know why it had happened.

Steph. She was a compulsive top. Everyone knew about her live-in subs. She'd scrounge around Zoe's bedroom and find a couple of flimsy scarves to tie Zoe's wrists to the bed. With only a little effort, Zoe would be able to free herself, but she wouldn't do it. When Steph drew her lips close to Zoe's and asked, "Are you a good girl?" Zoe would melt and say yes yes yes until Steph affixed the strap-on, wearing it like a weapon. Soon it would be down her throat and Zoe would bite down to create some friction and give Steph a thrill. Yes, she was good. Zoe would be so, so good.

Lily. It always changed. At a certain point there was no use speculating. Despite some close calls, it had never happened and it never would.

Zoe decided that she didn't care about the painting. If Lily had wanted Zoe to advocate for her, she would've shown some appreciation. Instead, she crunched her chips whenever Elena's brush touched the canvas and laughed to herself at every flinch. One day art historians might comment on the Zoe effect: one girl's ability to shift brushstrokes to the left or right by a tiny bit, transforming the painting. Or they would, if this painting was destined for a museum instead of hanging unsold in the city's third-worst coffee shop.

When Elena flinched and accidentally globbed some white directly over Lily's face, Zoe let a little bit of that internal laughter escape. Elena slammed her paintbrush down on the palette, splattering droplets of paint. The three of them packed up and soon Zoe had full control of her kitchen once again, but noticed too late that a speck of white had leapt onto her sweater—a stain she could do nothing about, which would leave its mark indefinitely.

# LILY

Sometimes Lily received very urgent texts from her friends asking her to come hang out, and she felt compelled to join them. One night, such a text came from Steph, begging her to go to Dicks's house because "Adam is boring the shit out of me."

Every time Lily entered Dicks's house, it looked different. This time, it was organized around one long hallway with about fifteen rooms branching off. Though the second and third floors were still visible from the outside—lights shone and silhouettes danced in the windows—the stairs were gone. A light shone down past the faded orange walls, a flicker of people animated in conversation. There were fifteen doors along her path to the end, most of them left open, and Dicks could be in any of them.

She peeked her head into the first one on the left. The floor was empty except for a straw mat in the center. Deep grooves lined the off-white walls, like the scratchings of an enormous claw. Within those gashes, gemstones of all colors twinkled under the bare, flickering lightbulb above. Lily spun herself around and around and the colors overtook the white and became a rainbow whirl around her. But she couldn't sustain the spin. The colors lurched back and forth around her dizzy eyes, and when she tried to sit down on the straw mat to regain her composure, she missed and smacked her tailbone against the wood.

In the next room, one person sat on the shoulders of someone who sat on yet another person's shoulders. They walked around the room, teetering and tottering as the middle one read a book and the top one reached down to scatter flakes into a vivid blue aquarium. Lily couldn't see any fish, but there had to be some. Why else would it be there? The person on bottom noticed Lily was there and step-turned around over the protests of the other two, but they stopped as soon as they saw Lily too. "Hi! Can you help us? We're very tired and want to go to bed, but the light switch is on the ceiling and we can't reach. Will you climb up?"

"Sure."

Their myriad hands gathered her up onto themselves. She'd expected a desperate bid to maintain balance as she ascended, but it felt just like climbing a tree. What were branches but arms? What was bark but skin? Once she got to the top and swung her legs over the shoulders of the person there, he clamped his hands down on her thighs and the ceiling grew taller until the light switch was just out of her reach.

"We've got you! Now you're stuck here with us forever, and the next passerby we lure in will sit on your shoulders. You fool! You oaf!"

The three of them cackled in unison. Lily hoped that reaching the light switch would change their minds, or at least help her escape, but when she lunged toward the switch, it disrupted their balance and all four fell toward the hardwood. Lily braced herself for impact. The hard floor was a better fate than a lifetime in their clutches, at least. But the ground gave as she hit it, and bounced her up like a springy mattress. Lily was unbroken and not in any pain.

The former members of the human stack were all laughing, joined in a pile of interlocked arms and legs grasping each other. "You fell for it! Why would we want to trap someone here? The three of us would never get to fuck if you were here all the time."

As she left, they asked her not to tell Dicks about their prank, but Lily reserved the option to tattle if she felt angry later. At the moment, she was annoyed and a little amused and certain to be more careful when peeking into the rooms. Dicks was generous with their space, but they weren't as careful as they should be about keeping the wrong people out. It was common knowledge: you'd meet the best people in Pittsburgh at Dicks's house, but the worst too. So many people passed through Pittsburgh as a shortcut to another city, or as a place to gather themselves before taking advantage of the limitless options beyond its borders. Not all of those people were good, or kind, but Dicks let them in anyway. Who found a place there wasn't up to Dicks; it was up to the house itself, they claimed. Whether or not this was a cop out was the subject of a debate that Dicks refused to participate in.

The next doorway was a trick mirror, which somehow reflected the hallway but not her. Would it feel like a regular mirror? Would it reveal its secret under pressure? Lily touched the mirror. A tentative finger went through without the slightest resistance, and then her hand. The barrier shimmered around her wrist, very far from giving up any of its secrets. Her earlier lesson about caution already forgotten, she stuck her face through. Her hand was safe beneath her, and the hallway looked the same in both directions. At the other end, a tangle of glowing white ribbons in the shape of a person bent through a doorway. Lily stuck her whole arm through and the tangle gained a new appendage. It waved when she did. But when she stepped all the way through, she was still wearing a red skater dress. Stylish, but it didn't glow, and neither did her legs.

Branching off right before the kitchen, a lavender room housed the most beautiful woman Lily had ever seen. Standing upright, Calamity was probably about six feet tall, but it was hard to tell because she was usually hunched over the table. Waves shone as they ran through Calamity's black hair, rippling every time she crunched another handful of blue pills into her mouth. Lily could smell femininity in the air, in the powder which escaped Calamity's ever-occupied jaw. Men and the masculinely inclined avoided Calamity's den, fearful of the rumor that the estradiol dust had a powerful feminizing effect.

Maybe so. Maybe that's what brought trans girl after trans girl to the room, to offer a few pills onto Calamity's pile in exchange for the possibility of a blessing. Here gorged the hungry goddess of transfemininity, and with her favor, a lucky girl's lips could swell into an alluring pout and her eyes could shift into a perfect almond.

Lily's offering, five expired pills, was less a prayer and more a courtesy. Though Calamity's perfect skin, which shone tight over high cheekbones, and her honey-brown eyes gave her an otherworldy beauty, Lily hadn't come seeking a goddess. She took a seat at the table, where the pile rose above her eye level.

Calamity nodded, acknowledging Lily, as she shoveled another handful of pills into her mouth, some halves tumbling to the ground. The two of them exchanged no words, but maintained a flicker of eye contact until a couple more girls came in. Each of them spilled a full bottle onto the pile, muttering about how they'd switched to injections. As if Calamity ever worried that her pile came from deprivation. One look at her, delicate curves on top of a pair of powerful legs that strained at her skinny jeans, provided all the justification for her appetite that anyone would ever need. Not that Calamity ever asked to be justified.

After some perfunctory conversation—Calamity gestured through her half—the girls shifted attention to themselves, each complimenting the other on how suddenly a shape was rounder or skin softer. Calamity rolled her eyes, pupils tracing a perfect circle, at Lily, who didn't know how to return the gesture. She smiled. That seemed to be sufficient.

More came and went. A beautiful femboy in a luxurious gown which trailed far behind his feet asked if she'd like to go on a date, but she waved, gesturing to her pile. One young woman, twenty years old and clearly at the beginning of her transition, kneeled in prayer, though she couldn't yet spare pills of her own to offer. Calamity smiled and caressed the girl's hair, who leapt up and took a selfie and wailed in overwhelmed happiness that her hairline was fixed. Lily saw no change, but congratulated her anyway. Calamity took a bow, the swing of her back and arm more graceful than the movement of any ballerina, her smile certainly capable of launching more than a thousand ships.

When Lily got up to leave after half an hour, Calamity gestured for her to come over. She funneled two scoops of pills into her own mouth and, once they were ground up into powder, kissed Lily on the forehead.

But Lily didn't leave that room transformed. She felt a light tingle, and nothing more. As she was, she remained.

Walking onward, she got to the kitchen. Dicks shoved a spoonful of red sauce into her mouth as soon as she entered. Their dog, Roxy, trotted up to Lily, pressed her flank right against Lily's knee and scratched at her skin with rough fur. Beneath little brown eyebrows situated amongst black fur, Roxy's eyes shone with adoration. She deserved nothing less than all the love Lily could offer, so she scratched Roxy's back and the dog tapped her back feet in an appreciative dance. Dicks said, "How's it taste? I'm after a vegan sauce that isn't all fucked up."

Savory, tomato, a nostalgic flavor that needed a bit more salt, but Lily didn't think she could back that up with anything solid. "Saucy."

"Not gonna be helpful? Give me my sauce back." Lily spit it back onto the spoon, and Dicks flicked the sauce into the trash can. "There's cookie dough coming later. You're not cut off, but you're on thin ice."

"No more fooling. Loud and clear." Lily refrained from a mock salute, even though it'd be funny. The cookie dough would probably be incredible, and she never gambled if she couldn't afford to lose. "Are Steph and Adam here?"

"Out back. Get to Steph. Get in her ear. Get her to stop." Dicks stirred the saucepan.

"What's she doing?"

"Backyard." Dicks shook their head and returned to cooking.

Lily stepped out the back door with Roxy close behind, and welcomed the cool air after the hot kitchen. Sitting up on the porch, a cigarette in each hand, Steph laughed and laughed. "Daddy's got enough guns to fight off the Colorado National Guard by now." She glanced away from Adam, whose year-round sandals were finally seasonal, and revealed the whites of her big eyes. "And that's not even accounting for divine protection. You know how many bullets God can stop?"

"So many that he couldn't even count them?" Adam thought he was being clever. It was in the little smile of his. He and Lily had gone on a date a few years ago, before either of them had really settled into their personalities. Back then, Lily still talked like the internet, and Adam started half of his sentences by clarifying that he was, in fact, a male lesbian. Now Lily put down the phone more often than she picked it up, and Adam had gotten invested in reclaiming the poetic roots of masculinity or whatever it was. Lily didn't talk to him that often, as expected after a date just mediocre enough to preclude a second. Roxy ambled over to lick his face, but he gently pushed her head away.

"You got it just right," Steph said. "And what's more, he could count them."

"Oh, hey Lily." Adam's smile faded into awkwardness. It was unclear how he survived in a community where everyone had been on a date with everybody and their least favorite ex. Maybe he didn't go on that many dates.

"Hi, Adam. Steph." Lily tried to borrow some of Dicks's sternness from earlier, but it couldn't stretch far enough to cover her uncertainty.

"What?" Two cigarettes dangled from Steph's lips, and her hands braced her as she leaned back over the railing. The light from the kitchen didn't extend far enough now that the door was closed, so she was illuminated only by those two cherries and the light of a thousand stars to the east, where Pittsburgh opened up into the Midwest. To the west, not a single star could yell over L.A.'s light pollution. Above, the clouds allowed only a single one to peek through.

Looking at Steph beneath the twice-split sky, it was easy to believe she was the daughter of god's chosen warrior. But the moment faded, as it always did, and once again, Lily saw her as the daughter of some shithead out west and east and north, more attached to his guns than to reality.

"Dicks says you gotta stop."

"Stop what, exactly?"

"Whatever it is, you gotta stop. I'm just the messenger. So, you know, don't shoot."

Steph pointed a finger-gun to Lily's head, still leaning precariously over the railing guarding everyone from the dirt and rocks ten feet below. If Lily pushed Steph over, something would save her. Maybe it would be god, maybe fate, maybe luck. But at worst, she'd brush some dirt off her pants and yell at Lily. No worse injury felt possible. Not that Lily would ever push her. Intrusive thoughts come and go, but it was a pleasant change of pace to have one met with the knowledge that no harm would come.

"Then just tell them I stopped."

"Did you?"

Steph interlaced her fingers on Lily's shoulder and leaned close, smiling so wide that Lily could see her gums. "You tell me."

"I don't know."

"Keep up and we'll find out. I'm proposing a heist. We break into David Bowie's house, shoot him in the head, and get the Jayne County performance that he ripped off for *Diamond Dogs* out of the vault." Steph turned her finger gun toward the wall, where an imaginary Bowie could plausibly be, and fired. She whispered "pow" under her breath, so quiet that it must have been meant only for her. Lily didn't know much about guns, but she saw the confidence in Steph's arms as she did it. How many guns had she fired? Had any of those bullets connected?

Adam said, "Bowie's dead already. That's what *Blackstar* was about."

"Rad, even easier. No one left is gonna care all that much."

"You'd have shot Bowie?"

"Right in the lightning bolt. You know the old recipe for omelettes, don't you?"

That was Steph not stopping, but Dicks could handle that. The most Lily could do was help move the subject along. "Hey, have either of you heard about Zoe's new movie?"

Adam poked his head up at Zoe's name like a puppy. Roxy burrowed her head between his arm and side and rested her head on his lap, which he permitted. "Yeah! With Sage Almstead, right? That's gonna be so good. She's gonna be famous famous."

"I bet you can't wait to be a movie star's best friend," Steph said as she picked up a beer can, squinted at it, shook it, and set it down after finding ash on the rim. Then she moved on to another, repeating the process until she'd eliminated all of the cans as unsuitable.

"I don't know. Things have been weird lately. Tense."

"Yeah, I was in that kitchen. I thought it might be something between her and Elena, rival claims to the artist's insight or something like that. But maybe it was you."

"Maybe it was her." Lily said, but she regretted it as soon as it left her mouth. It felt like a betrayal of all those years when it felt like it was her and Zoe, together against the world. Was Lily just becoming part of the world, leaving Zoe on her own?

Adam said, "I don't know what happened. I wasn't there. I mean, you two know that. You were there. But have you considered maybe, just maybe, that it's just stress from being an actress? Like I know it's hard work, long hours, huge career implications. That could be it."

"Not a chance. It's personal. I just didn't know who it was personal between. What you need is a special tincture. Daddy makes them. It'll get her to tell the truth without fear or resentment, even if she doesn't know it."

"No, no tinctures. It's fine. She was probably just having a bad day." Lily snatched one of Steph's cigarettes and took a drag. Maybe it was unfair to place it all on her. Lily must have contributed in some way, but she couldn't figure out how. So instead of confessing her own sins, she let the conversation pass on to Adam's succulents and how the true masculinity is one that cultivates.

For an hour, Lily dangled her feet off the deck and smoked cigarette after cigarette until her throat scratched itself raw begging her to stop, and Roxy had to go inside after barking too insistently at the darkness. The single star peeking through Pittsburgh's relentless clouds twinkled directly into Lily's eye as if it had some desperate message to communicate, with nothing but its own wavering light. Adam—deep in a rabbit hole about how masculinity is itself something that needs to be cultivated—stopped talking, smoothed his hair, and assumed a cool pose leaning on the railing with his elbow, shoulder nudged against the wall. Only one person could get into his head like that. When Lily peered back, yet-unlit and lung-undesired cigarette dangling from her mouth, she confirmed her suspicion: Zoe was in the kitchen, teasing Dicks by threatening to dip one of her fingers into their sauce. Dicks bore the antagonism gracefully, swiveling their body and moving the pot out of Zoe's reach, laughing the whole time. Lily couldn't tell whether Zoe wanted the sauce, or just thought flirting a bit with the host was polite. Either way, it came to an end, and Zoe emerged from the back door.

"How the hell did you smoke up the outdoors? It's like a cigar bar out here."

Adam laughed a little too loud, and Zoe started, but folded her arms back into the aloof-yet-inviting expression that Lily had watched her practice for years. Zoe crouched on the deck and laid down a little towel from her purse, then sat next to Lily. That placement, rather than next to her admirer or Steph, felt like an admission of something. Needfulness? Regret? Or nothing. It could be that Zoe just wanted to pretend that nothing was wrong in front of people she knew.

"Did any of you meet that Calamity girl? What's her deal? Is she...?" Zoe asked.

"She's trans," Steph said.

"Sort of." Lily felt the need to correct, despite the fact that Steph wasn't wrong. "She's not really a trans girl, but she's transfeminine. Transfemininity incarnated. I think. It's kind of hard to figure it out."

"No wonder she's so hot. Please tell me she's had work done." Zoe stared in the direction of Calamity's room, drawn to it as sure as Lily and every one of their sisters inevitably were. "With a really good surgeon or something."

"I doubt it. I think she's always been in that room, housing pills," Steph said.

"Wait, who are we talking about?" Adam asked.

"Calamity. The girl standing at the table with all the pills on it."

"What?" He laughed. "You're joking, right?"

"Just outside the kitchen, dude. Maybe you can't see her because of the whole masc thing," Steph said.

"No, men can see her. I saw a femboy come in, but maybe that still counts. How could you see her, then?" Lily said to Steph. "She's definitely here for trans girls, but you're not..."

"Suck enough girls off and you get a kick from the estrogen runoff," Zoe said. "The chaser's ascendance."

"Fuck off. I'm not a chaser."

"Yeah, guess you catch them too often for that." Zoe dug a suggestive elbow deep enough into Lily's side that she gasped for air.

"Zoe, stop it."

In an instant, Zoe's smile vanished and her eyes sunk into furious pits deep in her skull. "I'm just joking. I'm allowed to joke."

Steph said, "I wasn't laughing." Not helpful, but she'd borne the brunt of Zoe's jokes, so Lily couldn't expect her to be of much use.

Adam said, "Let's all just take a breath, remember we enjoy each other's company, and—"

"I'm trying to enjoy myself. But if I'm gonna get policed, I might as well go." Zoe stood up in one smooth motion, balletic in her refusal to admit to shifting and bearing weight. "Unless you want me to stay, Lily." Zoe's smile held in her eyes, until those eyes met Lily's. Then they became cold, reserved only for the unknown dead, a gaze for when you needed to see a person only as uninteresting meat. Eyes which Lily couldn't see, couldn't bear to be seen by, couldn't tell a lie to, and, ultimately, couldn't hide the truth from. "I see," Zoe said, after Lily cringed away.

"Well, I want you to stay," Adam said. "Let's work this out."

"No. I know when I'm not wanted." Zoe slammed the door into the house behind her. Dicks admonished her; she flipped them off, and left the kitchen even faster. The three remaining on the deck tried to resume some conversation, but after a half hour of false starts, Lily decided to leave.

When she got home, she was too tired to find Zoe and attempt to mend whatever had broken, yet again, earlier. All she could do was flop into bed. The light in the domed fixture flickered above her head, casting the off-white walls into intermittent darkness. One moment, the few framed pieces of art she had up were visible; the next, they were gone. She wondered if she'd be able to see them in the last moment before she went to sleep, but when the time came, she wasn't paying attention anymore.

# ZOE

The mall. Zoe was at the mall. Not since she was a teenage girl—she paused and dared her subconscious to correct her, but it wisely stayed silent—had she been so excited to be at the mall. She had bought a navy blue pair of straight-leg silk pants with ties at the bottom that she'd been eyeing for quite some time, but this had expanded into a whole spree. Some of the money from the movie had come through and the entire world felt like it had a price tag on it. Any item, only one big cartoon dollar sign. And she had so many cartoon dollars now. As she walked by the food court, the smell of buttery soft pretzels grabbed her. When she was a teenager, she had been able to eat whatever she wanted, whenever. A metabolism that had fueled endless growth upward, combined with a world which had few expectations of her body, and a mind which hadn't recognize the world's legitimacy, had allowed for a feast without limits. These days, she could barely look at food without inviting that tiny pouch of fat right below her belly button to come stay for a while.

But she was in a good mood. But it'd take work to undo the damage. But she was celebrating. As she wavered back and forth over the decision, the line in front of her dwindled and, before she knew it, the pretzel was in her hand. However it got there, throwing it out would be a waste. Zoe took a bite. As the butter suffused her taste buds, her mouth sprung to life like a dying plant after long-awaited rainfall. She stuffed another bite into her mouth and another until there was barely room for her teeth to operate amidst the dense bread.

"Oh my god! Are you Zoe Berger?"

Zoe huddled and chewed and chewed until just

enough of the pretzel had been processed to avoid any squirrel-cheek effect. Then she rose to her full bearing, nodded, and smiled with her eyes while pointing dramatically at her still-working mouth. Without lipstick or eye makeup, it was a wonder anyone could recognize her. Sure, she had almost-perfect skin—only a single hyper-pigmented spot from the early days of laser haunted her—but that didn't stand out on its own.

"I loved *Drama Dolls*. You were so good in it! Was it based on your real lives?"

This girl was six-foot-two and had the presence of an overgrown twelve-year-old. The braces didn't help, but some dolls never bothered getting their teeth fixed before transition. Why bother decorating a home you don't want to live in? She'd certainly made up for lost time, decking herself out in the finest that Hot Topic had to offer.

Though Zoe was hoping to reach a better class of fan with the release of the movie, girls like this would always be drawn to her. In beauty, in fashion, in the way she navigated the world. Freshly-out girls harbored certain illusions. I can be anyone; I can make a fresh start; I can be like her. None of these were true. Zoe'd turned out the way she had as a result of hard work, but also because beneath her boy-face had rested perfect bone structure and the mind of an acting genius. This girl surely had neither. Few are born to be the subjects of adulation, and many were destined to supply it. So this girl didn't deserve Zoe's cruelty or indifference. She was in her proper role, watching from the ground as Zoe climbed to attain her own correct position at the top of the world.

"No, we were too busy acting to live like that. Can you imagine? Exhausting."

"Of course. Duh. Anyway, I'm such a big fan, can I take a selfie with you?"

Of all days, this had to happen when Zoe didn't

have any makeup on. Usually she did a full face before going anywhere, but it hadn't felt necessary for going to the mall. Still, she nodded assent and bent her knees to make herself even smaller as the girl embraced her and held up her phone. A few clicks later, they reviewed the pictures.

The girl's joy overflowed her smile into rosy cheeks and crinkled eyes, while Zoe's perfect bone structure was all too evident; none of Zoe's flesh made as much of an impression as her skull lurking just below the skin. In each picture, she looked like a demon emerging from the melting body of the possessed, ready to discard dangling skin and animate her bones with fire.

"Oh, these are lovely. Do you mind if I post one?"

Zoe trembled. The dark circles under her eyes extended deep past the skin, past the eyes, into a void which ended fair beyond the back of her skull, beyond any sense of distance. But showing vulnerability to this girl so far beneath her would be just as bad as letting the picture escape onto this girl's tiny Instagram account. No way she had more than 500 followers.

"Fine with me, but I don't know if you should."

"Oh?"

"You're pretty new, right?"

"I guess. It's been six months. How could you tell?"

The short pleated skirt.

"It's just a sense. You'll get it too. You look great for where you're at. But do you see how this pose catches your jawline?"

"Yeah..."

"And here, at the brow. Again, you look great. I'm looking at you right now: six months, you're an angel. Learning your angles is a process, and it gets easier the longer you're on hormones."

The girl stared at the photos. With just a step, Zoe could disappear into the current of shoppers behind her.

Instead she squeezed the girl's shoulder. This was a kind of tough love, but someone had to give it to her.

"It's okay. The toughest part is the beginning. It gets so much easier. You can't imagine what a mess I looked like when I was six months in." Zoe brushed a fried lock of hair behind her ear. Why had she come out in public looking like this?

"Could we try some more pictures?"

"I'd love to, but I really have to run. Busy schedule, you know. But here—" Zoe handed over a business card. "—is my manager's information. I'd love to meet up with you again sometime and make it up to you. Take care of yourself."

With tears gathering in her eyes and the business card gripped loosely between her index finger and thumb, the girl ambled away. In the long run, she'd thank Zoe, who fished her sunglasses out of her purse and searched for the exit. For once, the fewer people who saw her face, the better.

# LILY

Most days when Lily was home alone, she spent her time blasting music or watching the hyper violent horror movies that Zoe hated seeing even a glimpse of. One movie, it's that the lighting is abysmal. Another, the direction makes no sense. Usually, it was that the actresses were terrible, that horror was a refuge for women who could scream but couldn't achieve true art. After a while, Lily gave up on trying to watch them while Zoe was around.

That day, Lily had to clean. It had felt kind of tense in the house lately, so Lily wanted to give Zoe some space, which meant she couldn't just run the vacuum through the entire house. The kitchen still loomed with tomato sauce encrusted in spots on the counter, dishes piled in the sink, trash rose higher than it had any right to go. Back when they had talked about moving in together, the two of them had discussed a chore wheel. Keeping everything equal because they, no matter what, were equal. That was before Zoe had gotten the *Drama Dolls* role.

When they had met, Lily was a year on hormones and just starting to come out of her shell. Her hair had hit chin length, which was life-changing. Zoe never talked about how long she'd been out, what she'd been up to before. All Lily knew at the time was that Zoe was gorgeous, and when the two of them ended up engrossed in conversation, Lily felt like the luckiest girl in the bar. The two bonded over a love of basketball. Both of them had played at one point, but neither pursued it anymore. Lily because she didn't feel comfortable on a court with men or women anymore. Zoe for reasons unknown. Maybe a fear of an elbow coming for her perfect nose. Lily's initial hopes to hook up with Zoe got dashed when Zoe said, "I'm straight..." and then muddied when she waved her hand and said, "except..." but didn't follow it up with anything. The night ended in a smear of intoxication, and Lily didn't know where she stood the next morning until she saw a text message from Zoe—which meant she'd gotten Zoe's number—and a message from three a.m. which read "we're getting coffee at 11 tomorrow bestie! meet me at the place that's like way too Italian."

Despite her pounding hangover, Lily showed up at Cafe D'Annunzio. Their friendship was forged over coffee and their mutual love of movies (that was when Lily found out that Zoe was a struggling actress). Zoe championed the French New Wave, while Lily advocated for the Japanese New Wave as a more interesting set of movies which adapted the techniques of the French to better purposes. Zoe lent Lily her vape to hit in the bathroom to blunt her hangover, and after coffee, Lily gave Zoe a cigarette. Wisps of their respective smoke intermingled and, in their joint haze, some bond was forged. From then on, the two of them never went a week without seeing each other.

Lily consoled Zoe after a couple of boyfriends amounted to nothing, and after she ditched one girlfriend, and Zoe offered Lily fashion and makeup advice, and even though their personal styles diverged as Lily became more of a visible dyke, many of the principles Zoe had taught her remained solid. It was a friendship to keep at the center of one's life, as each understood the other's whims and moods like a farmer understands the changing weather.

The decision to move in together was like a single domino falling in a line of many. They saw each other most days; Lily's roommates were way too dirty for her, and Zoe couldn't really afford to keep living alone. That was when they discussed the chore wheel, the ways that each could avoid disturbing the other. Zoe had smoked at the time and gave the okay to smoking indoors. As it was, they were in constant harmony. Changing the setting wouldn't matter much.

The two of them were lying on the couch, watching some Czech movie that Zoe had been begging Lily to watch for months, when a phone call interrupted them. Zoe had been cast in *Drama Dolls*. They wouldn't finish the movie. Instead, they went to the state liquor store and got three bottles of champagne and spent the night in a bubbly frenzy. Once those bottles were empty and they'd spent what screams of excitement their throats could afford, the two lay on the couch with Zoe's arm wrapped around Lily. Zoe said, "I love you, Lil," and their faces were close enough that a kiss might have happened. But it didn't. Those grazes with romance never went anywhere because each of them treasured the stability of their friendship.

The *Drama Dolls* paycheck allowed Zoe to completely redecorate their apartment. A new suede couch, art all over the walls, new dishes to replace their chipped plates and glasses from Goodwill. When Lily expressed some nervousness over how much Zoe was spending on their shared house and how Lily couldn't possibly match it, Zoe had said that she treasured their life together, and that it was money well spent, without expectations attached. That night Lily fell asleep on the couch and felt as safe as she'd ever known.

But when Zoe became the breakout star, and *Drama Dolls* became a bigger hit than anticipated on the back of her sudden popularity, something changed. She held herself more aloof around Lily, and when they watched a movie together they were no longer able to discuss the merits of it as art because Zoe always talked about how one actress or the other wasn't "star material."

It was fine: things changed. People changed. Obviously, a burst of sudden fame would change Zoe's personality. That would happen to anyone. No doubt Lily, too, had changed over the course of their friendship. Now, Lily wiped down the counter, but felt the strength drain out of her body before the pile of dishes stacked on top of each other. Towers of bowls and plates with cups wedged beneath them teetered and threatened to clatter at the slightest touch. Old water pooled in secret crevices, and brown mush that used to be food clung to Lily's hands. Maybe Zoe would wipe the counter when she got back from set. Or not. It didn't matter. Lily was done cleaning for the day.

# ZOE

Every time they wrapped for the day, Zoe deflated a little. Her character was a troubled young widow trapped in a marriage with her dead husband's half-brother—a trans man who had stolen his brother's identity as soon as he had died, binding Zoe's character to him—and it took everything in Zoe's soul to bring it to life. All the grief, despair, longing, and even flickers of desire and love as her captor looked more and more like her husband by the day. In that last scene, she had been reacting silently to her co-star, Tevin, who went off on a rant about control, about how life was finally his to grab. None of it would work without Zoe. A journey played out on her face. Skepticism, fear, a momentary thrill, and finally annoyance all emerged in the subtlest ways. But the day came to an end, and the vitality in the emotions she summoned left her body. Muscles slackened, eyes glazed over, and life dimmed along with the lights that switched off one by one.

"Bravo! Incredible." Sage clapped their hands and a few other crew members rushed toward Zoe in congratulations. She prepared to wave them off with just enough modesty to ensure they continued, but they crowded around Tevin instead. Maybe it was a joke? Pranks were often a sign of affection, after all.

Tevin's monologue was a ham-handed masculine tirade, devoid of even the faintest bit of nuance. Not that it was a bad choice. It was just conventional. Everyone had seen it before and audiences wouldn't mind. But it wasn't the artful choice. That was Tevin all over, though: play it safe, take the easy way out. Or maybe he just lacked the vision. Some accident of charisma buoyed his career in ways that his talent couldn't.

Sage ambled toward Zoe and clapped a hand on the back of her shoulder. "It's such a thrill to get to work with one of the greats, isn't it?"

Zoe could easily walk away and return to her dressing room, where she could take a deep breath, chug a bit of wine, scream into a pillow, beg Nate to put one between her eyes and put her out of her misery, throw all of her clothes into a pile, burn all her clothes, re-do her makeup in an anti-facial recognition pattern and then tell the director she'd become concerned with the movie's operational security, or leak the script to the most gossipy journalist she knew. It wasn't a big movie by any means, but it'd generate some buzz and force changes. Instead, she rolled her head toward her shoulder, where Sage's manicured purple nails, with purple and green plaid accent nail, rested on her shoulder. Zoe daintily poked out her tongue and licked Sage's hand, who flinched and withdrew immediately.

"What the fuck?" Sage brushed their fingers off on their distressed gray jeans, but it didn't seem to bring them much relief.

"I think we're all lucky to be working on a film with two such incredible talents in the leading roles," Zoe said. "Too many of my productions relied solely on my gifts, and that's a burden they don't tell you about. I'm enjoying shouldering a more reasonable proportion of this film's hopes."

"What, too much pressure in those commercials?"

"Fuck off."

Tevin gave the crew a quick bow, and Sage laughed and clapped once more. "Well, no matter what you think your burden is, he's gonna be the star of this picture. Adjust accordingly."

"One more take." Zoe stamped her foot. That so much determination could amount to such a little clap on the floor surprised her. She was inescapably feminine, even when it didn't benefit her. "I don't care which scene. One more before we wrap up."

"Too late. Everything's shut down for the day."

"Tevin! One more?"

Tevin froze like a deer in the headlights, hands caught in the middle of an emphatic gesture he was using to explain to the crew how he had brought such a tiresome portrayal to life.

"Let's do one more. I'm still feeling it. I know you are."

He shook his head, but after a few seconds of Zoe waving him over relentlessly, he joined their conversation. Whether he'd chosen to become an actor before transition, or just because he suddenly found himself a short man, he certainly had the face for it. Green and gold eyes that could grasp a sudden intensity, a slender but well-defined jaw, and a nimble, expressive mouth. "I'm beat, Zoe. That scene... well, you know. You saw it up close."

"I wasn't the audience. Tevin. I had just as much going on as you did. Facially."

"Sure. It's a dance. You don't have to tell me. But let's call it before we get too tired to do all the steps." The lively bounce in his hands as he mimed a dance belied his supposed exhaustion. He just wanted to go out on top. Tevin Cioti, king for a day. A more gracious co-star than Zoe would have let him do it, but grace didn't build careers.

"I can get Nate out here to put everything back together. The crew can knock off for the day."

Sage said, "They're union. Your little man isn't touching their equipment."

"They don't have to know about it."

"Zoe," Tevin said, grasping one of her hands with both of his. "We put together an amazing scene today. That last take was perfect. Let's leave it there. We're not going to do any better." With that, he walked off to his dressing room. A conversation indulged and concluded on his royal whim.

Sage chuckled and gathered their things, and Tevin waved goodbye. On the way to her dressing room, Zoe fantasized about what the scene might have been if she had been allowed to do it. Her genius had been suppressed. Zoe sulked while Nate brushed her hair in the turned-low light of her makeup mirror.

# LILY

Grapefruit. Breathe in, breathe out. Other thoughts passed through her head, but they orbited around the grapefruit for a while and returned to space. Probably around two hundred grams. Around three and a half inches across. In, out. Often a host for fruit flies, but probably not this one. She ran a thumb over the rind, traversing the soft bumps and divots, losing her focus in the paths she could imagine between them. This object, firm but plump with juice, could become something entirely different. She had to believe it. Lily tried to believe that she held a cube of obsidian. Its corners and edges would be crisp straight lines, and it would shine in the light. But as she ran her hand over the object again, she couldn't transform the supple rind into unyielding stone. Without that, the tattoo gun would be useless to her.

"Here, watch me." Sveta plucked the grapefruit from her hand, and held it squished between two flat palms at the center of her chest. Sometimes Lily wondered if Sveta was a statue given life: all her resting poses hinted at the kind of majesty you see atop a podium, and she wondered if that was why shifting states came so easily to Sveta. "You feel the grapefruit. That's there. But when changing it, feel for the possibility. No way you'll feel the stone. But the possibility of stone? That you can feel, just as strong as the rind's texture." She snapped the tattoo gun up from where it hung on her belt loop and passed over the grapefruit with it.

It still looked like an ordinary grapefruit. Sveta handed it over to Lily. It was much heavier than two hundred grams. "Have a snack."

Lily dug her thumbs into the rind. As they passed through the rind and into the flesh, the fruit gave just like she'd expect it to. But as she rent the two halves from each other, shining black peaks and valleys sprung up before her. She poked at each point. They were sharp, and one of them drew a little blood when she pressed too hard.

"Now close your eyes and take a bite."

"No way. This is going to obliterate my teeth."

"Trust me. Close them."

Lily worked a shard of obsidian free from the rind and winced as she closed her mouth around it. But instead of chipping, her teeth sank in, and tart juice spilled into her mouth.

Sveta laughed as Lily's eyes sprung open. "If you listen to the fruit, feel all of the things that could be there, it becomes your choice what to make of it. That's the secret."

As Lily chewed on another shard, she wondered if she'd be able to sense that at some point. Even now, she could only see the object in her hand, where it was rock. In her mouth, it was grapefruit. Those properties were what it had, and she could not feel the potential for it to be anything else, no matter how much she reflected on the plain grapefruit it had been only moments before.

The bell on the door jingled, precluding any further attempts at contemplation. It was Zoe. Here, in her tattoo shop. Not hers enough for Lily to be able to kick Zoe out, but enough for her to be angry. Everywhere, lately, was Zoe's space. She could swish into any room. Why this one, where she knew Lily would be?

Zoe avoided Lily's eyes and made a beeline for Sveta. She asked if there was time for a consult, in that way she does to make it seem like she's doing you a favor by letting you help her.

Send her away, please please tell her you're busy, you're booked solid. Lie and keep her out just long enough for her vengeful blood to cool. Lily's clasped knuckles were bright white as she hoped. But to no avail.

"Sure, there's plenty of time. Take a seat."

Zoe sat on the wooden chair in the lobby. Her legs crossed, hands clasped on the top knee, back straight. Proper, respectful posture. Even now she was acting. "So this shop can do anything, right? I've heard some wild stuff."

"Whatever you want, we can do."

"Okay, so this might sound weird..."

"Listen to me. I once had a man come in and ask to be changed into a school of fish. Didn't even want any water. He gasped and flopped his way out. Don't worry about me. There are no surprises anymore."

"Someone's always thought of something weirder, right?" She laughed, gentle and melodic. Zoe was so charming when she wanted to be, but she wielded it like a weapon. "What I want is to have my butt transformed into a face, with a mouth instead of a hole. And... you know, I hadn't really figured out a particular face. But your assistant's face is perfect for it."

"Zoe! What the fuck?"

"You two know each other," Sveta said, tone of voice even. She placed both hands on Zoe's face and pulled her close. As she stared into Zoe's eyes, Sveta said, "No. What you requested is not what your body wants. Get out. Both of you. You come back tomorrow, you come back when you know what you want. Goodbye."

Zoe protested, but Lily knew better. Once Sveta was annoyed, everything that caused this annoyance was ejected from her surroundings. The bell rang as Lily exited. She trudged a few steps in the direction of home, but stopped and looked back as Zoe rumbled out of the tattoo parlor, screaming hatred back through the door. Once it was gone and only breath remained, Lily decided to walk back the other way. Past Zoe and her heaving chest, emptied of all invective and too tired to come up with more.

Lily chose silence in the moment they were nearest.

It wouldn't last. No, what came after would surely be as loud as anything she'd ever known. But all Zoe could muster as Lily passed was a sharp glare. Then she started to follow. Lily didn't know where she was going, but any location would include a ghost stalking her. So she travelled down the winding sidewalks and through crowded malls and dirt paths patted down by hundreds of thousands of steps before hers, framed by the dangling leaves too low to hope for sunlight so they drooped to her shoulders, reaching for touch, for warmth, the embrace of life for life. Through the foliage she burst out onto the place where the rivers met each other. One was water. The other was stone and earth that rolled towards its destination.

Tourists flooded into Pittsburgh for an efficient getaway: three locations for the price of one, or else a convenient way to hop from New England to the Midwest to L.A. Trains moved through Pittsburgh constantly, and the highways were always clogged with eighteen-wheelers and minivans.

On the water side, western Massachusetts. On the land side, Nebraska. When Lily closed one eye, she could see water continuing to flow, surrounded by the beautiful Massachusetts forest. On the other, the flat plains and a sky that felt like it stretched forever. Some of her friends said they could see both at once if they unfocused their eyes, but no matter how Lily tried, she couldn't do it. Whichever one she thought of last stretched out ahead of her. Lily turned away from the river and looked back at the city. Shimmering skyscrapers, illuminated by three different suns, reflecting light through prisms until all of downtown was enmeshed in rainbow. Some architects had seen a unique possibility. Soon, it would be a one-sun evening, then twilight, then another night with the uneven stars.

The way Zoe leaned on the fence next to her was

so posed. Back arched, ass all the way back and legs straight. Half the people passing by would look at her, rather than the landscape. Instead of enjoying the majesty of nature, they'd spend a few minutes gawking and forget why they even came.

"Why do you treat me the way you do?" Lily said. It wasn't what she'd hoped to have come out of her mouth. But the urge for diplomacy was gone. She just wanted to know what was happening to her friendship. To her life.

Zoe laughed, but even she wasn't a good enough actress to make it seem natural, rather than an attempt to assert dominance over the situation. "I'm just having fun. It's fun to mess with your friends."

"That's not what you're doing."

Zoe dropped her smile. As soon as the act was of no use to her, she was ready to throw it away. "Oh, you know exactly what I'm doing? With your incredible insight? You don't know anything."

"I know you've been really weird and mean to me for so long. And I'm sick of it. I want it to stop."

"That's the thing. That's it. You've hated me this whole time. You have to be the coolest girl, you have to be the most beloved person in the room, so you put me down. You poison people against me. You do it all the time," Zoe said.

"I don't want to hate you."

"No. You're not gonna crybaby your way out of this. You're not the victim here."

Lily didn't want this fight. She didn't want the momentum built up over so many other fights to crash into the two of them here. But once things started moving all Lily knew how to do was to watch until they crashed or skidded to a halt or continued forward forever and ever, far out of anyone's sight. She squatted close to the ground, pulled her hair back, and let some vomit pour from her mouth. Once the last spit of it cleared her lips, it pooled in front of her, taking the unmistakable shape of Zoe's face, who held her eye contact as her heels clacked toward the puddle, and broke it to look down. At first calm, a sneer took over Zoe's face, then a snarl.

"Is this how you see me?"

"I don't know."

"Fuck you. I am the greatest talent in the world. I'm a star. I don't need the friendship of Pittsburgh's worst tattoo artist."

"I guess not," Lily said. No urge to disagree summoned itself. No desire to soften the blow. So the two of them stood apart for a long minute, then the sound of Zoe's heels grew distant. After a while, Lily accepted that Zoe wasn't coming back. No one last things, no wait I'm sorrys. Nothing. She turned her attention back to the rivers, and through the tears, couldn't even see one of them.

# ZOE

There was no substitute for having a useful little boy like Nate around. Earlier that day, he'd gone and fetched all of the paint, wallpaper, and other materials. Zoe hadn't had to lift a finger as he unloaded his overfull Prius—all she'd had to do was point one at the wall to get him started. Scampering all over the house, he taped down the edges, laid out the drop cloths, and filled the room with paint fumes. It was an unsatisfying trade with the coats of primer, but once the lime green on the right of the brick fireplace went up, she spurred him on. As the paint dried, Nate affixed the crumpled bronze on the opposite side of the fireplace. This morning, quantity, not quality, was the goal. Lily would be waking up at any moment and there was still so much to do.

While Nate was just one man, he was the most determined man on earth in that moment. Countless times he'd pledged his life to Zoe, begging for the chance to die for her. Every time, she'd denied him. But sometimes she followed that denial with the truth: a symbolic death would do neither of them good compared to Nate working himself to death. And so sweat poured down his face and trickles of blood from nails and sharp edges wound their way down his fingers. Zoe could set off an air horn, and his focus wouldn't break, but if she so much as whispered a word, it would tunnel its way directly into his consciousness and he would drop everything for her. A goddess is nothing without devotion, and Nate's devotion proved that Zoe was nothing less than a goddess. Figuratively, of course. They lived in the real world, where only real people existed. Divinity came with too many strings attached, and this way, Zoe could get all the perks without the burdens.

There was some rustling upstairs. Either it was a rat scurrying through the ceiling—not impossible, given the mess in the kitchen—or Lily was awake. The two did share some qualities: both were tenacious and both scavenged for every possible morsel or advantage they could find. Perhaps society might benefit from the eradication of either, but that kind of speculation was over Zoe's head. The creaks down the staircase answered her question well enough. No rat tread so heavily. She whispered to Nate, "Hurry, hurry, sit down. This is good enough."

Nate collapsed onto the sofa and curled up like a little dog. Zoe imagined that the morning had been hard on him, but the fruits of his labor were worth it; she couldn't look anywhere in the room without the clash of colors stinging her eyes or the shifting textures giving her vertigo. When Lily turned the corner from the stairs, she staggered in place. Her expressionless face delighted Zoe. The surprise which had reduced her to nothing but a pair of eyes searching for comprehension would inevitably morph into disgust once it sunk in.

But Lily only laughed. "This looks like shit. You get this from the movie set?"

"No."

"Good. Your movie would be in trouble if it was using this stuff." Lily sat down next to Nate. After their fight, she'd decided to be conciliatory. Despite all her machinations to diminish Zoe, she didn't have the courage to even complain directly about the new decor. Everything was always intended to lure Zoe into direct aggression, but she was too smart for it. While she hadn't read *The Art of War* or whatever, she knew that, in their circles, the person who initiated direct conflict was usually the enemy. No matter what provoked the outburst. Unless Lily's plan was to pretend that nothing had happened until it was too late to even complain about the fight. Then Zoe would be playing right into her hands.

Lily's face didn't reveal anything about her intentions, and Zoe didn't want to risk doing nothing. So she kicked her feet up on the couch behind Lily and scooted her off the couch. "Sorry, my feet were already there. Sit somewhere else."

"What the hell?"

"They were there! You sat on my feet! Why else would Nate be curled up there?" In his sleep, Nate's legs twitched. He must have been dreaming about chasing down the makeup artist on set.

"Are you gaslighting me now? That's your big revenge?"

"*Gaslight*? Oh, I love that movie. It's my favorite Bergman."

"He didn't direct that movie. You're doing it on purpose."

"Uh, I meant Ingrid Bergman. Some random Swede makes a few boring movies, and now the last name belongs to him? Kinda misogynist there, Lil."

Lily rolled her eyes and stomped into the kitchen. The clamor of dishes in the sink told her that Lily was looking for a pan. Lily called out.

"Where's the eggs?"

"Ate them," Zoe said, just soft enough that Lily would miss it the first time and have to ask again.

"What?"

"Ate them."

"The cereal? The bagels?"

"Ate them."

"You did not eat that much."

"Oh, you're policing my diet now?"

Lily didn't respond. The frustrated scrape of a metal spatula against a non-stick pan that had been flaking for over a year took the place of her words. Every screech invaded the peace that Zoe needed before a shoot, but Lily never cared about that anyway. Ever since *Drama*

*Dolls*, Lily had been rooting for Zoe to fail because then she'd tumble right back down into the unremarkable abyss where they'd met, where Zoe had wasted too much time already.

They didn't exchange any more words before Zoe left to go to set. By the time she got back, the sun had long since gone down and all the vivacity she entered the day with had been wrung out upon the film. All she wanted was some silence and some late 2000s reality TV to be empty with her, but when she got back, Lily was watching anime. The crumpled bronze that Nate had hung up was on the floor, but none of the other alterations were disturbed.

"Did you think I wouldn't notice this?"

"It fell."

"Bullshit. Nate doesn't fuck up. You took it down."

Lily slowly raised the remote to the TV and paused it, like she was demonstrating how calm and collected she was, how unreasonable Zoe must be by comparison. But there was no one watching. Just the two of them in a house that had suddenly become much too small. Zoe said, "I buy the furniture, I buy the dishes, I buy beautiful art to put on our walls. And I should be able to put something up and know that it'll still be up when I came back."

"I didn't ask you to do any of that. And it fell down on its own."

"Put it back up."

Lily gawked at her, maybe not expecting that Zoe would stand up for herself so powerfully. She was so used to getting her way, to steamrolling over Zoe's kindness, that this refusal must have come as a shock. Maybe she'd thought herself the master manipulator, and had only now discovered that Zoe knew the whole time what she was trying to do and had let her. In the name of friendship.

"Put it back up now."

Without another word, Lily abandoned the living room and fled upstairs. Fine. Zoe wouldn't follow her, scream fury at her, nothing so immature. The couch was hers, and Nate could handle the bronze in the morning. Zoe settled in, each grain of suede like a little finger brushing against her, all holding her safe in their collective grasp. A throw pillow beneath the knees, one behind the neck, a couple to rest her arm on, and soon, Zoe achieved the total comfort she deserved. All that was left was to turn on the TV, but the remote had vanished from its spot on the coffee table.

Lily had stolen it, and even after Zoe rushed up the stairs and banged and screamed at her locked door, she didn't return it. All of Zoe's invective washed up against the white paint and subtle wood grain like the ocean against a cliffside until there was nothing left.

# LILY

When Lily invited Steph over, part of her design was to create a buffer between herself and Zoe. Not that the two of them ever avoided fighting amongst themselves, but another person in the house might force Zoe to put a lid on harassing her directly. Clearly unwilling to just let Lily have some of the house, Zoe sat silently next to the two of them on the couch, occasionally laughing at something on her phone so loudly that Lily and Steph had to interrupt their conversation. Steph was going on at length about one of her subs—he was developing an allergy to his collar, but Steph didn't know if removing it or making him live through it was more appropriate—when one of these peals of laughter stopped her. It went on for so long that both Lily and Steph had time to check their phones, and rather than resume the conversation, Steph picked up the remote and typed a URL into the browser, letter by letter.

"What's going on?" Lily asked.

"Daddy's finally getting started." Steph laughed and drummed her hands against her thighs so fast it mimicked the rhythm of gunfire. "I didn't even know today was the day. I told him I'd help."

A stocky man, with black hair ringing the sides of his bald head, was on camera. He had a mustache and a soul patch and both he and a black assault rifle rested against a concrete wall. With wet brown eyes staring into the camera so deeply that Lily felt like he could see her, judge her, find her wanting, he said, "They believe they have come to snuff out our great movement, but they are the spark, and we are the kindling; and soon, we will burn across this land with a fury it's never seen."

"Not what I expected the messiah to look like," Lily said.

"He used to have a full head of, like, gorgeous curly hair. When I was a kid he always complained about how much harder it was to recruit once it was gone. But he wouldn't get a toupee or hair plugs or anything. God had a plan for those follicles."

Zoe shushed her. "We gotta focus, this is so good."

The camera followed Steph's father as he rose above the concrete barrier and fired off a few shots before he ducked back down to avoid the return fire whizzing over his head. Panning past him, it showed dozens of others doing the same. When no one spoke on camera, the sounds of gunshots and distant shouting melded into a wave of noise. Lily said, "Who's he shooting at?"

"The police, I guess. They have this whole thing about Daddy selling drugs; it's total BS," Steph said. "But that doesn't matter anymore. Soon there will be no police; there will be no law. With the divine order in place, correct action will be as natural as breathing and require no more enforcement."

After firing a few more rounds, her father's face returned to the screen. "This is the day we've been waiting for. No decisions of man can stand in the face of God's will. He has chosen this day for us. These guns, for us. Our only duty is to act as His conduits. Each of these bullets is a lightning bolt coming down from God to smite His enemies. When this day is over, our war will have begun, and all of you, out there, will rise to become His instruments, and—one second." He rose again and fired a spray of bullets. One shot appeared to go right by his head and he ducked down, exhaling like a tire with a hole poked in it. "Show them the rest of our righteous army. Come on." The camera focused on the rest of the gunmen, immediately depicting one of them taking a bullet to the head and collapsing to the ground.

"Woah!" Zoe cackled and stamped her feet. "I need popcorn. Who wants popcorn?"

As she hustled out of the room, Lily observed Steph. Her eyes seemed distant, but her face didn't betray any worry: the confidence that being the daughter of the messiah wins you. So Lily didn't feel too bad for indulging her curiosity. "What do you think he's going to do next, if he gets out of this?"

"Oh, Daddy's been in worse jams than this. First up is the Righteous Burning of the West: every building over two stories or which holds a business will be reduced to ash. Then everyone will be given the choice to join the army willingly or be conscripted. Or get killed, I guess. Then once the western hemisphere has been cleansed in fire, it'll be built back up as a godly, just society. From there we will carry the war across the sea. Then once it's done, we'll all live in peace and happiness." She wiped away some tears that trickled down around the corners of her smile. "I'm so excited that it's finally happening."

Little puffs of concrete dust and shards filled the screen behind the cultists as police bullets embedded themselves in the wall of their compound. Steph's father stood once again, straight-backed, the high sun illuminating his face, set against the bright blue sky. Certainty poured from him every time he pulled the trigger, and with each shot, Lily could see him believe, believe, believe. The messiah, armed with the idea that no earthly power could harm him, weighed his divine strength against the mortal state. And his strength was found wanting as a bullet pierced his chest and he tumbled to the ground. The camera stayed on him as he lay motionless on the ground.

Steph lurched forward. "Daddy? Get up." A few seconds passed. "Come on Daddy, get up. You can do it, it's just a miracle. No big deal." The camera moved away from his body and focused on the other followers. "Daddy no please no, no no no. This isn't right." The news of their leader's death passed like a wave through them, and all of them sat down and looked toward the camera. Toward him. "One little miracle; you've done it before. God wants your heart to beat, so do it. Please Daddy, please." Some of them scattered, others laid down their arms, others fought even harder, and plenty from each group cried. Steph pressed a hand on the TV where her father's body failed to move.

Zoe flinched. "Bitch, don't get your oils on the screen."

Lily grabbed Zoe's arm and shook her head. Zoe snapped her wrist away from Lily's grip and wrinkled her face in disgust, while Steph kept talking at the motionless image of her father on the screen.

"Get up, Daddy. You can do it. God's chosen savior can come back from the dead. It's not even new. Do it. Do it!" But the camera fell to the ground, then boots stomped past it. Two officers gathered around her father's body. One fired a shot into his head.

"Just to make sure."

Steph wailed at the screen and laid her head on the floor, sobbing. The sound filled all the space around Lily. She couldn't think or breathe outside of Steph's grief, while Zoe rolled her eyes and tapped at her phone. Lily crouched down beside her and rubbed her back. "I'm... I'm so, so sorry. I can't even imagine..."

Lurching away, Steph pulled her face even with Lily's, tears still streaming down it. "That's what you think I'm sad about? My dad's mortal flesh? He was always supposed to die. But he was supposed to bring us paradise first, and those fucking pigs just stole it from us. From all of us, Lily. I could kill them."

When she said that, the tears stopped and her eyes grew wide. Lily couldn't quite read the emotion. Shock? It didn't seem like sadness anymore. Even less, as Steph broke into a gentle smile. Uncertain of how to interact with that feeling, Lily rubbed Steph's shoulder. Steph said, "I could kill them. I could do it. Maybe..."

"Uh. Do what?"

"Usher in paradise. Daddy said he'd received a vision that he would be the origin of the new world. And he's my origin."

"Well, maybe you should."

Steph pushed Lily aside. "Sorry. Zoe, are you interested in a well-paying role?"

"No."

"You could be the face of a new society. The glory of our divinely ordained world."

"Have one of your cultists call Nate."

"They're not cultists. They're holy warriors."

"I'm gonna call them cultists if they're cultists."

Lily said, "Maybe just drop that one today. It's not important what we call them right after Steph watched her father die."

"Look, you bitch, I don't care how smart you think—"

But before it could escalate, Steph grabbed both Zoe's and Lily's wrists. "Please do not engage in conflict right now. This is, by nature, a peaceful universe. And we must condone only what fighting is necessary to set our world into a state of peace, which will continue forever. You two are not oriented towards peace or divinity."

As Lily exhaled, Zoe snatched her wrist from Steph. "Don't try the cult gimmick on me. I'm not a follower." She left them behind, stomping upstairs.

Lily had to admit, Steph had defused that situation well. Which did not, in any way, make her a messiah. But she'd never seen Steph deescalate anything, and the suddenness of it all disarmed Lily. Maybe this peacefulness had been within Steph all along, waiting for its moment. Only a few minutes later, Steph said she had to go attend the next phase of the holy war. Meanwhile, Lily settled onto the couch and waited for Zoe to rampage down the stairs. But she didn't, and Lily lost herself in the video still streaming on the TV. Fifty bodies that would never move, lost in a violence Lily couldn't understand. Among them, Steph's father, whose eyes still found her, invited her, included her in their vision.

# ZOE

Zoe could feel Lily's presence in the house at all times. It was a miasma. No filter could clean the air. Zoe would do whatever she could to get Lily out of the house, no matter what legal rights she had. Her first attempt was shrill, blaring music from every speaker. It didn't accomplish much. Lily took to wearing earplugs and giving Zoe menacing glares, which didn't affect her at all. Scorn was a weak defense.

The next week, Lily started to retaliate. Every night before Zoe had to get to set early, she'd invite some friend over. Dicks, Steph, Elena, any one of the people whose voice Zoe didn't want to hear. They'd yell and scream about some movie or some friend of theirs. Zoe didn't pay attention to the words. That would have handed Lily a greater victory by allowing her to annex territory in Zoe's precious mind.

Zoe responded by setting off the fire alarms with some smoke from a candle. The alarms were all connected, so the one in the hallway outside her bedroom would tell the one in the living room to screech, all while she retreated to her bedroom, where the smoke detector had, in a genius move, been disconnected long before. While Lily scrambled to shush the alarm and her guest covered their ears in anguish, Zoe could vape in peace. As she blew the vapor out her window, it always astonished her how quickly the haze faded into air. In mere inches, it was as if it had never existed at all.

Lily drew mustaches on all of the pictures of Zoe that were hung in the house. More fragile women would have pointed out that it was transphobic violence, but Zoe couldn't display any weakness. So she drew a mustache on her own face, took a selfie, printed it out and framed it and displayed it on the wall. For a week, cold silence wafted out of Lily's room from pure demoralization. A little empathy flittered in Zoe's heart. She could extend a peaceful hand to Lily and let the fight end. The two would reestablish some pattern of living together peacefully. But Lily would still live in the house. Still scheme about how she could be better than Zoe, how she could tear her down. It wasn't safe. Not emotionally, not physically. So Zoe started screaming outside of Lily's bedroom in the middle of the night, knocking on it as hard as she could whenever she left for the set in the morning, setting up robo-dialers to call her phone from different numbers every few minutes to render it unusable. Lily didn't bother fighting back anymore. She shrunk into the corners of the house, making herself seen only in jumps from shadow to shadow or in the kitchen at mealtimes.

One Saturday, Zoe went downstairs to fix herself some lunch and found Lily sitting at the table. She didn't say anything. Lily looked pale and her hand shook as she spooned some rice into her mouth. Her sallow eyes, dark rings lining them, glared at Zoe. Let her stew. It just meant Zoe was winning.

"Are you poisoning me?"

It was the first she'd spoken to Zoe since the mustache incident.

"Poison?" Zoe asked. "No. Why would I do that?"

"You want to get rid of me." She shoved the rice away from her, head wavering a bit. "Why not kill me? You seem like you want to."

"I'd never poison you, Lily. Can you imagine? 'Famous actress Zoe Berger kills nobody roommate'? It wouldn't make sense."

"Fuck you."

"I'm not gonna kill you, Lil. I'm not even going to hurt you. I'm going to make sure you never get a moment of peace. I'm going to disrupt every little bit of pleasure you can wring out of your time in this house. Until you leave. And then we're good."

Lily didn't say a word to Zoe for the next two weeks. It was something like peace, but Lily's continued presence demonstrated that it wasn't the real thing. She had to go. However much she tried to make Lily's life in the house worse, Lily seemed to just crumple in further and endure. How? Zoe could have found somewhere else to live weeks ago. The thought had occurred to her some time back. She could have afforded to live on her own, so why stay trapped in this miserable dance with Lily? It would have been easier to live in L.A. proper and avoid the commute.

But she'd never leave, never let Lily have the satisfaction, never for one second allow anyone to imagine that Lily had the power to make Zoe do anything. Not in the face of the art on the walls, the furniture, the new paint. In the course of a year, Zoe had transformed their house from a hovel to a palace. Lily's house was that grimy relic that now only lurked in the shadows, the basement, the kitchen sink. If only she were as imperceptible as the rest of it, but she had the audacity to pretend she belonged on the suede couch. To dare to kick her disgusting feet up on the reclaimed wood coffee table.

Somehow, Lily recuperated in her room enough to endure all of Zoe's attempts to force her out. Zoe decided she'd take it away that night. Lily didn't get to sleep until about midnight, long past when Zoe usually got to bed. Early mornings going to set and a disciplined sleep schedule to guard her beauty against the ravages of fatigue and poor health forbade late nights. But exceptions had to be made.

The lock on Lily's door opened with the insertion of a paperclip. Such was the assumption of everyone building houses, that once you got in the front door, you were free from the dangers of the world. As if families didn't hurt children, lovers didn't murder each other, roommates didn't come in conflict. Zoe turned the handle gently and crept into Lily's room. A streetlight snuck past the borders of the curtains, but all it could do was provide the gestures of shapes in the room. A solid dim rectangle, the dresser. Insubstantial scraps of nothing on the floor, discarded clothes. A mound, with little wrinkles jutting out at the borders of its plateau: Lily fast asleep. This little serenity all alone is what let her endure, while every night Zoe twisted her sheets into knots in anguish that she had to continue sharing a house with her. No more. Zoe pounced onto the bed, seizing each of Lily's wrists and screaming into her ear.

Lily struggled, but Zoe kept shouting and shouting. "Every night I will come for you and every night you will be afraid and every night I will not let you have one second of peace and every night you'll beg me to stop and leave but I'm not going to leave, you are going to leave." They struggled for a while, and then Zoe left Lily to a fitful night of sleep. The next night, she did it again. The night after, Lily's light was still on, so Zoe just banged on the door once or twice. Two nights after that, all of Lily's clothes were gone.

Zoe screamed with delight upon seeing the empty hangers dangling in the closet. For weeks she'd been dreaming of this moment, this exact feeling, but every morning hadn't dared believe it would come true. All the misery, all the tension, all of Lily's attempts to drag her down into banality, done.

Freedom swirled around her feet as she bounced down the stairs. Victory cupped its hands in front of her face and made her laugh a little louder. But it was tranquility which wrapped around her, turned her attention to every quiet corner of the house. Her house alone.

Zoe drew the curtains in the living room shut,

stripped down to nothing, and flopped onto the couch. The suede welcomed her bare skin, ecstatic that it was just the two of them together without that awful third wheel ruining the mood. The mere fact that it was an option drew her fingers down between her legs. With each flicker of pleasure, new visions of her post-Lily existence came to mind. Better performances, new friends, dinner parties (once the kitchen was clean), a home that was an actual place of rest rather than the battleground Lily chose for her protracted war against Zoe's success.

Soon her glory would come. More movies, more cameras, her hand twitched faster, better and better co-stars, awards and flashing lights and a name that meant something to everyone who heard it.

Her body begged her to keep going, keep going at any cost, but amid the heavy breaths and the warmth building in her chest, a vivid image of Lily—her high cheekbones, her almond eyes, her full lips—wormed its way into her mind and in a moment, she tumbled from her grasp near the summit down to the base of the mountain.

Zoe wiped her fingers off on the knit throw blanket. She'd have plenty of time to try again.

# LILY

As Lily walked down the sidewalk with a duffel bag dangling from her shoulder, the breach with Zoe felt wider and wider and stretched longer and longer into the past. When had it started? Had it always been this way? Maybe Zoe had only tolerated Lily all this time, a mysterious whim that had expended itself over the course of years and left nothing but bitterness when it vanished. Lily didn't want to believe that, but the intensity of Zoe's hatred after their fight couldn't have been born so quickly. Resentment is made like a pearl: layer after layer wraps the seed until it glimmers, ready for the world.

Lily had sent Elena a text earlier that she was on her way over, but wanted to have the conversation about staying there in person. If she said yes, it would be a relief that she longed to share with Elena. If she said no, better to see Elena's face and understand what she meant by it.

A bell tinkled as she turned the corner to Elena's block. The bushes to her left rustled, and Lewis emerged from the undergrowth. Without a pause, he pranced up to Lily and, before she could crouch down to meet him, stood on his back legs and nuzzled his orange head into her hand as if it had been shaped only with that task in mind.

"How you doing, buddy? Going on an adventure?"

Lewis trilled, then opened his mouth to drop a bleached-white bird skull into Lily's hand. Pets received and his messaged delivered, he scampered away to chase or investigate something beyond Lily's perception. She held the skull before her eyes, beak pricking the pad of her thumb. So much for the local ecosystem. Though she didn't know if Lewis had killed this bird himself, or had just brought her the skull. The cryptic intentions of cats left yet another mystery. She pocketed the skull and walked down the block.

Elena's house had transformed over the last couple months. The ivy no longer crawled wherever it pleased. Instead, it was confined to a trellis, and its leaves twitched constantly. Fresh planks and paint had replaced weathered wood. The rusted gutters with holes of gnarled metal allowing rainwater to pour in streams onto the front steps were gone, and the new ones could do their job. Not everything had changed though: the windows still had cracks all over them, and the rotten wood on the porch creaked beneath her steps.

Lily set her bag down by the welcome mat that had been there since long before Elena bought the house, so gray with dirt that no design could peek through. Maybe it said "WELCOME" or "HELLO" or "LEAVE." Or maybe it just had a picture on it, something cute like little fish or pineapples to put a guest in a good mood as they entered the house. The front door was now mustard yellow with three little windows peeking above Lily's head. Even if Elena got on her tiptoes, she would never be able to see anyone through them. Lily tried the doorbell. The dingy white plastic didn't look new, but maybe it held secret changes of its own. A few presses didn't do anything. When she knocked on the door, it didn't make a knocking sound. A chime rang in the house.

Lily's nerves knotted and bunched up into her throat. She needed more time to settle them, but the chime had already sounded, attention had already been called, and the patter of Elena's feet was already so close. A tuft of her bleach-blonde hair poked up into the leftmost window, then the door swung open.

"Lily! What's up? I got your text, what's going..." Elena's question found its answer when her eyes peeked over to Lily's massive duffel bag. Her whole face tightened as she returned her attention to Lily.

"It blew up with Zoe, Elena. I need a place to stay."

"Didn't think that was worth putting in the text?" They snatched a few locks of hair on the back of their head and held them tight, eyes closer to Lily's feet than eyes. "This feels like an ambush."

"You're right. I wasn't thinking. I just had to pack up and go right away and I should've called. I'm sorry."

Elena didn't say anything. Silence lingered and grew between them as the wind blew some of Lily's hair into her face. A bell tinkled as Lewis strutted between them on his way inside.

"I couldn't stay there. I didn't know what to do," Lily said. She didn't know how to convince Elena that it would be fine, that they would be happy living together for a little while. Honesty was the only choice. No lie would hold up, and its failure would reveal the truth in its shadow. "I was afraid you'd say no."

Elena exhaled a thin jet of air and finally met Lily's eyes, though those dark irises and dots of light didn't reveal Elena's thoughts. "Fine. Come in." They stepped aside. "You can crash on the couch for a week." Elena wrapped one of the multicolored ropes that dangled from above around their hand and pulled it so tight that Lily feared the ceiling might come down. But they let go with the house still unharmed and turned around and wrapped Lily in a hug. "I'm sorry this is happening to you. I'm gonna help you get back on your feet." They kissed the top of Lily's head and the two of them embraced for a couple minutes before Elena returned upstairs to their art projects.

Left alone, Lily wandered the house. There were twenty ropes tied to hooks jabbed in the ceiling, each a swirl of colors. The floor was shiny black vinyl, though the lighting wasn't strong enough for Lily to see more of herself than a few smears. Here and there, wood peeked out from the cracked plaster on the walls. She nestled her suitcase between one of those cracks and the couch—maybe she could take up so little space that Elena would barely notice she was there. Unpacking was easy enough, just a few piles of clothes along the baseboard.

Everything would be fine, unless Elena had strong opinions about what that corner of the room should be used for. What if she did some kind of important art there? No, there weren't any supplies around. Maybe it was performance based. Some kind of room-based dance. Lily ran up the stairs and found Elena, deep in concentration in front of a canvas as wide as she was tall. "Elena."

"Busy."

"It's important."

"Okay."

"Can I use the corner next to the couch to stack up my clothes?"

"Not important. Yeah. Who cares?" Elena touched a brush to the canvas, applying diagonal streaks of red in parallel down a delicate painting of a lake. The first was bold, but each one faded compared to the last until the last one was almost invisible. Lily returned downstairs and settled on the couch. It was lumpier than the couch at home. Her former home. But there were no stomping feet or shrill complaints. No constant tension in the air and no suspense over which Zoe would show up. Drafts blew in, chilling her oasis. Elena's steps creaked above her, but Lily soothed herself by picturing them pacing around upstairs in front of a future masterpiece. Frustration leading to insight leading to genius. Despite the noise, the effect of those last few long nights drew Lily into sleep.

A couple hours later, warmth awoke her. Elena's head nuzzled into her neck and their arms wrapped around Lily. She scooted into the crevice where cushions met to give Elena some room. They lay there for an hour—trading warmth and comfort and affection and providing a mountain for Lewis to climb and knead—until Elena abruptly broke out of their mutual grasp. "Do you want to come stay in my bed upstairs? Just for tonight."

Lily slept there for the entire week, and continued as the one week grew longer than planned. Each extra day was measured in the creep of Lily's clothes and toiletries out of the corner and across the room. It was empty space which she never saw Elena do anything in. Even though Lily was officially living on the couch, she never slept there. Each morning she'd bounce down to the room, giddy from a night of various kinds of affection, and grab her clothes for the day.

Every morning, she gave Elena a kiss on the cheek to announce that she was awake and leaving the bed so that Elena could sleep in for the next couple hours. The first few times, it elicited a gentle smile from their sleeping lips, but Elena started sleeping through it before long. Probably just a change in how she was sleeping, or bad dreams. Lily lounged on the couch for the rest of the morning. She had the day off, no tattoos or grapefruits or sweeping or anything to distract her from reading in the patch of sunlight the window above the couch allowed in.

Between pages, she let her focus wander to fantasies of Elena letting her stay in the house forever. Art fluttered up the sides of the walls, paint strokes snaked their way into expansive murals. Abstract sculptures bloomed from nothing as an experimental soundscape played in the corner. All around the two of them, the house sprung to life along with their love. That was the first time Lily had used "love" in her mind, around Elena. No, she wasn't in love. It would be silly to be in love. But was it wrong to hope? Love struck in all kinds of situations, and the notion that love could only exist within committed romantic relationships was ridiculous. So it was fine. Lily wasn't in love, but hoped one day love might arise. Reasonable and rational.

Elena grumbled down the staircase and managed a half-awake nod to acknowledge Lily before going into the kitchen. The coffee-first lifestyle. And they would find a pot of coffee, ready to go. They deserved quiet delights like that for letting Lily stay so long in their house. She kept an eye on the doorway so she could see Elena's perked-up face as she exited the kitchen, but Elena was downcast, tapping her fingers on the side of the mug.

"You know, I didn't ask you to make coffee all the time."

"I know. I did it on my own."

"But you don't even drink it."

"Not true! No, I drank one cup a few days ago. And another last week. So it's only fair."

"It's a bit stronger than I like it to be. Like, it's thick. I usually make it like diner coffee. Real watery so I can have like ten cups." Elena swirled her cup around and stared into the whirlpool she'd created rather than look up. "Okay. Thank you."

"Oh, got it. No problem." Elena went back upstairs, and for the rest of the day, Elena's creaks sounded muted and tentative, rather than the lively ones that Lily had come to enjoy.

# ZOE

Nothing prepares one for a day at work like a good night's sleep, and without Lily's hatred permeating the house, Zoe slept marvelously. As she walked onto the set, she bestowed random crew members with hugs, kisses on the cheek, winks, whatever signs of affection sprung to mind. Even the guy who smelled like freshly tilled dirt got a friendly handshake. On most days, Zoe wished him dead from ten feet away. But now that she was rested, she could be her best self. Cables and lights and chairs only provided slaloms for her fairy-stepped jaunt through the set, over to where Tevin and Sage sat on the facsimile kitchen countertops. A big risk, since they weren't built to last, but their lives were in their own hands. With a click of her heels on the tile, Zoe announced her presence to them. "Hi, friends!"

Each of them swiveled, made confused eye contact, before greeting Zoe in turn. Was her good mood so difficult to imagine? Everyone around dreamed of stardom, of possessing the indefinable quality that surged through her muscles like electricity. And yet they thought its bearer wouldn't be happy on occasion? Behind Sage and Tevin, a couple stout crew members duck-walked a fridge-sized box. If her life had still been composed of a chain of dull little miseries like theirs, the only surprise being what connective tissue would splice them together, she'd understand the reluctance to believe in something better. But Tevin had received a greater taste of stardom than Zoe thus far, so he should be well-acquainted with elation. No. He'd been seduced by the false promise of Art: that glory came in moments of quiet satisfaction. The grind of a pencil as it laid down a line exactly where it needed to be, a particularly soulful note sung in the lonely basement, the complex line reading delivered without any desire for recognition. None could withstand the light of glory or cries of adulation. Craft was the wire mother that lesser artists tried to suckle from after success left them to nature's whims.

"What's up your ass today?" Sage surprised her less. A middling director, who'd fluked their way to a peak from which the rest of their career dangled, helpless.

"Relief to a problem that went on for too long. What's on tap today?"

Tevin handed over the script like it weighed twenty pounds. "It's a rough one."

"Is it? I thought the kitchen scene was going to be fun." Zoe flipped through the lines. The same, the same, the same, and then... different. "Oh." A monologue drenched with melodrama from Zoe's character about how she'd been abused by someone who looked just like Tevin.

Tevin met her eyes as she looked up from the lines. "That's what they want. Time to get the tears going. Congrats."

Sage said, "I know you were prepping for a lighter scene. Think you can do it?"

"I'm a pro. This," Zoe said as she rustled the pages around, "is no problem. A child could deliver these lines."

They got into position. The lights clapped on, each one bright enough that a woman with less presence would have disappeared beneath their glare. But Zoe only became more real, more present and alive. She and Tevin exchanged lines; their characters joked amid simmering tension. Each rejoinder cut a little too far beneath the skin. Each smile, a little less animated by laughter and more by the thrill of hunting an animal whose blood dotted the forest floor. The original script left it with a retort just-too-true about how Tevin's character would be alone if not for Zoe's. Then he leaves the room and Zoe's character is the one who's alone. The new one compelled him to slam his hand on the kitchen table, rattling the salt and pepper shakers out of arrangement and onto the floor like an earthquake. Stage directions sent Zoe scrambling backwards, into a corner, where she would tearfully begin her monologue.

Except when she started, she remembered Lily's pitiful eyes, swollen with tears in the dark, and a perverse smile crept onto her face. "I've known men like you, you know. One. He looked like you. Talked like you. Fucked like you. And maybe he punched like you too. If you're going to, show me. When—"

"Cut!" Sage sunk into their chair as much as they could, but their elven frame sat on top of the taut fabric like a cloud. "Zoe what was that? Why were you happy?"

"I went down a road in my mind. Let's do it again."

"Are you going to do it right?"

"Let's do it again."

"From the start of the monologue. Action!"

"I've known men like you, you know." This time Zoe's voice wavered with the appropriate amount of fear. "One. He looked like you. Talked like you." Again, the image of Lily. Again, the smile.

"Cut! Zoe, what the fuck?"

"This is where I'm taking it!"

"It's supposed be dramatic and heartbreaking. Why are you smiling?"

"Because my character is amused. Look, we get new lines sprung on us the day of, and we're going with them. Why? Because you trust us. So trust us. Tevin?"

Tevin hemmed and hawed and looked up at the ceiling and rolled his shoulders around and explored his pockets and took a deep breath in and a deep breath out, and when he returned his attention to earth, Zoe was still waiting for him to answer. "I think..." Zoe could hear the reluctance, scraped up as she yanked out the answer from deep within his belly.

They started up again. And Zoe began her speech again, pulling Lily's image to mind just as she said, "... Fucked like you. And maybe he punched like you too." A bitter laugh came out like a gasp. "If you're going to, show me. When I saw you, I thought I had a chance to do it all different." Zoe summoned Lily's midnight sobs, audible through the thin walls. "But if it's the same, give it to me the same. Come on. Right here." Zoe tapped an impatient finger beneath her eye. None of this was in the script, but Tevin gamely tensed his fist and added a shoulder flex no more noticeable than a fish passing below the water. "Show me it hasn't changed."

Tevin raised his fist. Or his character did. And Zoe felt real terror, flinched out of character, and couldn't get the mood of Lily's departure back in time to save it. After the cut, Zoe waited for someone else to speak first. Even though she'd blown the take, the new direction had such richer possibilities.

Sage said, "I'm gonna get a writer. Where's the guy?" They snapped their fingers at their assistant. "The guy! I don't know his name. Writer guy. Get him."

"A writer? Come on, this is it. This is the way it needs to go."

"It fucks up the rest of the story, Zoe."

"Then let it. This is the only way I'm doing the scene. I'm not giving you other options." As the writer scurried into the conversation, Zoe and Sage were busy digging trenches.

Tevin said, "I think Zoe's right on this one, guys. It feels better than the other way."

Sage rolled their eyes and explained the situation to the writer, whose expression transformed from bemused to horrified over the course of only a couple dozen words. "No. No, no, no." His nasal voice was devoid of charisma.

Why did he think he had any authority once he stepped into the world of actors? The more Zoe looked at him, heard him, felt her surroundings burdened by his presence, the more she sympathized with bullies who shoved nerds into lockers. Everyone had a proper place, and for some, that place was simply out of sight. "In the writer's room we use something called the Relatability-Likeability-Empathy matrix to measure what the characters should be doing. The reason why this is supposed to be a sad scene is to increase your character's score on this matrix. That gives us momentum through the back half for catharsis at one hundred minutes. You see?"

"It's dull. I'm not doing it."

"You have to," the writer whined, and appealed to Sage like a child calling over the teacher to administer a punitive fairness. "You have to. Or—"

"Or what?" Zoe felt her smile become a shark's. Too much blood in the water, and no one else able to smell any of it. "You'll fire me? Do it. Fire me."

Tevin said, "Don't do it. Please don't fire her. I get that it's disruptive, but the scene's good. It's really good." He extended a regretful hand toward the writer, his eyebrows rumpled like a boy-band vocalist singing a regretful melody. "I'm sorry. I know it's not what you wanted."

"Are you going to fire me?" Zoe marched jaw-first into Sage's personal space, her hungry teeth telling her it was time to remind Sage who was taller, who was stronger, whose hands were tied and whose weren't. "I'm not going to do the scene any other way. Fire me now."

How long could Sage hold eye contact with Zoe? The full foot of height difference was never more important than at that moment. Their neck would ache. Their eyes would tear. Zoe's defiant eyes and blood-tinged smile would take up their entire field of vision. With a snort, they broke the staring contest and shoved their copy of the script into the writer's hands.

"We're doing it her way. Fix it."

"Fix it? We're going to have to change everything."

"Then change everything. This is the way the story goes now."

Stamping feet echoed through the set, still quiet from the tense miasma that had just surrounded the director and the actress. Zoe's cheeks ached from the breadth of her smile, and she said, "Let's do the scene. I'm ready."

# LILY

Glass shattered on the floor, and Elena threw the hammer that had done it across the room. From behind the open pages of one of the *Eragons*, Lily pretended not to be watching Elena. She flinched to create the illusion that she was startled a full second after the hammer wedged itself into the plaster. Lewis, curled up in her lap, didn't budge. He'd seen it all before. Dust already crumbled from the wound. From the couch, Lily couldn't easily get to Elena to comfort them. A canvas stretched across the entire floor with smears of paint and sketches covering it. But when she stood up to begin the journey around it, further shards of mirror tinkled as Elena stretched out their hand to Lily and arrested her in place. "Don't move. I'm onto something."

Lily didn't know whether that meant to sit back down, or if her just-risen pose had stoked Elena's inspiration. To be a muse would be the highest honor. Great paintings and music and novels would spin out into the world from a light between Lily's breasts, refracted through the brilliant mind of the artist. But Elena wasn't looking, so she sat back down. None of the tense workings of Elena's eyes were for her. In return, she pointedly denied Elena more of her attention, which included this copy of *Eragon*—modified so the titular Eragon spoke entirely with lines borrowed from Taxi Driver. The rest of the house had plenty to look at. The shards of mirror pasted here and there to reflect different parts of the canvas glinted wherever the blinds didn't protect them. By now the ropes dangling from the ceiling offered no intrigue. The thrill of discovery was gone. Lily stood again, and again Elena said, "Don't."

"I'm getting a snack. Is that okay?"

Elena grumbled, but didn't follow it up. She tossed mirror fragment after fragment on the floor in front of her as Lily circumnavigated the canvas. Only six inches separated the art and the wall. One foot in front of the other, just like she'd seen Lewis do a hundred times. Halfway through this high-wire act, she teetered to her left. Her whole body tilted, and she wished it was a cliff above jagged rocks rather than over the canvas. Better her body get smashed than covered in this paint. Muscles all over her torso held tight and her outstretched arms stopped their windmill panic. Her foot returned to its model's walk, and she passed by Elena, who was clearly still imagining the worst case.

The kitchen countertops were all memory foam. "Every spill should be remembered." Elena's voice ran through Lily's mind even when she left the room. Luckily there was little chance a banana would cause a spill. She'd been told once that rather than opening the banana from the top, the right way to open it was from the bottom. That's how the chimpanzees did it. They, not humans, were the banana experts. But Lily couldn't understand on what basis. Was it greater banana experience? Passion? Were chimps natural banana eaters any more than humans were? Lily opened it from the top and bit away the gross part right beneath it that got smushed. As she chewed on her snack, she hoisted herself up onto the countertop. Right at the spot that remembered her butt. Across from her, the fridge was the perfect illusion of a massive ice cube. Elena had spent weeks painting it, even simulating the kitchen light refracting through the ice. The only thing that gave it away was that it never melted and wasn't cold enough to the touch. Lily flipped the switch off, so that the light dancing through the cube no longer had an origin. Now it shone too bright for its surroundings, which begged it to come down to their level. But it was defiant. But it was just a fridge. Lily opened it and saw the ordinary racks with ordinary food packed on top of them. She tore a stick of string cheese off the rest and kicked it shut, and the fridge once more became an illusion.

With the tip of her fingernail, Lily separated the tiniest segment of cheese from the whole, laser-focused while Elena swore in the other room. Thread by thread, Lily consumed the cheese. Maybe after a few more bites, Elena would find a solution to the problem that was frustrating her. Maybe halfway through the cheese, Elena would burst into the room, elated by inspiration and dying to share their joy with Lily. Maybe. Fifteen minutes passed; the cheese was gone.

Nothing sounded different out there, and Lily didn't feel like having another snack, so she ventured out. Elena was laying on the ground, their face smashed against the canvas, neck twisted as far as an owl's to see the hand mirror that wavered in between their middle and big toes.

"Do you want me to hold that for you?"

After a sharp exhalation and a second's pause, Elena said, "Yeah, that'd help. Hold it so you're kind of catching my face by surprise."

Lily took the handle and moved the mirror as little as she could. "Here?"

"Mm. No. Little bit left and up."

"Here?"

"No. My left!"

"Here?"

"No. My up! Shit!"

"I can't really see what it's doing."

Elena slapped their hands against the ground, and frustration reverberated through the entire house. Mirrors tinkled in sympathy. The ceiling ropes bristled knowingly. Only Lily stayed perfectly still. Elena plucked the mirror from Lily's grasp and let it clatter to the floor.

"I'm done for the day."

"I'm sorry."

"My artistic failures aren't your fault." Once Elena trudged upstairs, Lily felt the living room contract around her. The canvas and the walls and everything in the house which so desired Elena's attention wanted to squeeze the life out of Lily for driving them away. Unable to bear the anger, Lily jogged up the steps.

Elena sat on the floor in the bedroom. Their head leaned back and rumpled the bedsheets behind them, while their arms dangled to the floor like an out-of-use puppet's. Elena's unfocused eyes didn't bother to find Lily. "I'm feeling kinda bad. Would you mind giving me some space?"

"Totally, yeah. Just... I am too, and really don't want to be alone right now. Can I stay up here with you if I don't say anything?"

All of a sudden, the puppet was gone. Elena's body surged with easy purpose as she stood. Gliding step after step carried them toward Lily, who wasn't sure if Elena would say anything to her or do anything to her or walk right past, until one of those confident hands slid up the side of Lily's neck and took fingerfuls of her hair. "Seems like we want different things. Wanna fuck about it?"

All Lily could muster was an enthusiastic little nod, and Elena tossed her onto the bed. Before Lily could shift into an alluring pose, they leaped on top of her and pinned her hands to the bed and kissed and sucked and bit at her neck. All Lily could do beneath the pressure of Elena's voracity was squirm against her grip and rub her trapped body up against Elena's.

"You're not going to escape," Elena said, as matter-of-fact as someone noticing rain outside the window. Just one of Elena's hands kept both of Lily's wrists immobile above her head, the other danced down the buttons at the front of Lily's shirt and down her jeans and soon, her chest was exposed and all of her was accessible. More kisses, bites, licks. At any given moment Lily couldn't tell if pain or pleasure would find her and so it all became pleasure.

When Elena's greedy mouth found Lily's nipple and supplied violence, Lily cried out. "Ow!"

The bite transformed into a tender kiss. Elena lifted their mouth, a thread of saliva connecting her bottom lip and Lily's nipple and said, "Shut up. No more words." Phrases ricocheted against the back of her teeth, but they dissolved into moans as Elena's other hand reached into Lily's pants. For an indeterminate time, Lily drifted until the pleasure faded to the touch of a fingertip, and then nothing, and then Elena's pussy blotted out the light like a meteor above earth and crashed into Lily's mouth, smothering any speech which may have remained and leaving her only the options of providing pleasure or nothing. Lily chose pleasure. Elena rubbed one hand on Lily's chest and another on their own. Lily discovered her hands were no longer captured, but kept them crossed above her head as if pinned by Elena's will alone as Elena's wetness filled her mouth.

When Elena came, they did so with a shout like a warrior charging into battle. Face-first, they tumbled onto the bed. Their sweat-drenched legs still engulfed Lily's head, who inhaled deeply the intermingled scent of pleasure and effort.

After a minute, Elena moved. Without putting any clothes on or saying a word, they trudged downstairs. This time, Lily felt the directive not to follow. As if Elena had tongued it into her brain moments ago. She idly pawed at herself in pretense that she'd finish what Elena had started, but she was unable to recapture the spirit of it now that she was alone with angry walls. A bell jingled, and she became aware of Lewis watching her. Those big eyes were as observant as they were uncomprehending.

Once futility outweighed pleasure, she curled up to take a nap. With closed eyes, none of her worries had to be real.

# ZOE

There's an art to dating. Actually, there are endless intersecting arts to dating, all of which contradict each other. Mastery of the subject requires mastery of its constituent arts, as well as the wisdom to apply them judiciously to mask those contradictions. Zoe was one such master. Though her beauty made it easy, Zoe refused to rest on her laurels. Mental agility, emotional intelligence, conversational acumen, patience were only a few of the skills one used in any given date. She was supposed to meet August, a guy she'd matched with on an app and had heard about here and there from friends: great at sex, terrible personality. These were qualities Zoe could work with. Personalities were liquid and containers could change. Sexual prowess was a gift.

Nate held the door to the restaurant open for her. Chivalry for hire never felt as good as the real thing, but as long as Nate's fervor was genuine, what difference did it make? Knights too in medieval times had gotten some kind of reward for their noble violence. The restaurant's walls had a burlap texture, like they'd scratch Zoe's skin if she brushed against them. A brunette with unsubtle blonde highlights smiled vacuously at them.

"Table for Baros? I'm a little late, so he might be here already."

"He is, but it says here it's a table for two, and..." She stared past Zoe's shoulder. Confused, Zoe followed her gaze until it landed on Nate.

Zoe laughed. "Oh, don't worry, he's not a guest. He's here as my assistant."

"Will he be eating?"

Nate said, "No ma'am, I'm taken care of." He fished a coconut-sugar sweetened and gluten-free protein bar from each pocket until all four were on display. The hostess nodded in the way one does when equally unconvinced that something is fine and that something is worth opposing. Zoe didn't like pushing restaurant workers to that line, recalling all too well how many times she'd made the wrong choice in her time under the dim yellow lights, trying to fulfill the needs of one hundred tyrants nestled into plush vinyl booths. As they wound their way through the restaurant, Zoe wondered if the hostess wasn't trying to show Zoe off somehow. Other patrons swiveled their heads and waiters swerved out of their path as Zoe towered over all of them. Tall though she was, the sudden feeling that she was a foot taller than everyone else shocked her, even if it was obviously not true; a man who passed them on the way to the bathroom was her height, but he too seemed to be looking up at her. Nate offered Zoe a stout plastic bottle of water out of his tote bag, but she waved it off.

Zoe's booth was all the way in the back. Rather than a grand tour of the restaurant, was Zoe being shunted off into its darkest corner? No, that didn't make sense. They hadn't seen her or known her name when they had seated her date here. Maybe he had angered someone. She took a deep breath to slow her racing thoughts. It was a full restaurant; none of the waitstaff were likely to engineer the seating arrangements to suit arcane beefs with people they didn't know. Her date certainly didn't seem to be entrenched in a covert war with the hostess. He smiled as he rose out of the booth, massive and powerful like a whale breaching the ocean's surface. Zoe fantasized about resting atop him: his back on the bed and her comparatively tiny body curled up on his solidity.

"Hi, Zoe. I'm August. Nice to finally meet you." He had the wide, insincere smile of a car salesman, which dropped as his eyes jumped from Zoe to her left. "Who's this?"

"Oh, don't worry about him. Nate's my assistant. He's gay."

"Huh?"

Nate said, "My husband understands how important my work is."

"Uh, okay."

Zoe slid into the booth, weight gliding from foot to hand to hip so that it barely rustled the vinyl. While August had certainly begun to appraise her physicality from the moment he saw her, she wasn't going to surrender any details without a fight. For all he knew, she was nothing more than smoke and mirrors: a computer-generated delight to feast on with his eyes as his hands hungered.

Nate tapped the hostess's shoulder, interrupting her turn to depart. "Do you have a stool? The shorter the better."

"I'll see what I can do. In the meantime, our booths are very comfortable."

"No, thank you." Nate sat on the floor and poked his head into his bag.

As he rustled through his items, Zoe said, "I hope you weren't waiting too long. The shoot today went over. You know how directors are."

"You know, I don't. I—"

"Here's some hand sani." Nate proffered a large bottle with a pump top. Zoe took some, then Nate swiveled toward August. "And for the gentleman?"

"No, thanks."

Zoe said, "Go on and take some. Nate gets a thrill out of it."

"I'm good." August smiled at Zoe, but kept glancing down at Nate. A problem seemed to be developing. Perhaps jealousy? Countless men had worked themselves up into a frenzy picturing the number of eyes that had found their way onto Zoe's body. Each leer came with a wish. To grab, to squeeze, to undress, to lick, to possess, to enter, to be. Even when they were closer than any others, the possibility of sliding back into the crowd of intentions proved to be too much to bear. So their wishes changed. They would scream. They would grab. They would try to hold fast someone who could be jailed no more easily than light.

"How do you find the movie business? Lots of excitement?" Despite August's best efforts, Nate seemed to be distracting him. Zoe considered dismissing her assistant, but wasn't sure how best to get the condoms from his bag and into her slim purse in a graceful manner. She couldn't make so much as eye contact with Nate while focusing entirely on August, in a bid to allay his concerns.

As she answered, she tried to sign to Nate beneath the table. Neither of them knew any real sign language, so she shaped out a circle and pointed to her purse. "Please. You know what you do on a movie set? The same thing, over and over and over again. The only way I can get excitement is in my spare time." While she beamed a sultry look into August's eyes, his found Nate rustling to her side. Without any subtlety, he'd scooted over to the booth and dropped a couple of hoop earrings into her purse.

Zoe grabbed two fistfuls of Nate's linen shirt; it flowed so loosely around his body that her pull generated barely any tension, but her intention brought him near and held him there. She whispered, "You little idiot, I wanted condoms so I could send you the fuck away. Don't you see you're weirding out my date?"

"Sorry. I'm sorry. Here." Nate dug through his bag and presented the condoms. "There we go, all better. I'm sorry."

In a flash, Zoe pulled them under the table. Had he seen? Did August know what they were fighting about? He looked slack-jawed and puzzled.

"Were those condoms?"

"Sorry about that," she said. "I'm not usually that forward, but as you can see, we're having a bit of a miscommunication here. Let me take care of it, and then I'll send him on his way and the two of us can get back to dinner." Zoe flung her hand into the air and the strip of condoms followed behind. Even in the dim restaurant light, the metallic silver wrapper flashed. She brought it down on Nate over and over. With each lash, he'd learn the cost of failure. Not just failure to follow her instructions, but the most grievous form possible: failure in his duty to present Zoe in the best possible light in all situations. After the first couple blows, Nate crumpled to the floor, but Zoe kept going. Each hit made awkward brushing noises, and Zoe wasn't entirely sure that they hurt. Still, Nate flinched each time. Zoe tried once more to hit him, but her wrist got stuck in place over her head. August's enormous hand, which wrapped around her arm and replaced all her ferocity with delicacy by mere juxtaposition, stopped her.

"Look. I don't know what's happening here. But I know this is no way to treat your pet."

"My pet?"

Everyone in that corner of the restaurant had their eyes trained on Zoe. Meek little animals observing the spectacle. But they were drained of all admiration. What kind of woman was this that would abuse her pet—did they all see Nate as a pet?—for a simple mistake? The answer was simple: a spectacular woman, who expected only the best service from those charged to perform it. August's reproachful gaze and powerful hand prevented her from standing atop the table to exclaim her beneficence.

"Your pet, your boyfriend, your guy. I don't know what this is. But you're not being kind to him."

"Oh, like you're kind. None of this would've happened if you hadn't been weird about it. That's right, ladies and gentlemen and others, he was being weird about the unique and productive business relationship I have with my associate. That's what started this whole mess."

"I still don't know what's going on. But I know enough to stop it before you actually hurt the poor guy."

Nate sprung up without any trace of soreness in his body. He'd been playing along. Though maybe he'd been so sure that Zoe wanted him to feel pain that he did feel it, despite the inadequacy of her blows. He dug his nails into the half of August's forearm exposed by the rolled-up sleeve. Nate's voice was an animalistic screech. "Leave her alone!"

August withdrew, nursing the trickles of blood unearthed by Nate's manicured nails. "You fucking psycho. I was helping you."

"By manhandling a movie star? Get away from her." Nate stole a bread knife off the table and waved it at him. "I know it's dull. I'm determined."

"I am out of here." Something in August's hands, the way they picked up his jacket with the casual sureness of strength, aroused Zoe. She imagined those hands all over her body, hands accustomed to being pleased with what they found and unsurprised by pleasure.

She squirmed past Nate and pressed herself against August. "Wait. Let's start this all over. I know I can be cruel... but I can be kind too." Zoe caressed down his thigh with one hand, but he nudged her away and shook his head. Then he was gone, merged into the faceless crowd, only differentiable by his total lack of desire toward her. Once he was gone, Zoe sat back in the booth, this time with a thump that crinkled the fabric beneath her weight. At her feet, Nate sat with the strands of condoms arrayed around him, clutching his knees in a tight embrace.

"Get up here. Come on."

Nate wormed into the booth opposite her with the condoms clenched in his hands. Even after her noble gesture, he wouldn't look her in the eye. "I'm sorry. I messed up the date."

A reciprocal apology was on the tip of Zoe's tongue. "You did. Mistakes happen. I trust you'll handle it better next time."

"Thank you for not firing me." Tears surged from his eyes. He grabbed the cloth napkin, but dropped it immediately in favor of the tissues from his bag. "May I use these?"

Zoe waved just her pinky and ring finger, while the rest of her hand held a glass of water. Reading her intentions correctly once again, Nate retrieved a couple of tissues from the pack and wiped his eyes, then blew his nose loudly. Everyone in the restaurant was still looking, listening, trying to sense what was going on at the dramatic corner table. But nothing more happened. Zoe had a salad with grilled chicken. The lettuce could've been fresher, but the tomatoes were lively. Nate had spaghetti with red sauce and a big meatball in the center, which he goggled at, but made a courageous attempt at finishing. On the ride home, Zoe spent the entire time lounged across the back seat, staring at the sliver of Nate's face as he batted the steering wheel and danced in his seat to the decade-old Katy Perry album on the speakers. What was it like inside his head? At the center was a shrine to Zoe, of course, but what floated around the margins? Besides prioritizing time with his loom. Maybe she'd ask him one day. The gentle rumble of the engine and the cool air flowing in from the window made Zoe feel like a child again. And like a child, she soon fell asleep.

# LILY

As the weeks went on, the area which Lily could occupy shrunk. The art studio had always been off-limits, but as it filled up with piles of glass and canvas and paint, Elena's work extended outward. The bedroom was out; Elena needed it to visualize the next stage of her art project, and any disruption in the way objects were arranged could throw off the entire process. Drying paint samples and open buckets of each color's wet correspondent dotted the entire kitchen, each like a family of paint visiting a dead relative's tombstone. Every time she walked in to grab a snack, or drink, she felt Elena's scrutiny no matter how gently and deliberately she stepped. One night, she and Elena got drunk and were fooling around and it felt like it did back when the two of them had hooked up at parties and then had not seen each other for a few weeks afterward. But before they could proceed toward ecstasy, Lily needed a drink of water to prevent the headache blooming in the wine's shadow. The wine had clumsied her feet and toe-heel deliberation gave way to the heat of the moment. She kicked a can over. By the time she righted it, frost-blue paint had puddled on the tile and Elena was already at the doorway.

"How did this happen? You knew this was important. What if I choose this paint and don't have enough?" The paper towel sacrificed its white to gather the blue.

"It was an accident."

"Accidents happen to things you're not paying attention to. Because they don't matter." Elena slithered between paint cans to the cabinet under the sink and sloshed some rubbing alcohol onto a fresh paper towel. Wrung to a point, the towel grabbed the scraps of paint which had snuck between the tiles and gripped onto the corners. "But it does. It's supposed to matter to you if you live here."

"I'm sorry." Would that it were a sobering experience, but Lily's head swam. All of the rambling lust from just moments ago deflated and weighed down her limbs, her mind. She wanted to go into the other room and sleep, to let nightmares trouble her instead, but didn't want Elena to think she was ignoring her or not taking her seriously.

"Look. I know you didn't mean to do this. But I need you to mean not to do it, you know?" Elena tossed out the paper towels. She peered into the paint can, frowning. Lily didn't know what to say, didn't want to apologize again, so the two stood in the kitchen until the waning power of the wine pulled them toward sleep. Elena clomped up the stairs to bed. Lily didn't follow her. Though the couch's scratchy fabric would leave her itchy tomorrow, something worse seemed to lurk up in the bedroom. The next day, neither mentioned the fight.

A couple weeks later, the canvas occupied the living room again. Lily had access only to the couch, the perimeter of the living room, the winding path between the kitchen doorway and the fridge, and the bathroom. The stairs up to the bedroom were also available, but she couldn't do much with that. Even with space freed up, the studio was Elena's exclusive area. Lily worried that Elena's art would make more annexations, rendering the house unusable for her, but she didn't say anything. It was Elena's house, bought and partially renovated for the exclusive purpose of Elena's art. Lily couldn't hope to supersede that goal. So she tiptoed around the canvas, didn't knock over any more paint cans, and abided by every guideline Elena offered to make their living space harmonious. The two hadn't fucked since the paint incident, but Elena's art captured her focus so deeply that it was a wonder she remembered to eat, let alone summon up the energy for sex.

One morning, Lily woke up with an arm dangling off the couch. The canvas had crept closer to her, and her sleeping fingers rested their backs against it, like a mother evaluating her child's fever. She snapped her hand to her chest, clasping it with the other. She couldn't bear to look. Instead, she stared into the middle distance. No paint. No paint. Please, no paint. First, she raised her other palm into her sight line. No wet paint had transferred from one hand to another. That was good. With a deep breath, she lifted the other, palm facing her. Nothing on that side, but she wouldn't expect there to be. The threat lay on the other side. She scrunched her eyes closed, flipped her hand around, and then, with pain, looked. Nothing. The terror shattered into elation. Lewis shoved his fuzzy head into her open hands, as if she'd summoned him by raising them.

"Hey, mister cat."

Lewis settled on her chest and purred for half an hour. Each time she tried to stop petting him, he stretched out a paw and tapped her on the cheek. She continued until some noise, imperceptible to her, prompted him to poke his head up, then sprint across the room in pursuit. Every time he ran on the canvas, Lily's heart stopped, but he never left a mark. Nor had he ever disturbed the arrangement in the bedroom, nor the kitchen. Somehow, he and Elena existed in perfect harmony.

With the cat gone, Lily got up and circumnavigated the canvas, careful step by step. When she reached the staircase, she and Elena almost collided.

"Good morning, love," Lily said.

"Shit. God damn it." Elena slammed her palm against the wall. "I was thinking. I had something. Lily, I had the thread of something so special right in my fingertips but then you scared me and then you said that word while I was trying to get it back. And now it's gone."

"Oh. I'm sorry. I—"

"This isn't working." Elena stared down at the floor, hands on her hips, eyes unfocused and confounded like she was looking at a chemical spill. "I can't live like this."

"What?"

"I need you to move out. I'm sorry."

"Elena..." Lily wanted to slap Elena. She wanted to scream, to beg her not to do it, but shoved those emotions down and, in a measured tone which only wavered a bit, said, "I know things have not been good here lately. I know that. But that's just because you're working on this big project. Once it's done—"

"How long are you planning on staying, huh? Another week? Two?" Elena stepped into Lily's space and made her back away into the perimeter, wobbling as she kept her feet in single file. "Because it sounds like you see yourself here for a long, long time."

"I mean—"

"So, what? A month? How long are you planning on abusing my hospitality?"

"I just thought we could be happy here." It came out like a whimper, the barest admission of a desire.

"And you decided you could just think that." Elena turned her back to Lily. Her shoulders were tense, and her fingers dented the soft flesh on each arm. A bare, tapping foot diffused all of Elena's furious energy into the room, which became more and more hostile toward Lily. The patterns in the exposed wooden beams reconfigured into angry faces. They accused Lily of spoiling everyone's happiness.

"Please..." Lily said, but she couldn't follow it with anything. She tiptoed around the canvas and retrieved her duffel bag. Elena knew how awful Zoe was, how Lily couldn't afford a place to stay on such short notice. But still, Lily was an afterthought. Worse, a non-thought, compared to Elena's precious art. Instead of taking the long way around one last time, Lily tramped through the canvas, careful to step directly on a portrait Elena had spent hours painting, and smeared it beyond recognition.

"What the fuck?" Elena chased after Lily as she stepped out the door, but when Lily looked back one last time, Elena stopped. A mirror glittered in Elena's wavering hands, high up in the air. In the shard of warped glass, Lily saw the portrait as though it had never been scuffed. By accident, she'd helped Elena, the one time she'd tried to hurt her. She was glad. She would've regretted it. But now the spite she thought she'd consumed lived in her stomach and gnawed at her lungs, her heart. If she could only vomit it out there on the doorstep, she could leave without sorrow, but it had no way out except into Elena. Lily couldn't reach her, no matter how she tried. A thousand potential reflections buffered her. So she closed the door and hoped Elena would miss her a little. Eventually.

# ZOE

The flash of the camera held little novelty for Zoe at this point in her career, but when a man with a well-kept beard, rare in an age of overgrowth, asked to take some pictures of her for a fashion blog, she was a little thrilled to acquiesce. She hadn't yet achieved the level of fame or fortune that allowed her to have a personal stylist, so this was direct affirmation of her exquisite taste. This wasn't even that elaborate an outfit, just a tank top and some pants, though the pants did tie in a knot around her ankle and the silhouette paired well with her strappy sandals. The photographer switched the flash off, and the camera went back to clicking. Compliments overflowed from the photographer. Usually I have to tell people how to pose, what angles to take to the camera, but you're a natural. Wouldn't it be funny once he googled her name, as he would to find out if she was single, and realized who she was?

What he wouldn't realize is that she was anything but a natural. It took work to get where she was, years of work to cajole her old body into its new, perfect shape. Work to learn how to play to a camera, how to play away from it. Work to exude sensuousness from her body like an alluring miasma. But that was the trick. Make it invisible, make it natural. A hundred hours of practice to make the flick of a wrist as natural as the sunrise. Let him think it is a gift from god. He's better off not knowing that there are great rewards at the end of labors he can't hope to complete.

"Zoe!" Some excited voice off to her side, scratchy with masculinity, called to her, but no one was going to cut in on her dance with the lens of the camera. When her instincts turned her around, she saw Adam's blond beard and his excitement in the momentary graze of eye contact before she settled just above the shoulder of the photographer. This guy was getting the best photos of his life, and he barely had to do anything. Point and click for spectacular art.

Another five minutes or so went by, the photographer said thanks and told Zoe the pictures would be up soon, and still Adam stood by her side.

"You didn't know how long that would take."

"How many pictures can one man take?"

"Ha, that's cute." That simple fool. Adam wanted to fuck Zoe so badly, but she wasn't inclined to let him. She started walking towards home and gave him a little wave to suggest he should tag along for the duration. Adam was at her heels without a pause.

"Funny to see you here. I was just coming back from the men's group, the one I told you about at Dicks's, remember?"

"Sure." She didn't remember and didn't remember asking.

"Today we were talking about the muse. This central figure in the lives of great male artists throughout history. Real or metaphorical. The muse."

Zoe had had a muse once, before she'd transitioned. A beautiful woman she'd pictured all the time: the Fount of Beauty. In every scene she'd acted, commercials or low-budget local theater, that had been the ideal against which all beauty and artfulness had been measured and always found wanting. Needless to say, she'd now been that woman for years.

"And you know, when I think of someone who's a lot like a muse, I think of you."

"I'm inspiring, then. Do you feel the urge to launch a ship?" Toying with a man when she was bored was one of Zoe's little pleasures in life. This autumn walk would have been too solemn with only the crunch of leaves beneath her feet, the ever-sparser branches whispering in the breeze above her head.

"Red sky at morning, sailor take warning. I saw it on my run at seven. Maybe tomorrow, if you're in a boating mood. Best I can do is a kayak though."

"I don't go on boats. They're a danger to actresses, historically. If you catch my drift. How's the mythical boys' club thing going?"

"Me and the other guys, we're really getting moving on this. Correcting some of the mistakes that the last guys made. You can't do all of that Native appropriation stuff. It doesn't fly. But we've got a campout next weekend. Don't be surprised if I come back a changed man."

They reached Zoe's porch, and Adam hung back at the bottom of the stairs. He knew an invite wasn't coming, that his cloying attempts to win Zoe's favor were futile. But he tried, and the spring in his step after Zoe waved him goodbye suggested that happiness lay in the attempt. There was something pitiful in the willingness to fail, which was maybe the root of what Zoe found unsexy about Adam. A man that can live without her does her no good. When a man encountered the possibility of Zoe, the glimmer of a chance he might slither between her legs, it should cleave his life into before and after, and if he wasn't worthy of a night with Zoe, let the rest of his life punish him for believing in something that could never be true.

Not that she could endure a man who had nothing going on other than her. Zoe settled on the porch, taking the chair just in the shade to protect her skin from the sun. No, he needed to have goals and dreams that defined his life, but even those wouldn't compare to the thrill of attaining her. She flipped the switch to turn on a fan hanging from the porch ceiling. Cool air whisked away the little droplets of sweat that gathered around her collarbones. A family walking a dog and a child in a stroller walked past, and the mom waved and tried to make eye contact with Zoe, but Zoe ignored her. They didn't have anything she needed. None of these people did.

# LILY

After she walked out Elena's door, Lily could have followed any of the roads that led out of Pittsburgh and landed across the country. So many places, so many new people were right outside Pittsburgh's multi-local borders. Why stay, then?

Part of it was money. Lily couldn't afford first month's rent and deposit anywhere, let alone if she gave up her job at the shop. And the disappointment she'd feel leaving the shop after surrendering the apprenticeship that she'd put so much of her hope into would be too much to bear. More than any of that, Lily pictured Zoe's smile at hearing that Lily had left town. She heard the glee in her laughter, and refused to let Zoe win. Why should she get to force Lily out of her home?

That defiance carried her to the doorway of the house she'd shared with Zoe for years. Lily had entered through the door a thousand times, and it had never been so forbidding. But it was still her house. She had the key in her hand, twiddling it as she listened for any noise inside. Nothing. Just a flickering light. Maybe Zoe wasn't there. If she was, Lily would assert that it was her house too, and she'd be staying as long as it took for her to find another place to live. Still, when the key turned in the lock, Lily expected alarms to go off, spotlights to find her. Zoe to appear with a posse of sycophants to carry her off the property. It clicked, and the door opened without a sound. Nate must have oiled it.

As she tiptoed into the house, Lily felt safer. But when she crossed into the living room, a spotlight snapped to and blinded her. It came from somewhere on the ceiling, but Lily had to keep her fingers clasped over her eyes to keep the pain away.

"What the fuck." Zoe's voice. Everything had gone so wrong, so quickly. "That's not yours."

The warm glow inside Lily's eyelids went away. Peering from between her fingers, she saw the light focused on Zoe, who waved her hand continuously to keep it from leaving her.

"It's a motion detector. Because I'm supposed to be the only person here. You left. You were supposed to stay gone."

"I'm back now. Until I leave. Why is there a spotlight in the living room?"

"All the world's a stage, bitch. It's my living room anyway, none of your business."

"It's our living room. My name's still on the lease." The horrifying paint and crushed metal were gone. Zoe probably took it down minutes after Lily had moved out. Instead, mirrors lined the walls. A thousand Zoes stood in the spotlight and another thousand Lilys lurked in the surrounding darkness. Faces just visible by the whites of their eyes and the little slivers of teeth visible by their sneers. An unwilling audience, infinite and forced to watch Zoe's show.

"Yeah, whatever. 'The law'. You left, that means it's mine. But your bed's still in your room. I didn't get rid of it. Because I'm a good friend."

There were no words to mend or defuse the situation, much as the mouse can't reason with the cat pawing it around for fun. Zoe's curt little smile and vicious eyes told Lily all she needed to know. "You're a great friend. The best. I'm going to bed."

Zoe's voice found her as she ascended the stairs. "Let me know if you need help clearing stuff off. I can get Nate here in a couple days. Maybe Adam too, if you don't mind seeing him. I know you two were a thing."

Lily had to lower her shoulder into the door and push to open it. Sandbags clogged the space between the door and the wall, but she was able to squeeze through the tiny crack she'd won. Christmas lights glowed white, strung around a massive round object sitting atop her bed. Deep shadows revealed cracks and divots in the surface. Grit crumbled onto the sheets when she touched it. A huge rock. Lily tried to flip the light switch, but neither direction did anything.

After a couple stomps back down the stairs, Lily paused. None of it was an accident, so why act like anger would solve the problem? If anything, it was Zoe's goal. And that bitch did not deserve to get what she wanted. One deep breath, and then Lily glided down the stairs. The spotlight found her again. Through her squint, she smiled and said, "Hey Zoe, it's pretty bad up there. Think you could help me?"

"This fucking thing. It's not built for two people. It needs, like, the self-driving car stuff for knowing who isn't supposed to get the spotlight."

"I think that's hard because there aren't different shapes. Speaking of, the boulder in my bed?"

"A star is a uniquely recognizable shape. Don't be silly." Zoe swirled her hand around, holding the light on her again.

"My mistake. The boulder?"

Zoe kicked her feet onto the coffee table, made entirely of mirrored glass. The floor, Lily could see now that her eyes had adjusted, was also mirrored.

"You noticed! It's so I can always look down and get a little upskirt peek."

"But you've still got a—no. Zoe, the boulder."

"Yeah, I do. You're right. I forgot I have a dick, thank you for reminding me. It's called negative visualization, Lil. Time to grow up and find out how stuff gets done." She took a sip from a huge margarita and pointedly looked away from Lily. It would be so easy to flip the table over, to rant and rage at Zoe for how awful she was being. But instead, Lily sat next to Zoe on the couch. Calm, collected, mature.

"You know. I bet we could lift it together. It doesn't seem that dense. Want to give it a try?"

"Nate can do it in a couple days. Don't sweat it. I won't charge you." Zoe smirked and her eyes zoomed up and to the corner, creating an illusion that they were bigger by revealing more of the whites. She was mugging for a camera that didn't exist. At least Lily could be sure that this was an act. Zoe's aversion toward verisimilitude was, for once, of use to Lily. Going through the process of elimination to figure out what Zoe actually felt was exhausting, but it reassured Lily that there was some kind of reality at the bottom of Zoe's actions. Delusional thrashing would be impossible to work with.

"Sure. But I thought it might be fun if we did it together. Zoe and Lily carrying a boulder downstairs and out onto the sidewalk. Wouldn't that be a wild time?"

"No chance, I don't lift. This body is finely toned for two things: expressiveness and sex appeal. Moving that thing around is neither. I'd obliterate my nails for sure."

"I know a lot of girls who think strong women are sexy."

"Great. I can get a bunch of lesbians clawing at my dick. That's not getting me cast in anything."

"What if Nate came by tonight?"

Zoe shook her head, her long blonde ponytail waggling behind her like a tail.

"He's got the night off. It's in his contract. He has a loom he weaves on."

"Sure, but this is an emergency, right? There's a... boulder."

"Boulder boulder boulder." Zoe flapped her hand like a mouth. "No how are you, Zoe, how has the last month alone been, Zoe. Like yeah, there's a boulder. Sorry, I guess. But that's not the only thing going on."

There was no winning. There wasn't even a strategy to pursue if Zoe refused to help in all scenarios. Lily went back upstairs, but turned right at the landing instead. Slow quiet steps gave way to a sprint as she lunged into Zoe's room, then whirled and wedged a chair beneath the doorknob. Within two deep, calming breaths, Zoe was pounding on the door. "Get the fuck out of my room."

No matter how much Zoe wiggled the doorknob or threw herself against the door though, the chair held fast. Lily sat on the bed and unzipped her bag, pulling out her pajamas. Unlikely that she'd get to make it through the whole night under siege, but she wanted to try. While she slipped beneath the covers, Zoe talked on the phone only a few steps away from the door. "Nate. Nate. She's in my room. I can't sleep in hers because of the boulder. Well whose idea was that? I don't give a shit about the loom, Nate. I don't. You can weave when I'm not in crisis."

Lily had won a victory in battle, but now the war stretched long and brutal ahead of her. Even Zoe's bed fought her, demanding Lily conform to the shape inscribed in memory foam which she couldn't fit. She wished she was back in Elena's bed, with the warmth of her lover—ex-lover—closing her in and sending her off to peace. Everything had been perfect, but for the fact of Lily. Another person could have so easily slid into that situation and it would have run like clockwork. But Lily was gum, and it had all shuddered to a halt as soon as she'd worked her way through the gears. Here, too. Zoe had been probably doing fine before Lily came back. Assuming Zoe even let her make it through the night without getting some people over to throw her out, Lily would try to find a new place to go first thing in the morning.

# ZOE

Gotta give her credit: Lily had gone and done it this time. Nate was on his way, as fast as his Vespa could bring him, so it would all get fixed in due time. But right now, there was something in her house that Zoe didn't have control over. For the last month, everything had been exactly as she had desired it. As a result, she'd been turning in her best performances yet: every emotion beautifully developed within the seamless flow of consciousness. Nothing too abrupt. Even outbursts of anguish felt like they bubbled up from deeper waters, giving the impression not of a sudden shift, but of a long-awaited eruption. Here, in her real life, she felt one such eruption beginning. Lily had been free to leave; Zoe wouldn't begrudge her that. But to come back unannounced was rude. It was just like Lily to enrobe herself in the technically correct, exploiting the rules of courtesy to disguise her actions. Locking herself in Zoe's room was too far. While Zoe could've been more helpful in removing the boulder, it wasn't her fault that it hadn't become a loom-interrupting emergency until after Lily had closed herself in.

After a few more bangs on the door, Zoe sauntered downstairs to rest until Nate arrived. The spotlight lit up once she entered the living room, but it only illuminated half her face. She tried to step into the center, but the spotlight tracked her movements. No matter where she went in the room, half of her body was shrouded in darkness.

It took weeks to get the spotlight system to work; weeks of begging electricians to figure out why it was going so wrong, and now it had degenerated further on a difficult evening. What if someone was surreptitiously taking a picture of her through an open window? They'd be devastated to find this half-vanished grotesque rather than Zoe's usual perfect glamour. It must've been thrown out of balance when it swiveled to focus on Lily earlier. Lily gets attention, Zoe gets problems.

She curled up on the couch. Nate would be there in fifteen minutes. Thunder sounded outside the window, and rain started to fall. Maybe twenty minutes. Zoe connected to the speaker in her bedroom and played a podcast interview she'd done a few months ago. Just because Lily could close a door didn't mean she could escape Zoe's perfect voice. Zoe tracked the time on the podcast app's playback, recalling the conversation. At 4:23, her voice lilted in a perfect, feminine way. A minute later, her voice cracked. The producer had promised to try and smooth it out in editing, but either he'd lied or it was so harsh a sound that no amount of editing could soften the blow. The replay in her mind didn't cooperate. As it continued past the ten minute mark, her voice became deep and gravelly. The words got lost in the static rumble of her voice. The whole interview became a spectacle, with the interviewer playing along and divining meaning from her unintelligible responses. Even after Zoe paused it on her phone, it played on in her memory and the spotlight was still half-lit and she smelled a trace of body odor in the air and couldn't be sure if it was Lily's or her own and what if she didn't get enough attention for her performance in this movie and what if and what if and what if.

Nate's polite knock on the door snapped her out of it. "May I enter?"

"Yes, come in."

His keys jangled and he burst through the door and ran up the stairs. The spotlight followed him, no matter how Zoe gesticulated to try and bring it back to her. It captured his motion fully, but once he was gone and it finally returned to her, its aim was still a foot off. She unfastened one of her heels and threw it at the spotlight. Her own aim wasn't much better. The shoe hit the television and bounced to the floor, heel up. The TV rocked backwards, then toppled forward, onto Zoe's shoe. At the sound of shattered glass, Nate ran back down the stairs. His alpaca-wool sweater was covered in dust and debris from the boulder.

"What happened? Is there a spill? Are you okay?"

Nate grunted as he lifted the big-screen TV back onto its resting place. Zoe's heel had punctured the screen, and the shoe was still attached. Nate clasped his hands over his mouth when he saw it. "Your television. Where you watch your performances... Sweetie, I am so sorry this is happening to you. We will get you a brand new TV right away."

"Thank you, Nate." Zoe wiped away a tear that had snuck down her face without permission. "Any luck with the stone?"

"I don't have the strength to move it. My pathetic twig legs have failed you. But we'll get it moved, I promise."

"Of course. I believe in you. And the bedroom door?"

"That, I should be able to take care of."

After he marched up the stairs, Zoe could hear the sound of a drill, then a thunk, then muted conversation. She couldn't discern the words, but it began with a series of quick and authoritative words from Nate. Then the pace slowed. Lily's voice sounded calm, while Nate's wavered with uncertainty. His momentum dropped off completely and he came downstairs, unable to look Zoe in the eye.

He'd failed, but it wasn't his fault. All of Nate's experience was in the bluster and hubris of show business. He knew how to face down powerful egos and refuse to yield, but whatever Lily's tactics were, they must have been unfamiliar to him.

"Lily has informed me that I cannot forcibly remove her from the room, because to do so would be an act of harm not just against her, but against the class of trans women broadly, of which you are a member."

Zoe kicked off her remaining heel. She squeezed her manager's shoulder and went upstairs herself. "You did fine. I've got it from here."

The door lay on the ground, propped against the frame. Lily hadn't attempted to block it any further. Good. She had enough sense to recognize inevitability. All of Zoe's pillows were scattered to the floor, and her sheets were in a pile. Everything was cleared off of her makeup table, her bookshelf, and her clothes were pulled from her closet and piled up too. On the bare mattress, Lily sat cross-legged, glaring at Zoe as she entered.

"Why would you do this?"

"I didn't know what else to do."

Zoe lunged for Lily and grabbed her shoulder, which slipped through until Zoe's grasp settled around Lily's elbow. Wrestling wouldn't suit either of them very much, but even with a foot propped against the bedframe, Zoe couldn't easily budge Lily. "You could leave me alone! You could not lock yourself in my room! You could not expect everything to be ready for you whenever you came back randomly!"

"You put a rock in my bed! I can't use it!"

"It wasn't your room anymore."

Lily screamed, and Zoe let go. "What? What happened?" She looked around for some kind of threat, but the two of them were alone in her disheveled room. A few drops of blood tracked down Lily's arm. "Oh shit, when did that happen?"

"You dug your nails into my arm."

"No, I don't think so."

Lily held up her arm, displaying the wounds right where Zoe had been grabbing her. But Zoe remembered her grip: finger pads down, wrists loose and elegant. She'd done nothing so inelegant as clenching her hand into a claw. "You might've caught it on something while you were trashing my room. Don't be dramatic." A loud rumble down the stairs interrupted them. When Zoe poked her head out of the door, a grimy Nate gave her a thumbs up. "And see? I took care of your problem. Be sure to wash your sheets; I'm sure they're filthy."

While Lily cleaned her sheets and Nate tidied Zoe's room, Zoe returned to the couch. She closed her left eye so that it would feel like the spotlight was on all of her. It worked well enough as long as she didn't look down. The light started to buzz and vibrate, shaking the boundary of the darkness just inside her vision. Was this how everything would be now that Lily was back? Beneath the flickering light, the stiletto dangling from the TV looked alive, as if every moment it was burrowing itself deeper and deeper into the shattered glass.

# LILY

Lily and Zoe sat on opposite sides of the room. Adam placed a yellow legal pad on the coffee table and lined it up to parallel the edge of the table exactly. Then a pencil above the pad, again, parallel. A blanket draped over the spotlight, which clicked and moved whenever it thought it sensed movement beneath the shroud. Adam held his hands clasped in his lap and said, "So, I'll be mediating this dispute between you two ladies. First, I'd like to acknowledge my personal relationship with each of you. Lily, we went on one date. It was alright, but we're just friends now. Does that feel like a fair assessment?"

Lily didn't know if "friends" was appropriate, but didn't think correcting him was the right move. She'd heard Adam was an excellent mediator and wanted to give this an honest try. The way Steph told it, the Thunder Ridge punk house would've erupted into violence without his deft conflict resolution in the stolen rolling tobacco incident. So Lily was willing to give him a shot. Anything to make the time before she could find a new place to live bearable.

"And Zoe. The two of us are good friends. Is that fair?"

"Am I under oath? What are the rules?" Zoe narrowed her eyes at Lily.

"No, nothing so dramatic. Though I encourage you to tell the truth. Otherwise, you may find this session to be less productive than you would've liked."

"Good to know. Anyway, yes, we're good friends."

"Let's get started. What are your goals for this session? Lily, you first."

"I want to live in this house without feeling like I'm constantly trapped in conflict."

"Zoe?"

"I want Lily to move out and also move out of the city and maybe go live in a cave."

Lily buried her head in her hands. "This was a waste of time."

"Lily, please. Let me mediate. That's what I'm here for." He scooted closer to Zoe and summoned the finite charm contained in his apple-cheeked smile. "Zoe. Can you phrase that in a way that's more concerned with the experience and tone of living here that you'd prefer?"

"Of course. I can do anything. I'd like to live here alone. I'd like to go through my life in the city without seeing people that aggravate me because their presence reminds me of all the ways they betrayed me. Is that better?"

"Yes, that's much better."

Adam peeked down Zoe's shirt. What was happening here? He said, "Lily, is there anything you can think of that would make this situation easier for Zoe?"

"I just want to be left alone. I'm happy not to speak to her or whatever."

Shaking his head, Adam stood from the couch and paced around the room. "Not talking? That's no kind of relationship at all. Conflict like this happens because there is a natural order, a balance, which any given relationship can achieve to be harmonious. The problem is that people act in ways they're not supposed to, do things that aren't true to their nature because it suits their desire to benefit at the expense of another, or because they want to destroy relationships. I'm here to get to the root of that."

Adam placed a hand on Zoe's shoulder. His fingers grazed her sharp collarbone. Maybe he was finally about to ask her a hard question. Something that would take her to task, make her reveal how she'd tormented Lily to make her leave. But he only looked at Lily and said,

"Can you think of anything you've done which may have harmed Zoe?"

The hands, the glances, it was all so obvious now. This was a trap, not a mediation. They were creating a record of Lily as the villain, and if she got up and walked out, Zoe and Adam could claim that she didn't even try to resolve their differences. There was nothing she could do, other than try to pierce the horny veil over Adam's eyes and convince him that Zoe was the problem. Lily said, "She's made it very clear. Do you want discrete actions? I could list things like walking, eating, and breathing. Those get mentioned."

"Lily. Please try to get through these questions without disguising insults. Stay calm."

"I am calm. I think there was an incident at a show a couple months back, but I don't really know what happened there."

"Bitch, you do."

Adam just smiled at Zoe. His eyes shone with adoration. Permitting her to act as she pleased gave him passage to gaze upon her for just a couple seconds longer than usual.

"And then it turned into a whole mess. She pissed off everyone there. People still talk about it."

"But I was right. Write that down," Zoe said. Adam took a note.

"Can you think of any other harmful actions you've done?"

"I didn't do anything. I was just trying to have a nice night out with Zoe."

"Are you sure? Zoe, how do you feel that Lily has harmed you?"

Zoe took a deep breath and wiped away a few dishonest tears. She was acting. Partway through, her voice would crack because she was just so emotional. "Where do I start? She pulled that shit on me at the show; she clomps around here so I can't get any rest—" The crack came to rest, but Adam didn't register how obvious this all was. "She talks shit about me to every single person she knows—"

"I do not."

"—Am I allowed to finish? I thought it was my turn to speak. Do I not get to talk?"

"Lily, it's important that you show Zoe an appropriate amount of respect. She's making herself vulnerable in an effort to address these harms you've done, to fix things." Adam crouched, elbows propped on his knees, wrists dangling between. Like he was coaching a child who had thrown a tantrum at soccer practice. Lily threw up her hands.

"Fuck this. I don't care what you say about me. You're thinking with your dick and I'm not doing this anymore."

Zoe gasped and Adam leapt to his feet. "You do not talk about her like that. No matter what her particular genital situation is, that is not an appropriate way to speak to a trans woman."

"I was talking about you." Lily picked up her duffel bag, barely unpacked after the night before. "Please consider that you've made this all worse, all to still not fuck a girl."

She lit a cigarette and blew smoke in his face, then left. As much as she wanted to say something cutting to Zoe, something that would turn all her joy and satisfaction to frustration, she couldn't think of anything, couldn't bear to meet that gaze.

The fallout would come quickly enough. Steph had vouched for Adam, so she might be willing to house Lily out of guilt once she heard how it had all blown up. Low-hanging tree branches caught the smoke Lily puffed into the air. While she watched it whirl and catch on the leaves, she tripped on a chunk of sidewalk that roots had pushed up. Fair retaliation, given the smoke. Lily placed her forehead to the tree bark. The pain of sharp edges gave way as she got used to it, though the sensation of roughness didn't leave. Above her, the leaves rustled in the wind and it sounded like music.

# ZOE

Within thirty seconds of Lily leaving, Nate barged in. Zoe had instructed him to wait outside and hide behind his Vespa. As ever, he was the consummate professional, even as he dusted dirt and road grit off of his sweater. "I can't believe it worked so fast!"

"Why not? I told you it would."

"Of course. I'm sorry. You were right, and I never doubted you for a second."

Zoe liked laying these little traps for Nate. While his devotion was never in question, she worried that he might one day become complacent. Any slip-up on his part could push her off of the high wire that any emerging acting career balanced upon, so she couldn't let him get lazy.

"I see. You were using me," Adam said.

Maybe he hadn't been on the same page after all. Zoe had to flash a smile and giggle and bat her big green eyes and watch as Adam's lost their focus.

"Oh, no. Of course not. But I had a feeling that she'd throw a tantrum and storm out. It's what she does."

"That's true." His faux-studied nod, the hand on the chin. Every movement of his body was designed to pretend some kind of erudition, but he was a worse actor than he was a mediator, and his pretensions disgusted Zoe, and her disgust made him more attractive than ever. She wanted to pin him to the couch and revile him, slurp him up and see if he tasted the way "mouthfeel" sounded. Adam said, "Lily has always struck me as a very toxic person. That's why there was never a second date."

Nate clapped his hands. "Thank you, yes. Every single personality test," he said as he dug out a folder from his bag, "Enneagram type: 6. Meyers-Briggs: INFP. Astrology: Scorpio. She's a nightmare across the board."

"What were my results in those little tests?"

"You're an angel, light itself. Tests can't measure your virtue."

"My astrological sign. I was born, wasn't I?"

"You are reborn moment to moment; the pure radiance of creation."

Zoe smiled and nestled herself into the pile of throw pillows on the couch. Long, soft threads tickled her wrist; a canvas pillowcase on the other side scratched at her shoulder. The pillows settled into place and, for a moment, she was exempt from gravity. Zoe was pretty sure she was also a Scorpio, given how near her birthday and Lily's were, but her acting skill allowed her to see every aspect of her own personality for the performance it was and adjust it accordingly. The mind allows the stars their influence, and the mind can forbid it too.

Adam said, "I see. How did you get her to take those tests? My experience with Lily is that she's resistant to doing what you ask her to."

Zoe laughed. "Did you find that out on your date?"

Adam laughed too, but it came out a little tight, like a gasp. He tried to sit casually on the arm of the couch, near enough to Zoe to express his interest, but far enough for plausible deniability. But his back was too stiff; his hands sat on his thighs too self-consciously. "No. I mean, it was—it wasn't a good date, but—"

"Miss Berger is teasing you," Nate said, gravely serious. "You should be honored."

"So if you two are experts on the human condition... think she's coming back?" Zoe didn't care much about their answers. She knew the truth: Lily was gone. Never fight, always flight. Maybe someday she'd be willing to dig in, and she and Zoe could finally come to some kind of agreement about their intertwined lives. Until then, Zoe would have to keep pushing her. All patience got her was scorn and belittlement.

Adam, much less informed about Lily's personality, but ready to pretend that their one date gave him insight, said, "It's hard to say. She's unpredictable." Wrong. "Everything she does is hidden behind this layer of... pretense." Adam was more accurately describing himself. He approached manhood like a dance you do to summon rain. If you go through the motions, something real will show up. "At a base level, she's jealous of you. But she'll come back. She only understands herself by measuring herself against you and seeing where she doesn't match up." Lily had transitioned later than Zoe, but thought she was the most beautiful and desirable girl in the city; thought she was Zoe's social better, that she could make fun of Zoe whenever she pleased to impress whoever was around. If she was only jealous, that would solve everything. That's a dynamic that made sense, one which Zoe encountered on a daily basis. The way Lily saw Zoe, however, was much more pernicious. Adam's eyes pleaded with Zoe, waiting for her response to his analysis.

"I'm sure you're right," she said, but was unable to resist following up. "Nate, do you agree with him?"

"Oh, not at all. She's a rat. She's making for the coziest little hole she can find. That's not here. You are a glorious, long-coated feline, and the only thing she fears more than your claws is if your beautiful eyes looked at her and didn't care. She can tell you're over her whole thing, and she's running."

"Really."

"That's right. You'll never see her again. Her big, dramatic return blew up right in her busted face. She won't try it again."

Zoe said, "I think she's quite beautiful. Someone once asked if we were sisters. It was at some kind of trans thanksgiving thing. Everyone who's lonely goes into a room and is lonely together. You bring the worst vegan dish you can imagine and talk to people sadder than the dead."

"Whoever asked that is an idiot. Her bone structure is still laden with the curse of her origin, while yours has always been that of a goddess, waiting to break through the skin. A gift to the world, waiting to be unwrapped."

"I met a goddess, once."

"Oh, was this that Calamity person?" Adam seemed happy to find his way back into the conversation. "I couldn't see her. Too masculine." He said this as an aside to Nate, clearly hoping to find some shared purchase in masculinity, but Nate's rapt attention to Zoe overrode whatever interest in gender he might have.

"She was gorgeous," Zoe said. "I kind of wished I could wear her skin. Not the whole Buffalo Bill, I'd fuck me, sort of song and dance. God knows we've got enough of that. But her skin was so warm. I wanted to know what sunlight felt like through it."

"No better than the sunlight feels through your flawless skin, Ms. Berger." Predictable. But then, no one hires an assistant on the hope that they're full of surprises.

"If you had her skin, you might be invisible to me. And men, generally speaking. That would be a shame." Adam even flirted like a little worm. Zoe wanted to tear his clothes from his body and threaten him, watch him stammer and squirm and get sweatier and sweatier as his little t-dick got rock hard. Not that she was inclined to follow through. Men should see her as a distant light on the horizon and use her to push themselves through deserts as sand scours their faces. To think of her as their grip begins to weaken on the lone rock in the middle of a river white with anger; to push themselves through the agony of each step, higher and higher up the infinite mountain because the only pain greater than the one that courses through their blistered feet and shattered bones is the one of spending a single instant getting no closer to her. Only by proving themselves capable of greatness should men be allowed to lay their scratched and callused palms on her soft flesh. Could Adam prove himself? She looked at him with the attitude of someone evaluating whether her time would be better spent napping, rather than that of a woman considering a sexual partner.

She said, "Maybe I would vanish. Imagine the intrigue! Zoe Berger, superstar actress, invisible to men! What a sensation I'd be. Poor little closeted girls, realizing they can see me. Men, who've heard tales of my beauty, injecting themselves with estrogen just to get a glance. Could be nice."

"So, being invisible to men could open up some horror roles for you."

"Don't be an idiot, Nate. I can't wear her skin. She's using it. And I'd look grotesque." Again, the practicalities. His sharp eyes saw only the path from point A to point B, and he'd believe whatever she told him those points were. Useful. But she had hired him so that she wouldn't have to think about such matters, so she could focus on becoming a transcendent talent and honing further her otherworldly beauty. Every time Nate's mindset revealed itself, she felt the mud of the world bubbling up around her knees. No matter how tall she became, her feet would be down there in it. "The important thing is, we can all agree that Lily's not going to keep trying to live here. It's not working out. She has to know that."

"It's obvious that she'd be better off anywhere else, where her problem with you doesn't matter," Nate said.

"I agree. I had hoped to resolve this problem, but her resentment was much deeper than I'd expected. It's a shame. I used to think she was better than that. But sometimes, you see new sides of people. It's a shock. It's a tragedy. We all have to face it." Adam paused, his final word caught up in the tangled strings of inevitability. If he'd had more dignity, more self-respect, he'd never have said it, but he was a creature of the mud and would act accordingly. "Together."

God, he was vile. Zoe couldn't wait to suck his dick.

# LILY

Between sending a message to Steph asking to crash at her place and receiving an affirmative response, Lily fantasized about burning down her old house (once), driving Zoe out of the house with violence or subterfuge (three times), leaving town and starting over under a new identity (once), and lying down by the side of the road and sleeping until she didn't have any more problems (continuously). She'd also floated the idea of crashing in the tattoo parlor, but Sveta responded, "No, it would be poison for the mind and the walls." Lily couldn't bring herself to ask what that meant, and whatever it was wouldn't matter.

Now, she flopped her duffel bag onto a bench in the middle of Arsenal Park. The park was a little corridor of grass between two busy streets, with a concrete walkway down the middle, and an ankle-high wire fence separating the people walking through, from the grass. Signs said, "Don't step into the grass, you might not come back :)". Whether it was true or not, the people in surrounding Lawrenceville believed that if you stepped into the grass while no one was looking, it would take you to some twilight between the world and nowhere. There you'd live, a shadow of a shadow of a shadow, until by chance someone looked into your eyes. It probably wasn't true, but there was no one around, and the brush of the blades of grass against her ankles would be so pleasant; the thin life of a shadow would ache so much less to carry. But her phone vibrated with Steph's assent, regrets, condolences, and suddenly, she had somewhere to go.

Lily hesitated once she got to Steph's door. How long would Steph's guilt hold open space for her? Maybe she'd be better off withdrawing all her money and finding the most threatening room for rent on Craigslist. But no, that would be stupid, and she probably didn't have enough money to cover even that. So she knocked.

Four people crowded the entryway as Lily walked through the door. One of them wore a collar around their neck, while three others wore white cloth ribbons around their wrists. The overhead light for the entryway shone red, hiding the four greeters' eyes in shadow and lending a demonic presence to their ready hands. Not a single crack of the wall could peek through the framed pictures lining the foyer. Each of them was a different nude picture of Steph, finding her from some other angle, in some other light. Taken together, the viewer could understand the totality of Steph's body upon their first step into her apartment. For now, Lily didn't focus on the pictures too much. It would feel strange in front of these people, whose relationship to Steph was a mystery to her—though the collar on one of them was a clue. She'd come back to look later.

She loosed the duffel bag from her shoulder and walked into the living room. Couches, chairs, end tables, bookcases, filled every inch of wall and floor space, and little staircases allowed access to the higher places to sit, read, or think. Low magenta light peered out from where the furniture met the walls. Another person in a collar descended one such staircase, with a bong atop a ceramic plate in their hands. Steph lounged on a white couch at the top of the stairs in a paint-spattered hoodie and tiny mesh shorts. She blew pungent weed smoke into the air and coughed while she said, "Lil, you made it. Thank god."

"Hi, Steph. Thank you so much for letting me stay with you. I love the decor. It's very... you. Where are Ronnie and Jen? I was looking forward to seeing them."

Steph leaned over and pulled the chins of the two people reclining beneath the couch toward her. "They're not around anymore. I needed some new subs that befit my status." Turning their faces toward Lily, she said, "Look at them. The same face, different bodies." One of them was lanky and smooth, while the other bristled with hair all over his enormous, powerful body. But their faces were exactly the same, somehow. "They're not twins. It's not gross."

"Your new status as cult leader?"

"Messiah. This isn't a cult," she said, as one of the wrist-ribboned brought her a drink. "Everyone is free to come and go, and I don't do any indoctrination. I've lost a lot of Daddy's old followers." The three stood at the foot of the staircase, backs to the wall, gazing up at Steph. "But everyone who stayed is so much more dependable. The Clenched Fist of God will be just fine."

"Is it just them? Hi, I'm Lily by the way." She waved, but all three of them stared at their leader, unwilling to break their gaze to acknowledge Lily.

"Oh, no. I have people all across the country. Daddy's fate, though his martyrdom is glorious and an inspiration to us all, has exposed some of the flaws with the compound strategy. I want something a bit more distributed." Her head cocked up, and she rose from the couch, carrying the attention of everyone in the room. "Smells like dinner is almost ready. If you'll excuse me."

The three cultists followed her, but the subs remained, so Lily scooted a bit closer to them. Part of her wanted to sit on the couch and see what happened, but taking big risks while relying on Steph's kindness seemed unwise. "Is there a TV or something here?"

The twink sub said, "No, Mistress doesn't let us have entertainment. It would take away from our time contemplating Her."

"Okay, but what about the cultists? Same deal?" Afraid to seem nosy, Lily wanted to strategize how she asked her questions. Curiosity, not gawking. Otherwise, they'd shut down.

The bear sub scoffed. "Sharing the apartment with them sucks, dude."

Lily leaned forward, as the twink sub shushed the bear sub. Lily said, "Hey, I don't want to get you in trouble or anything."

"She's Mistress's friend, she's going to tell Her!" The twink sub yanked fruitlessly on the bear sub's leather harness. "If you get me in trouble, I'm gonna—"

"Don't worry," the bear sub said as he lay down on the floor. "I can tell she's not into the cult shit. Right?"

"It's... better if I don't say anything." Lily was in Steph's thrall now, in a way. A bed doesn't buy as much as salvation, but Lily's silence came cheap.

"I'm right." The bear sub closed his eyes, assured. "It's fucking weird. I'm devoted as hell to Her, but at least I get fucked about it."

"Mistress says that She inspires many kinds of devotion. She deserves it all."

A cultist with a burn mark on the side of his face walked stiffly into the room. Looking into his eyes felt like staring into the little black domes on grocery store ceilings. Everything was obscured but for a dim reflection. "Our Lady has informed me that dinner is ready. Please join us at the table."

The table in the center of the dining room was a modest oak table, with a leaf shunted into the middle to make room for everyone surrounding it. Chair legs scraped against each other and thighs bumped thighs. On the walls were identical tables with an identical array of dishes jutting into the space; corners threatening Lily's head as the cultist led her to the other side of the room. Another table dangled from the ceiling, with a hole carved out of the center to offer the overhead light a tunnel. Only the occupied table had food on it; every other one stood empty, anticipating they wouldn't be used in time for this, or any, dinner.

The cultist showed Lily to a chair at the opposite end of the table from Steph, whose smile prompted everyone else to smile with her. Lily's chair was higher than the ones the cultists and subs sat on. Maybe Steph had considered that Lily would feel some discomfort and wanted to assure her that they were still equals, despite Steph's messianic status. Better treatment than she'd gotten from Zoe. This was strange, but manageable. As long as everyone there was on board with how they were being treated, Lily had no room to complain. At least until she found her way into a more permanent situation.

Steph raised a pink plastic cup toward Lily. "To our new guest, Lily. I'm sorry for how it happened, but I'm glad you're here. How are you doing?"

"Not too bad. Elena's art show is next month and I'm thinking about going, even with... everything. I want to see it, want to show her I'm okay."

"You couldn't catch me dead at that show. I like art, but not its people."

Lily smiled, spooned some curry onto the rice on her plate. She didn't know what to say. Whether she was one of the people who Steph meant; what a person lost in Steph's eyes as they wandered into a gallery.

"I bet none of you know how Lily and I met," Steph said.

"No no no. They don't need to hear that."

"Oh yes they do. So, when I met Lily, it was just—wait a second." Steph looked up at Lily. "Is it okay if I explain the context? Yes? So, she's trans. And the story you're about to hear takes place like three months into transitioning. Before." She gestured towards Lily's face and hair. "She became the angel you see now. Okay, here's how it went: I see this girl, she is absolutely the drunkest girl at the party. Not easy, at that party. And she's dancing on top of a table."

"With other people. I wasn't doing it alone." Lily remembered the smoke-filled air of the night, the tobacco and weed combining with the odor of cheap liquor to create the quintessential party aroma.

"But you were doing it the most. Here she is, with this cute little pixie cut and these tiny tits. Her top was off when I showed up. I don't think I ever saw her wearing it." Steph laughed and gripped the burn-faced cultist's arm, whose eyes widened in shock.

"Ugh, it was such a cute little sheer top with stars on it." Lily pouted, putting a little extra into it for show. She felt like she was performing with Steph for an audience, though admittedly a forced-favorable one.

"Anyway, she sees me and decides she's in love with me. She spends the entire night sitting in my lap, whispering in my ear. You would not believe the things she offered to do for me that night."

Lily shrunk down in her chair. "I was drunk!"

"So I didn't take her up on the offers, but every so often I like to tell her one of the things she whispered to me."

"Come on, not in front of them." Lily blushed.

"Please, they can hear this. In fact, I order you all to be okay with hearing this." The cultists and subs nodded in unison. "She told me, that she... would love... to move in with me and my followers and toys. Incredible foresight, that one." The glass of wine sloshed in her hand as she laughed. With a fake shocked look on her face, she stage-whispered to one of her subs, "Maybe she's a prophet."

One of the cultists, who had a little soul patch, said, voice trembling, "A prophet?" He turned to Lily. "I would be honored to witness your prophecy."

The burn-faced cultist scoffed. "Our Lady was joking. She's not a prophet."

"I'm not a prophet," Lily said.

"Right, she's an angel," Steph said. "Anyway, the

story ends with her puking in my car and me nursing her back from the brink of death during her hangover. We've been friends ever since."

The cultist with a soul patch said, "Surely being a friend of Our Savior must make you a person of some cosmological significance. Perhaps a saint?"

"Didn't you just hear that story? I'm no saint."

All Steph did was cock her head and smile. The bear sub waded into the silence, nudging the twink sub and saying, "Don't you have some opinions on saints?"

"Oh I do," he said, clapping his hands while his face lit up like a child finally given an opportunity to talk about Pokémon. "I think St. Simeon was the most fuck-able saint. Imagine, someone who could live up on that pillar could probably edge for days."

"What about St. Francis?" Steph asked.

"Ugh, no. Didn't he have animals hanging around him all the time? I'm not trying to bang a zoo."

The conversation stayed in that arena for some time. The cultists kept silent while Lily and the bear twink argued about the Virgin Mary. Meanwhile, Steph drank her wine. Soon enough, Lily was tired, and Steph ordered the burn-faced cultist to guide her to a room. The two of them trudged down the hall in silence, but after the cultist opened the door and dropped her bag on the floor, he said, "I hope you have a pleasant sleep, and reflect on what it means to drag Our Savior down into vulgarity."

By that point both drunk and sleepy, Lily said, "What?"

The cultist left, and Lily flopped onto the bed. Vulgarity. As if their meeting had been grotesque, rather than sweet and messy. Lily understood that the cultists needed to preserve a certain vision of their savior. But what contamination could Lily have accomplished that the subs didn't?

She tried to contemplate it further, but her best attempts couldn't wave away the fog enclosing her mind, hugging her still and into a fitful sleep.

# ZOE

Everyone talks about party-crashing, but no one ever defines the terms well enough. Weddings are unambiguous, events tightly controlled by invites, given out on the basis of connection to the hosts. Birthday parties are similar, though a bit looser. Nothing stops you from bringing ten different friends to a party, but if they're not fun, you pay the price. But what about a regular house party? Is it crashing if you just walk in? Even further, it seems impossible to crash something like a gallery event. Especially if you're arriving with someone who was invited.

Adam held the glass double doors open for Zoe, and then hustled ahead to open the next set. He'd settled into a servile kind of chivalry over the last month, which Zoe found unattractive, no matter how much Adam blabbered on about how the man's place is to shape the world—to create the path for the other genders to walk through peacefully. But Adam didn't have to know that she found it unattractive. The night wasn't about him, anyway. As the elaborate mirrors scattered around the gallery demonstrated, it was Elena's night.

A few glances caught Zoe directly. Others used the mirrors to scope her out. The untalented would be unable to detect those, but Zoe was better with mirrors than any of them were. Already, she'd identified three fragments, each suspended about ten feet in the air and angled downward, which would be most flattering to her. As she navigated her way towards one—if people were going to sneak looks and gossip about her, they would need to do so under the full weight of her beauty—she came upon a bronze circle on the floor with a black arrow pointing towards the left. Feeling no need to struggle against the art, Zoe stood and looked in the direction it suggested. Mirror into mirror into mirror into mirror into nothing. Same as ever; Elena needed to play a few clever tricks to elevate her art. Other shapes accompanied by other arrows decorated the floor. A puzzle for the intrepid art-lover to solve. Zoe parked herself beneath one of the favorable fragments. In due time, she'd move on, but not until she got her use out of it.

Adam asked, "Do you want to come get a drink?"

"You go get them, please. I'm fine right here." So far, there wasn't a tremendous amount of whispering or gesturing in her direction. Zoe didn't know how close Elena's audience was to her own social circle, though unlike actors, visual artists often had a tight correspondence there. Such was the curse of the medium. Not everything spoke to the masses like acting. Instead of evoking despair or excitement with the flutter of an eyelash, Elena had to distort and ornament everything to prove some intellectual point. But it was probably a very good one, which Lily would breathlessly parrot as soon as she figured it out. Though she didn't see Lily anywhere. Lily's stay at Elena's had come to an abrupt end, but Zoe hadn't considered that the two of them might have broken up.

She stalked through the gallery in search of either Lily or gossip. Here and there, mirrors revealed flashes of hidden images: wailing beauties, mournful landscapes, abstracts with swooping, dynamic lines. Elena hadn't gotten a show by accident; everything was competently to exquisitely rendered. Standing on a pink triangle, facing away from the direction the arrow pointed, a set of reflections—each showing the jagged edges of the next mirror in the series—featured a set of lips and a hint of chin which Zoe recognized as Lily's right away. Those lips were what she envied most of Lily. Fillers weren't too expensive, but the perfect angles down from the cupid's bow and the way they settled into a coy pout were inimitable. No surgeon could give her that.

Adam returned with drinks. Zoe sipped some wine, but her eyes stayed sharp. "Is Lily here?"

"Is that a problem?" Adam puffed up his chest. Again the chivalry, but in a fighty way that at least got Zoe's juices flowing a little.

"No, of course not, darling."

His eyes sparkled at the pet name. He'd be enthralled for the rest of the night.

"She's in the other room, back there."

"Are she and Elena...?"

"They're talking to each other."

"Interesting." Zoe confirmed Adam's scouting when she entered the room, then got distracted by the display. A dome of mirrors surrounded them, and an illustrated pillar stretched from floor to ceiling in the center of the room. While looking directly at the painting didn't feel like much, the distortions in the mirrors stretched and pulled different aspects of the pillar. What looked to be a smear of colors became, in one mirror segment, a self-portrait of Elena with a mouth that stretched uncannily wide. Animals frolicking in one mirror became shards of angry color hurling toward a vulnerable woman when viewed through another. Despite her stardom, her prodigious talents, Zoe could never put together something so complicated, so majestic. As Zoe marveled at it, a collection of neon-yellow hair and wallet chains ambled toward her.

"Incredible, isn't it?"

"I've never seen anything like it." When Zoe's gaze lowered, she saw blurs of herself and this stranger intermingled in each other. Other mirrors stretched her face, squashed it, accentuated her stomach, and put her through other unflattering transformations. If Nate were there, he would've smashed every single one of them that caricatured her form. But that's why he wasn't invited. After a quick tour of the room, she'd return to one of her spots and everything would be back in order.

"You know, I helped install the mirrors. I'm Damien, by the way."

"Damien." Out of the corner of her eye, Zoe saw Lily notice her. It had taken long enough, but then Lily always was obstinate about recognizing her glamour. "Like the movie about the haunted child?"

"Exactly! But I think the kid was the Antichrist. I don't know if I have the mark, though." Damien leaned his head toward Zoe, prompting her to peek through their hair for a cluster of sixes. Lily was watching her, so Zoe leaned forward and idly brushed through the strands colored like finely shredded caution tape. Searching for nothing and finding nothing.

"You're clear. Neither christ nor anti."

"Whew, lots of pressure either way. Glad to have some spare time instead." He stuck his hands in his front pockets and shrugged upward in a shy skater-boy way that still struck a chord with Zoe, evoking her high school romances soundtracked by pop punk and flavored with energy drinks. Boys that weren't gay until she got their dicks in her mouth; boys that stopped being gay after she swallowed. But that was high school. That was another life.

Adam slid up next to Zoe, back from a tour around the pillar to scout what Lily was doing. "She said your name, but whispered the rest when she saw me nearby."

"Then you shouldn't have been seen." Zoe returned her attention to Damien. "Damien, Adam."

"We've met. He's not a good man." Adam's tight-lipped grimace didn't hide much. Had there been a falling out between the two? Were they past lovers? Ex-friends? Bitter rivals?

"Whatever, dude." Damien maintained an unbothered smile.

"Whatever? See, a man who doesn't have any cares in the world has no stake in it. No responsibility. Pathetic."

Damien rolled his eyes and leaned close to Zoe's ear. He whispered loud enough that Adam certainly heard him. "Is he always like this?"

Adam asked, "Did you know that Damien is a rape apologist?"

"Fuck off." Damien shoved Adam's shoulder, and a murmur surrounded them. Zoe wandered away and circled the pillar. A masculine pissing contest would be fun to watch, more so if she was the prize, but she didn't want everyone to think that she'd had a hand in organizing it. Better to let the boys figure it out for themselves, especially when she could come back the moment it got entertaining. Zoe stopped at a combination of shards. One of them reflected half of her face, the other a section of pillar which became another face, this one unfamiliar. Its eye was closed and Zoe felt like she was winking. Sensation crept over into the painted cheeks and lips. When Zoe opened her mouth, the reflection's still-pursed lips jarred her. It seemed like it should have come alive and acted as the painterly correspondent to Zoe's own, and its refusal to do so was an active rebuff to Zoe, to anyone standing in her place. It continued, stubborn, until Zoe moved on and it became just another blur of color.

From the shouting on the other side of the pillar, it sounded like Adam's famous mediation skills had failed him again. She merged into the crowd to watch the two of them fight and ended up right next to Elena and Lily. They'd certainly expect her to say something devastating, which she easily could. But though the crowd was distracted, Zoe's natural star power meant that everyone was ready to shift their attention onto her if she did something interesting enough. Wary of the eyes of the crowd surrounding her and Lily, Zoe opted for a curt nod and an insincere smile. Elena narrowed her eyes and Lily averted hers.

Screams begging the fight to stop overwhelmed

those for it to continue, but the grunting at the center told Zoe that it hadn't. So she strode through the crowd, which instinctively parted to make room for each of her steps. The two boys were on the ground, pulling at each other's shirts and hair. Zoe cleared her throat. She had one chance to deliver the line with appropriate gravity. Something understated, which would communicate to everyone how far beneath Zoe their actions were. How far beneath themselves.

"Are you two done?"

They didn't let go of each other's shirts, but broke away from their enraged staring contest to peer up at Zoe, chastened. That was all it took: presence. Everyone in every room and every situation yearns for a focal point. All day, people trudge through an artless world. There's plenty of beauty in a tree or a sunset or a row of charming renovated houses, but no art because they lack a subject. No tree has a message, but starting the moment that Zoe spoke in such an authoritative-yet-dismissive tone, the gathering in the room became entirely about something. Elena's art was fun and appealing to the crowd, but everyone was in that room for different purposes. Some came to appreciate the art, true. Others were desperate to be at a social event where they could be seen—Zoe's own motivation. Some wanted to use the event as a chance to flirt, which appeared to be Damien's motivation; or to impress others, Adam's. But now, everyone was united in their attention to Zoe. Unity was the true bedrock of art, not the fragmentary novelties that Elena had constructed in the gallery.

Adam quivered and let Damien go. Damien responded with a quick punch in the ribs before doing the same. He brushed himself off and walked out of the gallery while Adam writhed on the floor. How lonely he must have felt down there, knowing that he'd made a fool of himself and secured only pain and embarrassment as companions. Zoe crouched down, but didn't rub his back or offer a hand up or any words of comfort. Instead, she whispered, "Any man on a date with me who gets in a fight better win it."

She waited for him to rise and accompanied him to the door of the gallery, but didn't follow him out. As the prize beyond all prizes, she wouldn't let people think she could be won by a loser. But now she was unaccompanied, and another quick tour of the gallery didn't turn up any men who'd be a suitable fill-in date. Zoe hung around anyway. It was something about the way she looked in the mirror fragment dangling from the ceiling. After years of being filmed, photographed, and even painted, Elena had finally found Zoe's best angle. One which made her look like the divine had bound itself into human form—a form that couldn't quite contain its energy. So it glowed and shaped itself into something greater than human. She couldn't very well walk away from the one mirror that finally did her justice.

# LILY

Before Lily walked into the Irma Freeman Center for the Arts that night, she brushed the soft, furry exterior of the building. The founder had once said that art was a living thing, and galleries needed to be alive too. The building never moved, never breathed, never ate, never drank, never wailed, never laughed, never sighed, never moaned, never whispered anything so sweet to its loved ones. When it wasn't in use, the walls were plain white. But it was warm beneath her touch, and the interior smelled like an animal. Would it bleed, if Lily pricked it?

Her goal that night was just to say hello to Elena, hang out with her casually, and pretend that even if they were broken up, they'd never really been dating so there was no reason they couldn't talk to each other like friends. It went well enough, though she and Elena could only trade a few words at a time before one admirer or another interjected with compliments or questions about the art. Then Zoe arrived.

Surely Zoe knew that she was standing in the perfect spot to reflect herself all through the exhibit. The red X on the floor was, as Elena told it, meant to underscore the gravity of doing so: that the endless reproduction and overexposure of oneself would aggravate others, dilute oneself into nothing but thought. Not that Zoe cared. Digital reproductions of Zoe flowed through the internet constantly, so what threat could some mirrors pose? Lily hid on the blind side of the pillar, where she couldn't see or be seen. Adam was cruel to bring her, but Lily couldn't work up much animosity after he had gotten beaten up and embarrassed like that. Zoe was probably the mastermind behind the entire thing, and had engineered it to rattle Lily, who could just run out and surrender the evening to Zoe. She'd done it before. When Zoe had walked into the post office last week while Lily was trying to send a package, Lily had sprinted out the door rather than spend five minutes in the same line.

But this time, she didn't. Instead, she sidled up to Elena, who glowered at the spot on the floor where the boys had been wrestling. "Who gets in a fight at an art show? Surrounded by broken glass?" Elena gestured at the mirror fragments enclosing them, and all of them gestured right back.

"You know it was Zoe's fault."

"I don't know, Lil. She stopped them. If she had wanted them to fight, why would she break it up?"

"Like she wouldn't set it up just so she could be the hero? You know that's something she'd do."

"I'm just glad it's done."

A couple of Elena's friends stopped by, but neither of them talked about the art. Only the fight. Elena didn't mention it, but Lily could tell that Elena was annoyed at her thunder being stolen.

Lily said, "Hey, let's drop it. It happened, but we're here to appreciate this incredible art."

"No, it's fine," Elena said. "That fight was wild. Obviously, people are going to talk about it."

After Elena shot Lily a displeased glance, Lily questioned whether she'd misunderstood something while Elena and her friends continued their conversation. If she didn't have the ability to read Elena's emotions, could she be sure that the glance was of displeasure with her? It may have been that she had wanted to communicate to Lily how unhappy she was that she had to talk about the fight, but needed to do so for social reasons. Eventually, the friends moved on, and the two of them were alone. Lily said, "Look, I can go talk to the gallery owner and we can get Zoe kicked out. It'll be fine."

Elena shook her head and walked over to the other side of the pillar. Her reflection and Zoe's intermingled into a mosaic of adoration and frustration all over the dome. Lily wanted to socialize—Dicks's jacket with shoulder pads up to their ears promised some intrigue—but the threat Zoe posed to the art show was too great. Why else would she be standing in that particular spot, if not to impose her image all over Elena's vision?

But when Lily went to convince Elena again, Elena flinched away the moment she saw her coming. Lily said, "Oh. I was just trying to..."

"I know. But don't."

Lily reached a hand out to feel the magnetism that would always draw her and Elena close to each other. A relationship like theirs was built on faith that the forces which compelled them to each other would always be present, and so no assurances were needed. No one makes plans about how they'll coordinate if gravity vanishes. But gravity had vanished. Elena wandered out of sight again.

Rather than follow, Lily sulked through the door. The fluttered reflections of Elena gave way to more and more Zoe until Lily was in the front room and under the gaze of the real thing. Lily tried to meet her stare, but burst into tears as soon as she tried. Humiliating. Weak. She ran for the doors and felt Zoe's huge green eyes follow her the entire way, like an owl watching from a branch.

The cool outside air did little to loosen shame's hot grasp. The long walk back to Steph's provided many opportunities to relive those moments: Elena's flinch, the tightness in her shoulders, the hardness in her eyes. Lily wouldn't forget them.

# ZOE

Her phone vibrated for the fifth time that hour, and Zoe wondered why she didn't just block Adam's number. Surely it was no mystery to him why she'd dumped him: revulsion was sexy, but he'd looked so pathetic on the floor, his fancy boy clothes torn by Damien's powerful hands, that Zoe had started to feel bad for him. Pity was the least erotic emotion, no matter how many people had sex because of it. Zoe wouldn't subject Adam to it, so she thought it better to avoid his calls entirely. It was a kindness.

If he thought that, after that fight, he didn't deserve her pity, then he was delusional. That wasn't sexy either. On most people. Zoe was almost certain that Don Quixote could get it. The only variable was if he smelled weird in a hot way or weird in a bad way. Another buzz. Blocking Adam's number was too forceful a rejection; it would be a total rebuke, expressing that Zoe didn't even want him to be a person anymore, and that wasn't true. She had no reservations about seeing him around town. She just didn't want to suck his dick anymore.

Given the way Lily had stormed out of the party, it seemed she'd suffered as bad a fall as Adam had. One last- ditch chance to get back into Elena's good graces, foiled by her obsession with Zoe. It's pleasing to see the right consequences—humiliation, isolation—fall on the right people for the right reasons. Like the final piece of a jigsaw puzzle settling into place. Zoe had picked up that Lily was crashing at Steph's place now. How like her to open her door to a desperate trans girl. Lily's legs were soon to follow, if Steph got her way. No matter how much a fetish greased the wheels, it would blow up from the stresses of being around Lily all the time, and then the cycle would repeat until she had nowhere to go and had to leave the city and disappear into the unknown.

Another buzz, this time not Adam. Lots of people had been reaching out to Zoe over the last week. Like most requests to hang out, to catch up, accompanied with lamentations that they "haven't seen each other in forever," they were people looking to elevate their own status through association with her. A famous actress, soon to be the most famous, at your birthday party or your karaoke night, communicates that you have a piece of that glamour which resonates with hers. So then people flock to you, and your station is higher than it was before your simple ruse. Most of these messages went unanswered or were referred to Nate's email address. One had lingered in her inbox, from Damien. It read, "sup? got your number from a liar. you busy tonight?" She had been busy the night it was sent, as well as all the nights that followed. For all he knew, she'd ignored it completely. It felt like dangling him by a string he didn't even know existed: at any moment, she could respond with a single word, "no," and upend whatever plans he had for the evening, whatever sense he had of his relation to the world.

No time for dates or games while they were shooting the last few scenes of *Somnolences*, though. Zoe spent what little free time she had honing herself into a sharp blade that could cut through the weak writing and bleed the truth from it. But one day there was a break in the schedule, so she texted Damien and asked him to lunch. He replied immediately, which was an unattractive quality unless it communicated some degree of carelessness with which he navigated the world. In that case, it would be hot, but guys like that rarely got into fights with little pigs like Adam. Zoe also pictured men like that without phones. Instead, they should just wander around town, and if a message finds its way into their hands, they should receive it with pleased indifference.

The cafe that Damien suggested was in Pittsburgh, so Zoe took the train from the set back into the city. The train cars were only five years old, built for passing through Pittsburgh more than for navigating the city itself. Normally, Zoe eschewed the moderate crowd in the train—she'd have to sit next to a girl who smelled like onions—but the gap in her schedule wasn't big, and a car would have been caught up in the always-horrendous traffic. Plus, the cafe was only a couple blocks from the station. So she sat still for twenty minutes and passed the time by wondering how many people in the compartment had recognized her. A young guy, clearly some variety of gay judging by the denim vest and slender frame, kept stealing glances at her, but whether it was her fame or beauty that lured his gaze, she couldn't know. The girl on the other side of the aisle was watching Zoe out of her periphery. Maybe she'd tell all her friends later who she saw, spinning up a round of excited squealing that would peak hard and valley harder after the emptiness of their lives became all too clear in the wake of the momentary joy Zoe's presence had brought them. This is why she needed to be in more movies, on more screens, so that her gravity could lift the tide and all these little boats with it.

When she got off the train, she jogged up the stairs. A tiny bit of sweat gleamed in the sunlight, enhancing her unworldly beauty. Part of that beauty was luck, part was the pocket of estrogen sitting in her thigh muscle and dissolving into her bloodstream day by day, and part was pure effort: every little trick, every optimization no matter how silly it was, needed to be pursued. Even if each barely moved the needle, together they had a profound effect.

Only a block away from the cafe, Zoe realized she was going to pass by Lily's tattoo shop. Not Lily's. Sveta's, whose patience with Lily defied all reason. No one Zoe knew had complained about Lily's tattoos, but Zoe had seen them. They were technically competent with clean lines and no scabbing, but completely soulless. She never took the curves of the body into account, and so the tattoo and the body it was on never became a unified aesthetic whole. Not that Lily ever listened to Zoe. Instead, she just got mad that Zoe wouldn't let Lily practice on her perfect body. As if receiving a bad tattoo had no stakes for her at all.

The last thing Zoe needed was to have Lily's bad vibes clouding her mind on a date, so she flipped off the shop as she walked past. The hostile energy was expelled, and by the time she reached the table where Damien sat, Zoe was all smiles. The two greeted each other, went through the ordeal of waiting in line to order food—a distinctly unromantic activity; an aberration from the cafe's airy, minimalist vibe—and before long, Damien was taking enormous bites of a vegan sandwich while Zoe poked at a salad.

"Can you explain something to me?"

The safe answer was generally no, but sometimes trans boys wanted a smart girl around. Still, Zoe was going to do the right thing, treat Damien like any other man, and fail to provide an explanation for whatever he had in mind. But first, she had to nod her assent so that he'd continue with his line of questioning.

"Why do cafes put such weird stuff in vegan sandwiches? Do they think we'll just be happy with anything?"

"I'm sure they're trying their best."

"Look," Damien said as he peeled the sandwich open, revealing a layer of sunflower seeds affixed to the bread by a layer of hummus. "Both of these choices are insane. Hummus is a dip, right?"

"I've never seen sunflower seeds in a sandwich. Maybe for protein?" Her own approach to the conversation was boring her. Forget a successful date. It was time to stun him with the luminous intensity of her full personality. "Here's what's happening. It's not shop owners who have no idea what they're doing. It's vegans who, whenever they eat, taste the justice of their meal more than any of the ingredients. So shop owners can throw together some absolute bullshit, and it'll taste great to them. Not to you."

"Oh, are you one of the 'vegans are obnoxious' types?"

"Vegans are right." Zoe shrugged. "Pretty obviously. I just don't have the time. You hate the sandwich because you're not excited about justice."

"Begrudging acceptance here. It's cheese I miss the most."

"God, same." Before Damien could object that she wasn't a vegan, Zoe gestured to her industry-standard body and he nodded his head in acceptance. The rest of their lunch was pleasant, if uneventful, and though Zoe didn't find in Damien the careless wanderer she had spent the morning envisioning, he was sharp and had a wide smile, and Zoe wanted to see more.

After the two of them finished their meals, in the hazy interregnum between the end of eating and the end of the date, when conversation's grip was loosening, Adam walked by the table. Had he been stalking her? Probably not, or he would've interrupted as soon as they'd started having fun. A shame: that kind of dangerous fixation might've gotten Zoe hot for him again.

"Oh, this is great. He assaults me, and you get lunch with him?"

Zoe smiled. "Everyone makes mistakes. I'm sure Damien is sorry for how things went at the art show."

Rather than play along, Damien scoffed. It would've been so easy to just be contrite, but Zoe had led that horse as close to water as she could, and now Adam was stamping his feet, nearing a tantrum. "This is so unfair. You won't return my calls because I get attacked for no reason, and now you're supporting the man who assaulted me. Great! Just great."

"I'm sorry that you're hurt." Zoe's smile creaked beneath the effort required to maintain it.

"No. No sorries. I just want everyone to know how fucked up this is."

"Fuck off, dude," Damien said, standing from his chair.

The last thing Zoe needed was another fight embroiling her past the time she needed to leave, so she used her gleaming eyes to grab ahold of Adam's attention and said, "Look, you little worm. I stopped seeing you because you embarrassed me. Do you think your little tantrum is helping the situation?"

"But—"

"It's not fair. Sorry there's not an ethics committee that decides who gets in my pussy. Leave."

When Adam didn't get the hint, she seized his shoulder and dug her nails into it. He winced, but still didn't move. So she pushed him away. "I only slept with you because you're disgusting, and that works for me. But I'm not into adult babies. Go find someone with some diapers and complete the costume."

She got up and walked away from the table. Adam didn't follow, but Damien hustled after her. He said, "Hey, sorry about that. I should've gotten rid of him for you."

Zoe sneered at Damien. He wasn't careless. He was clueless. "I have no use for a man who makes things more difficult for me. Lose my number." The sudden, shattered expression on his face oozed between Zoe's lips like melted chocolate. And then he was gone, and she was on the train again, satisfied by her lunch. Thwarted desire and wounded pride were such delicious flavors; no wonder she was always hungry.

# LILY

The tattoo gun buzzed in Lily's hand as she brought a perfectly straight line around her client's back and across his stomach. In their consultation, he'd explained: this was the exact point below which he could lose his entire body and have a decent chance of surviving. When pressed, he explained that what he really wanted was the exact 50-50 line. The inability to measure the exact state of his current health or forecast how he would heal kept him from certitude, so this line was the best estimate they could manage. Lily's job was to bring it across without a single imperfection. In the absence of certitude, her client wanted to present an illusion of it.

Heavy bass rumbled from the other table, but Lily kept her line straight through the vibrations. Six hours ago, Sveta's client had barged in the door and said, "I want to become loudness." After a few clarifying questions, Sveta had cleared her schedule. A shrill whistle had pierced Lily's ear drums. When Lily had started her appointment, Sveta's client was still visible, but the shape of his hands had started to pulse and waver.

Total disembodiment intrigued Lily, though she'd spent far too much effort on her own body to ever want to give it up. To be unconfined sound, generating and spreading more and more of herself over the world until little scraps of herself wormed their way through everything, sounded like true freedom. Would her consciousness remain without a body? Sensation without comprehension made her skin crawl. Whether the experience would be confusion or terror, she wanted no part of it, even though a third possibility seemed like true peace: each moment, every feeling, in all their multiplicity as her body expanded, taken in with no judgment whatsoever.

Lily exhaled, then connected the line. Perfect. Her client bounced over to the mirror and yowled in excitement. He buried a few punches in his body's new non-essential section. "I love it!" He handed over two hundred dollars in cash, every twenty dollar bill damp. As he walked past Sveta and her client, he pumped his fist and said, "Hell yeah, dude." The client raised his hand, now mostly invisible but still dense enough that the sound waves distorted everything behind it.

Lily's client, still shirtless, walked out into the street and immediately got hit by a convertible. Brakes screeched. Blood and viscera splattered as his body broke in two. From the shop's door, Lily could only see the separate lumps of flesh that had previously comprised her client, plus the horrified face of the driver, platinum blonde hair speckled with blood and other fluid. No doubt she couldn't see that one of the lumps had risen onto its hands. The rupture had occurred just below the line. Lily's client hand-walked back onto the sidewalk, smiled and winked at Lily, and then went on his way. So now the half-corpse out front was the shop's problem. Meaning hers.

She'd have to wait until Sveta was done. An amalgamation of construction noises vibrated out of her client. Over her shoulder, Lily noticed that the tattoo gun was completely still, and the client's body vibrated and pulsed beneath it. "You're here. Good. Watch." Sveta let go of the tattoo gun, which stayed in place while the activity below intensified. Lily worried the client's turbulent form might burst, spraying them all with noise and blood and sending the tattoo gun flying. Cutting a seam in reality. "Do you see? Intention guides it from here. I'm only here if he tries to hide." She gripped it again and slung her other arm around Lily's shoulder. "But that's not likely now. Is it, Sami?"

Sami opened his mouth to speak and released the

deafening sound of fanfare. Neither Sveta nor Lily spoke for the rest of the session. Cacophony rattled against the walls of the little shop, and soon Sami's clothes slipped off of his no-longer-corporeal form. The noise faded—passersby outside covered their ears in sudden agony—and Sveta turned off the gun. She picked up Sami's shorts and fished a wad of hundred dollar bills out of a back pocket. "See, it's good to trust your clients. I could have demanded and gotten this up front. But I if do that, there's no trust. Very tricky."

"What if he had lied?"

Sveta's eyes lit up and she waggled a finger at Lily, signifying that she'd made a good point. "Yes, what if I just let people come in and tell me they've brought the money and then they're vapor? I need to keep my shop open." With a tap of her finger, she played a recording of Sami. "Alright honey, payment's good. I won't keep you here." The honks of a flock of geese sounded before she pressed the delete button on the recording. "I've been in this business a long time. I know more about their new bodies than they do."

After Lily scooped up Sami's unneeded clothes—an incongruous combination of punk-band–patched denim jacket, mesh tank top, and slim-fit khakis which indicated that he'd never had any idea what to do with his fleshly body—she sat and stared at the tattoo gun. Before long, Sveta wandered over.

"What are you doing?"

"I'm meditating on what it can do."

"No, you are ruminating. I know the difference."

"It's just..." Lily wanted to pick up the gun. To hold it in her hands and feel the weight of potential once more. But Sveta had gauged her mindset and wouldn't allow it. Not that Lily had any hope of accurately translating her vision to reality with it. "Why couldn't it just be used to give me the prettiest face in the world? Like, the kind that no matter what room I walked into, even if someone was on stage. Doing stand-up, a catwalk on the runway, whatever. Even then, what if everyone felt compelled to turn and stare at my beauty? Why couldn't it give that to me?"

"It could. As a theory. But if I tried, you wouldn't get it." Sveta mashed her fingers into Lily's cheeks. "What rests beneath this face right now is uglier than you could ever be on your own. Don't ask me to bring it out." Eyes downcast, Sveta returned the tattoo gun to its locked case. The two of them didn't speak for the rest of Lily's shift, and once it was done, she ran out instead of hanging back to try and assess the damage.

The only thing that distracted her on her sprint away from work was Indisputably Coffee. She slowed and lingered at the door, sweat dripping and heart pounding. It would be so easy to walk in and pretend like everything was normal. She could say hello to Elena, get a drink, and be on her way. No kiss, though. Not even one on the cheek to rile up the other customers. The experience of that cleavage between past and present felt like the sword of Damocles dangling over Lily's head. But she ran onward, and the sword stayed at the coffee shop.

By the time she had reached Dicks's house, Lily was no longer running. Heavy steps carried her through the door, through the hallways that now curled like a labyrinth. Next to the open doorway to Calamity's room near the center of the maze, Lily slumped against the wall and slid to the ground. The sweat mark would evaporate in just a moment. Beyond the door, she could hear crunching. Calamity hard at work. A better version of Lily would walk in self-possessed, proposing a bargain with Calamity as near-equals. But they weren't, and Lily knew it. So she pushed herself up onto her rickety feet and calmed her breath just enough, without bothering to repair the damage sweat had done to her makeup.

Just like last time, Calamity greeted her with a pill-riddled smile. Unlike last time, Calamity invited her to sit where she had last time. Perhaps this was a preoccupation of godhood: a desire for circularity, inviting repetition in significant enough numbers to achieve meaning through quantity. Lily accepted, despite the worry that, in doing so, she had made an agreement without knowing the terms. Time dribbled onward as Lily gazed at Calamity. Her skin betrayed no flaw, no wrinkle, but gave the unmistakable impression that it had once been pock-marked. The triumphal aura of attaining perfection rather than always possessing it only enhanced the effect. "Calamity. I know you're not up for much conversation..."

Calamity smiled and chewed, meeting Lily's eyes warmly.

"But I have a specific request for you. It would be an incredible gift if you would help me become as beautiful as you are. Or even anywhere close. I want... I need the aura. The gravitas that comes with it. It'll solve a problem I'm having." The problem, for the day, was that Zoe's shoot ended at eight p.m., and it was already pushing seven.

Instead of waving a glowing hand or crumbling estradiol dust over Lily's head or any number of things she imagined might happen, Calamity took two full hands of pills and poured them into her own mouth. She raised a finger, imploring Lily to wait as her jaw churned. Then, accomplishing whatever she'd hoped to by chewing, she caressed Lily's cheek and kissed her. A pill-encrusted tongue crept into Lily's mouth, shedding all of the powder and fragments inside. Calamity's tongue didn't feel particularly different than anyone else's. Wet, flexible, energetic—that much was flattering, at least. After it withdrew, she missed it more than most.

Calamity guided her face to a mirror. She stroked

Lily's cheek with the backs of a couple fingers. What would Lily have to give up to feel that perfect softness down her face forever? But it went away when those fingers again prompted her to look in the mirror. Though it was clouded by blue dust, Lily could see the same face she'd always had. "Nothing's changed."

With a pleased smile, Calamity returned to the table for more pills. Maybe all of that was just an excuse for her to go in for a kiss. But when Lily offered a glance to suggest that she could return for more, Calamity radiated the same old beneficence. For the second time, she left Calamity's room the same as she had entered it.

On the walk home, Lily gazed at her reflection in every window and peeked into every car mirror. Could it be that she was already perfected? Maybe she was drawn to Calamity because Lily was the counterpart to her: the feminine goddess trapped in her ideal, and the feminine manifestation, free to traverse the world. Unlikely, given her failure to captivate Elena. More likely, she was just the best she was going to get. In the window of an abandoned storefront, now empty but for a few hangers scattered about the floor as if they'd been left in a mad dash to escape with the store's remaining goods, Lily examined her face more closely. Surely she was beautiful enough already. That was Calamity's point. And Sveta's. Neither of them would give her what she didn't need, when radiant beauty was already at her disposal. A crack in the glass disrupted the reflection of her smile.

# ZOE

Pictures of Tevin staring off into the distance soulfully, letting a single tear roll down his cheek, covered the walls of his dressing room. There were enough different costumes and settings that one or two photo shoots couldn't have covered them all. Bad enough, but the display wasn't even out of some misplaced vanity that they made him look beautiful. That would've made sense. Instead, whenever Zoe asked about them, he claimed that they were reminders of the great pain inside him, which it was his responsibility to guide out into the world. If it weren't for his talent, Tevin would be just another guy at the bar crying after his first beer. A laughable shadow of a person. But his talent was undeniable, his fame grew year by year, and every phrase that poured from his lips came out like honey, which was why Zoe had decided that the best way to pass the time between takes was to sit atop that gifted mouth.

Its gifts were not limited to speech. Hidden in darkness, his lips and tongue performed impossible feats which Zoe couldn't resolve into coherent movements as pleasure invaded her. After a couple months stuck with Adam's routine, fucking a guy with some confidence felt like reaching an oasis. As she got closer and closer to climax, her hips came alive, grinding her pussy into Tevin's face. Everyone in the hallway could probably hear her moans, but she didn't care. His soft hands seized her thighs and pressed her even tighter against his mouth and she was so close, she just needed one little push.

"Oh I'm gonna come. Say I'm the star."

Tevin's mouth and tongue paused for a second, but then resumed even faster. Little ripples of flesh rose to the side of his tightening grip.

"Please. Do it. Say I'm the star. Say it right into my cunt."

Zoe couldn't hear anything, but felt the whisper of speech in her vulva and that was enough. Pleasure blinded her and stole her breath and, for a moment, she was nothing but sensation.

Once she returned to herself, she scooted down Tevin's body and rested her head on his chest, her legs wrapped around his waist.

"I didn't say you were the star. I said you were the co-star."

She slapped his chest as hard as she could, but said, "Whatever. No take-backs."

"What's the point of all of this?"

"*Somnolences?* It's supposed to 'resituate heterosexuality as a place of emotional complexity and depth, absent the shallow wedding-catalogue baggage it's accrued over the course of the last few decades'." Her best Sage impression wasn't very good. She couldn't achieve the throatiness that Sage spoke with. Like there was always just a bit of phlegm in their throat modulating their voice.

"No. I meant acting. Movies. Sex."

"Fun, glamour, power. Reaching a pinnacle."

"Which goes with which?"

Zoe waved her hand dismissively. Someone needed to convince Tevin that just because he was drowning didn't mean his thoughts were deep, but that didn't need to be her job. "Hey, if fame is dragging you down, give it to me. I'm always up for more."

"I can't. It's chained to my soul. It and I are bound for the same destiny—the same rotten hole the earth has prepared for me."

"Just talk me up. Say I'm the real talent here. You'll seem kind, that makes you feel better. I get famous, that makes me feel better. Everyone's happy."

Tevin clutched his face with both hands. As he dragged his fingers down past his mouth, he stirred some of Zoe's pussy scent into the air: sweet and acidic. Not quite grapefruit. "Do you ever wonder if divinity is a blade waiting to cut the earth in half?"

"It'll get stuck in the ground. The dirt will be here forever." She sat up and spun her feet to the floor. Her hands couldn't brush her hair back to perfection, but it'd undo some of the matting. "The dirt wants us back so badly. You and I get to soar above it for a while. Let's enjoy it."

"I can't. God has some purpose for me I can't understand, but these hands are meant for something."

"Give me half an hour and you can put them on me again. There's some purpose."

Tevin rolled over, face buried in the crevice between the cushions. If he wanted to lose himself in despair, that was his business. His quest to find something deeper, more true than the place where he excelled seemed like a desire for self-defeat. Even the thought of a greater purpose than beauty sickened Zoe. Tevin's malaise might have the same source.

Desperate to shake off her uneasiness, Zoe stepped in front of Tevin's dressing room mirror and turned the lights on. Rather than illuminate her body in the soft light glow she expected, harsh fluorescent light revealed every pore, every blemish, exaggerated any bit of fat on her body. Zoe screamed as she turned it off. Within seconds, Nate was pounding at the door, begging Zoe to tell him she was okay. She ignored him and wrested Tevin back from the crevice of couch cushions. He gave no resistance and didn't look at her, his pupils instead following gravity down.

"Why the fuck are your lights like that?" Zoe asked.

"Every day, I need to know that this skin is nothing but a covering for what's beneath. It is artificial meat housing the soul, from which my art blossoms."

Her mistake for fucking Tevin. She slipped on her robe and walked out the door, finding a sobbing Nate who tagged along at her heels as soon as she snapped her fingers, even though he hadn't gotten ahold of himself yet.

When she reached her own dressing room, she locked Nate out and took off her robe. Her mirror was friendly. The soft lights caressed the gentle curve of her hips, smoothed out her skin, begged the viewer to take hold of this delicious fruit. She rubbed her fingers along her waist, tucked her hair behind her shoulders. Every inch of her skin drank up the light and glowed with satiety. Deep breaths in and out; her round breasts rose and fell. The mirror reflected the only truth that mattered. This was the seat of meaning. Beauty existed on earth, which the dirt below could not possess, but only nourish anew again and again and again.

# LILY

Lily's plan, to the degree it was a plan, was to find some way to upstage Zoe on her set. Some total humiliation when Zoe was at her strongest, to put to rest the idea that she was special, that she was above everyone else, once and for all. Yesterday she'd wasted too much time failing to get help from Sveta and Calamity, so she decided to wait until the morning. This struggle of theirs had been going on for months, what was another night? Without a perfect face like Calamity's, her scheme had a new lynchpin. One thousand sequins meant to dazzle beneath the lights adorned Lily's dress, which she'd only worn on three previous occasions:

1. The time that her ex-boyfriend was going to show up at Steph's birthday party and she needed to make him regret everything he'd ever done and watch her make out with whoever she could find. In the middle of the party, he'd asked to get back together with her. By the end, he'd gotten kicked out for jacking off into the upper tank of Steph's toilet. A qualified victory.

2. When she had to do karaoke for Dicks's top-surgery fundraiser but didn't want anyone to remember how bad her voice was. Afterwards, everyone congratulated her on an amazing performance, when she'd only danced and gyrated without singing a single line.

3. That night when she was lonely and horny and didn't have anyone to call, so she wore it to a dance party and had terrible, bitey sex with someone with a girl's hands but a boy's mouth.

The results mostly lined up, even accounting for chance.

A security guard stopped her at the boundary of the studio lot where Zoe's movie was being filmed. Thirty-foot- walls with "no peeking ;)" written on them surrounded the interior buildings. Lily scoped it out looking for a way in, but only found one: past the little hut where the security guard lived.

She explained that she was Zoe's best friend and emergency contact, and that she had to get in right away. No luck. The guard offered to summon Nate to pass her message along, or she could beg him to let her by. But how could she convince the man who attended to all of Zoe's needs that he'd missed something? The pleading girl routine wouldn't work. She was a couple inches taller than the security guard, which undermined any attempts to be a damsel. While she waited for inspiration to come to her, the clouds parted. Sunlight beamed down and she took it as a sign; the moment her jacket slipped past her shoulders, the security guard was blinded by a flash of reflected sunlight.

The guard clutched his eyes, and Lily snuck past after stealing a clipboard, making sure to refasten her jacket. While the dazzling lights were useful in that moment, they also attracted attention. She didn't need that until she got on set. So she assumed a brisk, purposeful walk with the clipboard out in front. That way no one would bother her as she wandered around the set while she looked for the building that contained Zoe.

Which was a perfect white cube. Lily circumnavigated it and, when she pressed her hand to its side, it leeched some of the color from her fingertips. She recoiled like she'd been shocked, then held her fingers up to the sunlight. Little gray caps sat atop the rest of her fingers, which retained their flesh color. After a few seconds, color started to swim in from the edges and then it was like nothing had happened. Even so, Lily didn't want to touch the wall again.

Soon she found a line of people walking into the cube. They marched two-by-two into the wall and they were decorated with headphones, microphones, cameras. After a second inside the cube, the crew was transformed to total grayscale. Would they get their color back in a few seconds on the other side? Toward the end of their march, Lily hopped to the end of the line. She worried that the cube would be gooey to pass through, that losing all of her color would be painful or enervating, and that with it, she would lose all will to humiliate Zoe.

A sound technician in front of her—the headphones gave it away—turned to Lily. "Hi. Are you new?"

"Yeah. I'm a new assistant for Ms. Berger."

"Oh, thank god. You have no idea how bad the last guy was."

"Um, no, I don't think I'm replacing him." They must have meant Nate, who Lily could never imagine leaving Zoe's side. At Zoe's funeral, they'd probably dump Nate into her coffin to be buried with her. His request, of course. Zoe would never write a will because that meant acknowledging that one day she'd die, which required conceiving of a world that existed without her. The spark of hope in the technician's eye faded as they entered the cube, and their brown-and-gold iris faded too.

Lily held her breath. The cube wall felt like aloe, soothing and gelatinous. Color left her body in tight curls which spiraled and loosened and faded into the stark white walls. Her lungs cried out for air but there was only jelly all around her, and she couldn't breathe jelly, but she couldn't breathe nothing either. When she gasped and expected to get a mouthful of the cube she found that none had invaded her mouth. Air in, air out, its origin a mystery. By the time she had emerged from the wall, her body and everyone else's was in total grayscale. So was the crew's, the director's, and the set and gear all matched. They were shooting a black and white movie. While the crew unpacked their things and set up, Lily peeled off and hid behind a mound of crates with just enough daylight between them that she could peek through. Without color, she'd be even harder to find. And her dress would still shine brilliant white. It was all better than she'd planned.

After an hour of setup, the lights in the studio were all pointed at Zoe. Somehow, she had retained some faint semblance of color. Was she just stronger than everyone else? Her co-star had some left too. Did they simply have more of it in them, so the cube wasn't able to leech it all? Maybe they recovered faster. It would take hours to find out what the truth was, and Lily had other goals.

The director said, "Action." Zoe stumbled around a bathroom, scattering pills and toiletries everywhere. If Lily remembered correctly from all the times Zoe had recited her lines at home—no matter who else was there or what they were doing—this was her big scene. Perfect. Everyone in the studio was transfixed by Zoe's overacting. Lily skirted behind them. A few glances found her, but none that could have any confidence that she didn't belong there. Soon, she was crouched around the side of the set. With one step, she'd enter the light that was meant for Zoe. Her jacket fell to the floor. Even in the darkness, the dress sparkled beautifully. But in a moment it would become like the sun.

A razor clattered to the floor and Zoe said, "I just wanted you to see me."

Her co-star said, "I see you."

Before she could reply with her line—"This isn't me" —Lily stepped into the light. Twenty hot lights fixed upon her and she gleamed so brightly that the grout between the tiles, the contours of the pill bottles, even

Zoe's tearful eyes, vanished in the light. Zoe's failure in her quest to become a star was to take it too figuratively. What beauty, what talent, could compete with light that blotted out all of its surroundings?

Lily couldn't see out of the shine. The sequins sent up bands of pink and green light to ornament the blinding glare. Whatever the cube's power, it couldn't stop colors generated inside it. More and more color radiated from her dress. Such a thrill could only be compared to a witch triumphant on the pyre. No matter what death they had hoped for her, her power stretched beyond it. She was the aurora borealis. She was the sun. No one could compete with her vividity.

"This... isn't me." Zoe's face cut through the light like the bow of a ship through water, more radiant than light itself. Her eyes caught and reflected all of the light from Lily's dress, transforming it into sorrow and regret. Beneath Zoe's face, a convincing mask of anguish, Lily could see that vicious, hungry smile like a shadow.

Lily fell to her knees as security guards rushed the set. Their rough hands and interrogative shouts meant nothing to her, even as they hoisted her up like a bag of old produce. With a single word, Zoe could have stopped them, but Lily didn't want to ask for her help. She knew what the answer would be.

The crew applauded Zoe's performance through Lily's disruption. Just as Lily got dragged out the door, Zoe met her eyes, and Lily saw all the colors she'd created swirling around in her irises, now at the disposal of her enemy.

# ZOE

After Zoe overcame Lily's interruption, she assumed dominance over the set. Neither Tevin nor Sage believed they could have performed a similar feat and so deferred to Zoe's radiance. Crew members, or fans, or stalkers, or any other category of unknowable person, filled her dressing room with flowers. Each of the makeup artist's brush strokes circulated the scent of them around Zoe. A convenient Elysium, brought right to her. Once the makeup artist finished, Nate burst his head out from between some sunflowers and roses.

"Oh! I didn't know you were in there," Zoe said.

"I took a nap and when I woke up, I was buried. All I could see was the color of different petals, and your voice muffled like it was at a long distance. I thought I was dead, in heaven."

"Good news, you're alive. What's on my agenda?"

"You have an exit interview with Sage in half an hour. Otherwise, you have the rest of the day off to celebrate wrapping the movie." He rifled through his notes, as if another appointment might come fluttering out from between the sheets. "Should I put a celebration on your calendar?"

"Let's wait. I want to see what Sage says before I decide what mood I'm in." After *Drama Dolls* was done, the creator had gone on a tirade against Zoe. Every flaw in the show had been her fault; every scrap of tension had been because she hadn't been a good enough actress, or because she had mishandled some interpersonal beef that she hadn't even known about. Even problems with the editing had been because she had supposedly pressured the team into making decisions that benefited her rather than the entire show. Beneath the red face, what the creator had really been angry at was that Zoe had become the star. But what had she expected? That the acne-riddled writer dork the fans never even saw would become the favorite, rather than the beautiful woman who brought them to life? Coming out of that incident, Zoe had resolved never to make someone else's unrealistic expectations her problem. Not that other people stopped trying it.

Even as the meeting with Sage loomed, a bigger threat muscled into Zoe's imagination. What would she do, now that the full days in front of bright lights were over? "Do I have any interesting offers for new roles?" She turned to Nate.

"Not right now. A few people have expressed interest, but those were for other web series roles. No movies."

"So go get me a movie."

Nate didn't say anything. He scribbled some notes.

"I'm sorry, Nate. But if I don't move forward after this movie, I'm headed way back."

"Yes, Ms. Berger. I know. I won't let that happen."

But what power could Nate's spindly little hands exert on the world? Would he act with the utmost urgency? He made a little more money if she was in movies, but would get paid even if she was stuck online forever. An actress who got these low-prestige roles with ease might even be the best outcome for him: he could get paid without doing any work. Deep in her peripheral vision, she scanned his face for deceit. He pecked away with his index fingers at the laptop balanced on his crossed legs. For so long, she'd thought nothing but devotion lay beneath his skin. But now, it felt like she'd find stone if she stuck a needle through his cheek.

After twenty more minutes of tweaking her makeup to perfection, she walked alone down the hallway to meet with Sage. They'd requested privacy—specifically, that Nate be absent. At first Zoe had refused, but Sage had pointed out certain contractual details that mandated both this meeting and its privacy, as well as certain clauses that could be invoked if they weren't met. Zoe hadn't really followed the conversation, but the message she'd gotten from it was "if you don't like it, get a lawyer." Zoe hadn't liked it and she had gotten a lawyer, who had advised her that it was a waste of time and to just go to the meeting. Her second and third lawyers had recommended the same, so Zoe was out about a thousand dollars and still had to go to the meeting.

When she entered the room, Sage greeted her with a smile and asked her to sit down. It was a departure from the groans, rolled eyes, and malicious shouting which had been their primary modes of communication on set. Zoe sat, tucking her dress beneath her thighs tight enough to stress the cloth where it curved beneath the weight of her leg. Sage handed her a slender can of premixed Bellini and opened one of their own. They took a long drink that drained half the can. Zoe set hers down on the table, unopened and unworried that Sage might notice.

"So we've got a problem," Sage said. "It's not a new problem, or a difficult one, but it's a problem that you see all the time when an actress and a director have the kind of contentious working relationship you and I have had."

"We're done working. Problem solved."

"That's where you're wrong, actually." Sage settled onto the couch next to Zoe and placed a firm hand on her shoulder. Her mind raced with stories and memories of directors grabbing, coercing, worse. But those were moments stolen by directors with leverage, at its highest, during casting. Over the course of the production, it trickled away slowly as each scene was filmed and the cost of replacing her rose higher and higher. Only future productions and their connections in the industry gave them power now, and they both knew that Zoe wasn't signing on for Sage's next film. So, how many friends did Sage have? How far did their word go? Sage said, "We just have a new problem. What are we going to say about each other?"

"Say whatever's in your heart. I'm not afraid."

"Ah." Sage waggled a finger at Zoe and smiled like she'd just answered a riddle. This was what bothered Zoe the most about Sage. The pretense toward wisdom. A year and a half with a gender, and they thought they knew something Zoe didn't. "And you say yours, and we let the chips fall, huh? Let's go with positivity. You were a pleasure to work with, I was a pleasure to work with. Better for both of us." A dark shadow hid beneath the spot where Sage's thumb dented their can. One foot pedaled the ground.

Zoe said, "I'd rather we both tell the truth. If you're not sincere, people will be able to tell. You're not an actor, after all."

"I'm just trying not to make this a hassle, alright? Do you want a back and forth, people talking about a feud instead of our movie?"

"I don't think there'll be a back and forth."

"Whatever, get out of here then. We're done, thanks for your fine acting." Sage grabbed the unopened can from the table and tossed it back into their mini fridge hard enough to dent the can. Zoe made sure her heels clacked with each step as she walked over to the fridge, reached past Sage, and removed the can. She cracked it open and took a sip.

"These are so much better than you'd think."

She left the room so full of Sage's white-knuckle fists and clenched jaw and enjoyed her drink on the walk down. The hallway was full of people smiling and saying goodbye to her, and she returned each bit of affection magnanimously. What a joy to be among rapture, to be at the center of it. So many months together, all hands on the same rope, hauling out from the depths of non-existence a work of art until finally, they'd hoisted it up and the last drips fell and it was beautiful. Few ever get to feel that burn on their palms. Fewer still the tension from the depths to the rope, to the muscles to the bones, of being the first person in the line, whose strength more than anyone's determines whether it rises or falls. But they all knew what that first person had done for them, and everyone in that building knew that person was her.

When she got back to her dressing room, Nate was gone. She ruffled some of the flower petals to dispel the silence. On her vanity, she found a note written in his wide, looping handwriting. "Had to run to a meeting. Good news. Three auditions. Movie deal sure to result. Yours in good health, Nate." Zoe laughed as she ripped the note up and tossed it into the air. As the little snow came down, she danced in her fan-made meadow. Stardom was at hand, and no one could stop her from grabbing it and holding it close with all her strength.

# LILY

Lily awoke to a less-than-a-knock. A gentle pawing at her door. Her phone told her it was seven a. m., and that at four a.m. Zoe had sent her a middle finger emoji. She lurched to the door and wondered how she could have been awoken, who could wake her, why they could do this, in a house where everyone was only allowed to do what Steph wanted, when Steph would never do this to her. When she opened the door, she found the twink sub, collar obligate, but wearing a white V-neck and boxers instead of the more typical leather and chains of his station. Glamour still slept just after sunrise.

"What do you want?" She didn't want to sound grumpy. The twink sub was always nice to her, especially when the cultists were brusque—though they didn't dare to be outright rude as long as Lily had Steph's favor.

"Hey, I'm sorry, I know, I shouldn't have woken you up." He set a tray with a bowl of muesli, topped by a drizzled lattice of honey, on the ground.

"Sure, yeah, whatever. What's up?" Drawing more apologies out of him wouldn't accomplish anything, and Lily didn't get turned on by groveling.

"I just wanted you to know that the cult guys were being weird last night. I got a vibe, and I wanted you to know about it." The twink sub's eyes, wide open and earnest, communicated how sincerely he needed Lily to know about the vibe. A sweet little man, who smelled like moss. Affection washed away the momentary thrill of annoyance.

"Thank you for passing along the vibe. They've been extra weird over the last month. What's their deal?"

"They think She's touched by God, what else is there?" With that, the twink sub wandered off. Lily picked up the tray and sat down, resting it atop her crossed legs. Dates and bananas hid inside the yogurt, beneath which the oats soaked and had become pleasant to eat. Had the twink sub make this for her? Or had one of the cultists? Whether or not it stemmed from an order—or implicit desire—of Steph's, it could've been made happily or begrudgingly. Though he certainly occupied the lowest position of power, except for maybe the cultist whose face Lily couldn't quite remember, it was useful to know that he sided with her, not with them.

Once the bowl was empty, Lily embraced wakefulness and took a cup of tea to the balcony at the back of the apartment. Ten chairs crowded the thin cement landing, and several more were thrust forward on individual sub-balconies that jutted out from the main one. Ferns and wildflowers bloomed all along the ground, so that each chair could have sprouted directly from a jungle floor. She found the unremarkable cultist, whose facial features seemed to average out into a blur, sitting and reading a book in the corner. Vines dangled between him and the pages. He brushed them aside every time he turned a page, and they swung and returned to their resting spot in his line of sight.

Hoping to blunt some of the cultists' resentment of her, Lily sat next to him. They said good morning to each other, but neither found the will to begin a conversation. Instead, Lily looked out at the alley below the apartment. A car drove past, slow enough that the engine only whispered, the crunch of gravel below its tires a token complaint. Otherwise, the alley was still. No wind, no animals running around, certainly no people. A frozen picture of clapboard houses and backyard gardens and cars lined up in gravel driveways and trash piled in and around dumpsters. She tried to sense if there was tension next to her, but couldn't tell if the cultist was rigid, or avoiding looking at her, or pretending to read and just imagining the words "Lily sucks" running down the page in two columns. So she ignored him and drank her tea and went on with an uneventful day.

When she returned from work that evening, Lily opened the door and smoke poured out into the building's hallway. Not enough to set off the detectors out there, but the interior was obscured beyond a couple of steps. Lily didn't know if she should call the fire department, run away, call for Steph to see if she was alright, and in the end decided on none of those and just walked into the smoke, daring it to keep her forever. It tasted like artificial fog. Intentional, no cause for concern. She ambled into the living room and found Steph seated on the floor. A chalk circle surrounded her, with lines drawn from the edges back to the center at which she sat. She was naked except for a blindfold with two bloodshot eyes painted on it. The cultists bowed on the floor in front of her.

Lily had hoped to relax and read for a bit now that she was done with work, but that obviously wasn't going to happen. Instead, she leaned against the wall and admired the view. Though she'd seen Steph naked a few times before, none of those times occurred during a ceremony, so there was a novelty involved in this. And maybe she'd say the name of god or absolve all of their sins or something, and Lily didn't want to miss out on that.

Steph rose to her feet and whirled around. Currents in the smoke followed her outstretched hands and wound around her into a veil, until Steph was a soft-lit silhouette among blurs and impressions. A powerful exhalation cleared the smoke from around her face, then she said in a harsh, strained voice, "Three ends find three mighty warriors. Escape, and time, and memory. Hold salvation in your hands, fools. Or find it lost when you need it. A thousand waves roll upon the shore and each one of them brings death. Be sure yourselves to bring something worthy of it." And then she fell, a tree careening down into a misty forest. Lily flinched forward, but she was too far away, and the goatee cultist slid under Steph instead and broke her fall. As he rubbed her hair, the burn-faced cultist rose from his bow. Lily felt like she could see a thousand feet of thread coiled beneath his shirt, his skin, all tied up without an inch of give. He marched toward her, eyes staring into hers.

"You are not at the Hand of the Lord. Those prophecies were not for your ears."

"Oh, you've got her prophesying now? You're gonna wear her out, dude. But fine, I'll go."

Lily raised her hands in mock surrender, but he yelled after her.

"You carry an unearned revelation. May it corrode your mind like acid."

In the kitchen, Lily found the bear sub eating some crackers. He picked one out of the bag, examined it and, once he found it satisfactory, ate it.

"Hey. Does Steph usually fall over when she does one of these things?" Lily asked.

"No idea," he said, one half of a cracker's worth of crumbs spewing from his mouth. "This is the first time it's ever happened. She just rumbled into the living room yelling that She was gonna do a prophecy. She fell?"

"One of the cult guys caught her. I think she's fine. I guess she's savior and prophet, all in one." Lily grabbed a cracker and popped it in her mouth.

"Dangerous behavior, friend."

Lily chuckled, happy at least that she'd established some kind of rapport within the apartment. The situation with the cultists felt tense, but it didn't present that many challenges. As long as she had Steph's favor, it didn't matter what they thought of her. Steph told them what to think, what to do, and they would just have to deal with it. Until then, Lily wanted to forget about it.

There was nothing she could do: no amount of good times or bonding sessions could make her join the cult. In time, the cultists would understand that, and they'd reach a tenuous peace. In the two months since she'd arrived, the strange ecosystem of the apartment had started to feel like home. Maybe the cultists would one day recognize that she added something to the dynamic of the apartment. Enriched it in some way.

She closed herself in her room, grateful for the space to get away from the density of the common area. Since she'd gotten there, she hadn't bothered to decorate. It would be pointless to put up art and buy furniture for a temporary stay, but Lily had begun to think more permanently. Steph hadn't said anything about her leaving, or someone else needing the room. The blank off-white walls would look good with a tapestry over the bed, some prints around the window. Maybe a rug. It would be hard to match the multiplicity of decor in the rooms outside, on her paycheck, but over time, she'd manage it.

Until then, she could flop onto the bed and take up space in peace. After an hour of aimless social media, she wondered what Zoe was doing. Lily couldn't dislodge the hot stone of resentment from her chest, but when she pictured the house in shambles, Zoe crying as yet another appliance failed to start, she felt no pleasure. But when she replayed the image, with a note saying "Lily broke this," and imagined Zoe blaming her to Nate, still locating her at the source of all her problems, her pity curdled into anger. She and Zoe lived in different worlds; they couldn't even see the same reality. It's not like it had been years ago, when it had felt like they were two halves of the same mind, when their difference in perspective had been only the amount necessary to see in three dimensions. If Zoe had been dropped into Steph's house, she would have immediately alienated everyone involved and been kicked out while screaming. All while her gay little manager stammered some wild misconceptions about property law. If only Lily had managed to hold onto the house, Zoe's journey out into the couches and guest rooms of the world would have been such a disaster. But maybe Zoe thought the same thing. Maybe she'd laughed when she'd heard that Lily had moved into Elena's house, then laughed again when she heard about Steph's apartment. Who cares? Lily put Zoe out of her mind, until she opened up Zoe's Instagram profile. Her main account was blocked, but Lily had plenty of alts.

Zoe's life looked the same, for the most part. Self-promotion, pictures in full makeup whenever she was on set, pictures with carefully crafted "no-makeup" looks in her spare time at home. Those ones used to be taken all over the house, but now they all came from one corner of the couch. A huge mess must have been lurking just out of frame, consuming the house until only that scrap of couch was safe. Otherwise the only difference was Lily's absence from the pictures. Lily scrolled down and found the last picture she appeared in. September 8th of last year. Things hadn't been perfect between them back then, but the tension had been still only a seed, just beginning to sprout. Deciding enough was enough, Lily tossed her phone away and reclined on the bed.

A few hours later, after evening bloomed into night, she realized she hadn't heard from Steph since the fall, and ventured out of her room to check on her friend. On the quick walk down the hallway, Lily didn't encounter any of the subs or cultists, and the emptiness felt like death in the air. When she knocked on Steph's door, she feared the silence she might get in response.

"Who is it?" Steph sounded annoyed. Maybe she'd sent the others away, would send Lily away too. But at least she was fine. Visions of ambulances and hospital rooms faded from her imagination.

Lily said, "It's me."

"Oh, come in." The tension in Steph's voice vanished, and Lily slipped in the door, closing it behind her with barely a tap against the doorjamb. Before her, Steph reclined on her mattress, which was laid on top of three other mattresses, with a pillow between her head and the wall. Ten more pillows were scattered on the bed and the floor. She was topless and hunched over her laptop, a far cry from her decorous perches around the apartment.

"Ah, sorry!" Some pretense of surprise that Steph was topless felt necessary. As if this was new to Lily, or as if Steph hadn't known her tits were out when she had invited Lily in.

"Whatever, c'mere." Steph patted the mattress next to her. Lily climbed in and Steph scooted just enough that their bodies were pressed against each other. "Look at this. Someone's been doing video analysis of when my dad died."

"Oh?" Lily looked down on the laptop screen and returned to the moment she saw Steph's father die. A lust for violence in his eyes. His head jerked backward as he tumbled to the ground. Where did all of that intent go when the bullet passed through his brain? Maybe it dissipated like mist into the atmosphere and carried through the windows, distributing the bloodlust among the nearby towns. While Lily speculated on this topic, Steph pressed closer, one of her breasts now smushed against Lily's arm.

"Yeah, their analysis suggests that, from the angle of his head when he goes down, it couldn't have been a bullet from the police. But obviously, if a bullet had come from the other angle, we would've seen the exit wound."

"So... not a bullet?"

"One theory is that it was an invisible heat gun. Fried his brain from a hundred meters. But this user, GodsWill69, thinks it was divine intervention." Steph laughed. "They think that God killed my dad for some reason. Like the cops weren't about to do it."

"Sorry to ask this, but what was his body like when you looked at it?"

"Dude, it was full of bullets. Like they definitely shot the fuck out of him after he died. No doubt. But, wow, people are going hog wild about him."

"Does that feel bad?" Lily rubbed a hand against Steph's back in a comforting circle, and couldn't help noticing how soft and smooth her skin was. How her own fingertips felt compelled toward Steph's shoulder blade and the gentle bumps of her spine.

"It's whatever. I'm mostly laughing about it. There's one theory that maybe someone in the cult poisoned him and like, weakened his power, which is why he didn't do any miracles when the cops showed up. I buy that one. It's why you don't see me in a compound." Steph leaned her head into Lily's shoulder. Her hair smelled like cinnamon.

"You mean you don't want a hundred of those guys around you all the time?"

"No way. I'm not trying to get poisoned."

"Okay but what if, instead of being poisoned, one of them has a secret lightning device, which invisibly shocks you and makes it seem like you had a stroke."

Steph laughed her halting, raspy laugh, completely devoid of any grace or elegance. "No no no. I got it. He's got a tiny little gun, and it like shoots a sharp little bullet that's so small it's invisible. But it goes through my brain and damn, I'm dead."

This time Lily cackled, and the two of them cuddled up closer. "I'm glad I got to spend some private time with you. It's weird out there."

"I know. I have to do so much for those dudes. I never get to relax except when I'm here: my sacred temple."

Lily looked out from the mattress. Food wrappers and beer cans and clothes all over the ground created their own kind of topography. Ridges and pathways where she could pass or where she had to climb a bit.

"Truly you have offered me a blessing, by allowing me in," she said, closing her eyes and clasping her hands solemnly to her chest. Unable to see, she tried to feel Steph's response through the contact with her skin.

But she didn't have to try that hard because Steph shoved her and groaned. Lily shoved back and soon the two of them were wrestling for position and laughing, and then Lily straddled Steph and pinned Steph's arms to her side. Both of them breathed heavily and stared into each other's eyes in the little corridor that Lily's dangling hair curtained around them. Lily brought her face closer, and Steph closed her eyes and leaned up and her lips felt as warm as home should.

The door burst open and the twink sub rushed in. "Mistress, are you alright? Did you fall again?"

Lily could have jumped off of her, but it was too late. So she stayed there, her hands still digging into Steph's fleshy upper arms, while the cultists and the bear sub soon followed the twink into the room, all stammering and inquiring if everything was okay, only to fall silent once they saw what was happening.

"Oh my god. What are you doing to her?" the twink sub said.

"Everyone, out. Now." Steph pointed at the door. The cultists filed out obediently, and Lily saw the hint of a smile reaching out to the borders of the burn on the worst cultist's face. The other subs backed out of the room, eyes wide and mouths agape in disgust. Even though she was the clothed one, Lily felt like their eyes had just seen every fold of her flesh, the curve of every bone, and hated everything they'd seen.

Only once the room was empty did Lily dismount from Steph. "Mood's a little killed, huh?"

"Ugh. Little bit. But you know what? Gonna do some

discipline, then I'm back. I'll see you later." Steph kissed Lily's cheek and stormed out the door. Lily assumed it would be a few short seconds: a quick reprimand, and then she and Steph would go to work delicately rebuilding the moment they had stumbled into by accident. But seconds stretched on into minutes, and Lily grew more and more nervous and less comfortable alone in Steph's trash palace. After half an hour, Lily left. Steph would know where to find her.

Two hours later, she did. With a gentle knock, Steph asked permission to enter. Once granted, she walked in, head bowed, with her full retinue flanking her. All of them glared at Lily. Even the twink sub looked like he wanted to flay the flesh from her bones. Lily didn't know what this crowd intended to do. What they thought of her. How it had come to this. All she did was sit on top of Steph and kiss her. How, in an apartment full of cultists and subs, had that been so wrong? Steph kept her hands tucked behind her back and said, "So, a lot of hard conversations have been happening. I didn't really understand how much having you here was going to mess things up for these guys."

Steph glanced up, her eyes begging Lily to say something, but she didn't.

"So the problem is, they can only handle living here when I'm in charge. Just me. So I thought maybe..." She stepped forward, though she remained closer to her cultists and subs than Lily. Her hand finally emerged from behind her, holding a pink collar. Spiked, with a heart-shaped ring on the front. "I know it's not what you expected, and I know you won't join us in the Clenched Fist of God, but it might be nice. You'd still be special, but I'd be in charge, formally. Like I am with all of them."

Lily could see the strings now. Each one, gossamer-thin, trailing from the subs' and cultists' fingertips. Alone, those strings weren't capable of much. But Lily saw the thick rope they wrapped around Steph's neck.

Considering the offer, Lily imagined her future here. A simple life, dedicated only to following directions and providing pleasure. No more concerns about roommate squabbles or angry cultists. Nighttimes with Steph's manicured hands on her body, or chains and ropes holding her in place. Her lips trembling while the rest of her craves more and more. But the faces behind Steph, all stern and displeased—the burn-faced cultist openly scowling—told her that peace wouldn't come with the collar. The pink color and design differed from the uniform black leather collars the other subs wore. To set her apart. They all knew it. Future struggle and anguish came with it, and even so, Lily's fingers twitched when she thought about accepting. Even with all those problems, if she said yes, she would be home. No more wandering, no more uncertainty. That pink collar would decide everything for her. Lily would need only to follow directions and stay in her place. She held the collar in her hands and ran a finger along the smooth leather. One of the spikes pricked her and drew a little blood, and Lily handed the collar back to Steph and shook her head.

The rest of the crowd muttered half-hearted goodbyes and barely concealed their smiles. When they were alone, Steph gave her a hug and kissed her on the cheek and whispered she was sorry and left the room. Once again, Lily packed her things.

With her duffel bag dangling from her shoulder, Lily walked down the familiar sidewalk, here cracked, there uneven from a tree root breaking free. Maybe there was nothing but returning. Each attempt to venture out brought her back to her orbit around the old house with Zoe. Like a comet, she'd keep coming back until she flamed out in the sky.

Every window of the house streamed vivid white light, so bright that, once she turned the corner, it appeared to become daytime again except for the dark midnight sky above. The kind of light that erases the borders around your body. Makes you no different than the wall. She didn't think she could stand up to that kind of light; she just wanted to lie down and rest. Lily could hide from it in her room, beneath a pillow, beneath a mound of blankets and a blindfold and curtains and all of her clothes. Thin strands of light escaped the seams of the front door and even out of the keyhole in the deadbolt. Lily blocked it by sticking in her key, but a few rattles later, withdrew it. She knocked on the door. "Zoe!

The window to her left slid open, and a pitch-black silhouette blocked the light. Zoe's shadow slithered closer, every detail of her face still obscured by the powerful backlight, but the sound of her hair rustling and the smell of her perfume were the same as ever. In a blur, she grabbed Lily's wrist and squeezed much too tight.

"Stop it." Zoe's smile shone white, even amongst the bottomless shadow of her face.

"Let me go."

Still just a smile and an even stronger grip. Lily's muscle ached and bulged beneath it.

"I don't want to be here. I don't want to come back."

As she tugged and tugged against Zoe's grasp, the smile grew wider and whiter. The lights streaming from the house pulsed to the beat of Lily's attempts to free herself. The house itself mocked her for coming back. Too often a temporary home, less hospitable each time until it, too, had become her enemy. Lily slipped her wrist through the gap between Zoe's thumb and fingers, and withdrew. Ribbons of light wrapped around Zoe's face and body until her demonic smile vanished into the light. Until the light vanished into her smile.

The light faded as Lily staggered away. She couldn't go back. Zoe had won. It was hers. It had always been hers. Lily had fooled herself for years, thinking it was a home the two of them were building together, rather than Zoe's space with some little crevices Lily could nestle herself into. So long as she let them distort the shape of her body enough to fit. The only place left for her was the house where every straggler and shithead passing through Pittsburgh found a place to stay, if the house made room for them: Dicks's transforming house. If any house in the city would make room for her, it was that one.

# ZOE

When a knock on the door came, the spotlight trembled and sparks flew from its housing. The blanket that Zoe kept draped over it smoked, and she pulled it down and stamped it out in perfect rhythm with the insistent visitor's repeated knocks. The spotlight illuminated the area two feet to her right and she threw a coaster at it, and it clanged off and now pointed even further away. Why wouldn't whoever was at the door just leave? Did their Mormon god or whatever really dictate this relentless a pursuit? Zoe would buy nothing, convert to nothing, sign nothing, and yet whoever stood outside that door felt it necessary to engage her in the pretense that she might. Zoe decided she wasn't home, and sat down on a blanket on the floor. Burn marks dotted the light gray cotton. Each scorch, an insult. A couple minutes went by. Still, one after another, knocks pummeled the door. Quiet but insistent.

Enough. Zoe clomped over to the door. Each step was louder than the knocks, so whoever it was knew she was coming; still, their soft hand hit the door until it opened. At first, Elena's eyes met Zoe's with a ferocity that blunted her clenched jaw, softened her angry fist, calmed her beating heart. But then Elena softened, and Zoe regained her grasp on fury.

"What do you want?"

"Is Lily here?"

Zoe leaned back against the door frame, her foot propped against the opposite side, to make an obstacle of herself. "You know Lily. She comes, she goes. One day she's living here, the next she has a big tantrum and storms out to go chase another doomed relationship."

Elena winced. Hidden within her closed mouth,

Zoe worked her tongue in a circle around one of her canine teeth. Hers were particularly prominent and sharp. Once, a makeup artist had told her that she might be able to play a vampire without any dental prosthetics. But she'd never take that role and her teeth went unused except for the rare times when Zoe needed to rip into a piece of tough meat and tear flesh from gristle and watch the string of white fat connecting the two glisten in the light.

"Sorry. I forgot you two used to..." Zoe said.

"Yeah. We did."

"You can come in and wait for her, if you want. I think it's a waste of time, but it's yours to waste." Zoe removed her body from the doorway and swept her arm to the door. A perfect imitation of a butler she had learned back when she was a male actor. Her roles had been so much worse before she'd accessed her beauty. Still, the body remembered.

Elena walked by without a word and kicked aside the burnt blanket. The spotlight found her and the mirror fragments sewn into her jacket glittered. Maybe it was their height difference. The spotlight might be worse at tracking taller women. Or maybe the mirror fragments were helping it track Elena better. Though that didn't explain its other problems. Elena sat on the couch, feet placed politely on the ground facing forward like she was in a waiting room. Zoe crossed in front of her and absorbed the spotlight, casting her shadow over her guest. "If you want water or tea or something, you know where everything is. I'm going to go take a shower."

Elena nodded. She didn't respond much to Zoe's movements about the house, but every noise outside sent her eyes to the front door. As if Lily was worth that kind of interest. Upstairs, Zoe stripped off her clothes and tossed them in the hamper, except for her top, which she folded gently and returned to its shelf. It had another wear in it. Washing every time when her body barely exuded any but the sweetest odors wasted water and shortened the lifespan of her expensive clothes. She traveled from her bedroom to the bathroom completely nude. Not that Elena had any reason to come upstairs, peek into the hallway, and wait for those three seconds where Zoe's unobscured beauty was visible. But the fact that she could gave Zoe a little thrill. It tickled at parts of her that she hadn't been able to express for the longest time. Ever since she'd gotten her first handful of fame, enough eyes were on her that she had to give up certain exhibitions. Fun was in the risk of being caught, not the inevitability. But she missed the cold air that danced along her ass as a boy pulled out of her in an alleyway, and the warmth as he thrust back in, his flesh and hers flush against each other once more. The danger of moaning too loudly as people walked past the dressing room, the irresistibility of it as pleasure mounted. These days, the most she could get away with was walking around without underwear. Once *Somnolences* came out and some paparazzi got on her trail, that would have to stop too.

Near-scalding water seethed fog into the bathroom. She stepped into the shower and her world shrank to those three tile walls and the one glass. She imagined strained eyes peeking through, catching glimpses of her hips, her tits, wishing they could tear the veil of steam to shreds with their hungry fingers. The sex scene in the movie had been fun, the audience of the movie seeing her topless had excited her, and even now sent her fingers tracing down her stomach, but they stopped short of their destination. She had almost fucked Tevin again that day, but after the scene, he'd started babbling about the cruel tasks that birth obliges him to and the vibe was smothered in an instant. None of the other men she knew were suitable either. She'd learned that much about Adam. But here was someone with a butchy, masculine vibe just downstairs. Her broad shoulders would do the trick, in a pinch.

Zoe exited the steam and returned to her room. Normally, she'd just apply all of her nighttime goops and oils and lay in bed, but this time she applied a little eyeshadow, some tinted moisturizer—not enough makeup to call attention to itself, but enough to elevate her face to a functional performance. She slipped on a tiny bathrobe which exposed half of each breast. White lace lined the hem and the bottom of her ass cheeks peeked through its little gaps. Not a subtle approach by any means, but the situation called for a blunt instrument. Zoe descended the staircase with loud steps to announce herself, but when she came down, Elena was still looking at the door.

"You're still here?"

"I want to see Lily." Elena took one glance at Zoe and returned her gaze to the door, but not before it got tied up in Zoe's cleavage, then down at the hemline. Eyes on the prize. Yes, Elena would do nicely. Zoe flopped on the couch next to Elena, and the impact jostled the bathrobe's shoulder down, exposing all of one breast's delicate slope. Sure enough, Elena looked.

"Oh, you know how Lily is. She'll go out late, lead a few guys on—all genders, I'm sure you've experienced this—and then come back once she's gotten what she wants. Not that it's impossible she comes back with someone." No one was immune to the fires of jealousy. While Elena's attention was on the door, Zoe would act as the bellows until the furnace deep in Elena glowed red-hot and begged her body to do anything to relieve it. To hurt Lily for making her feel that way.

"That's fine. She and I aren't together."

Zoe couldn't see her face. Most observers would hear the cool tone of her voice and assume that she was unmoved by Zoe's efforts, but a studied eye could see the truth. The voice artificially even. The little swallow.

The eye twitching towards its periphery in Zoe's direction. Tapping her foot, adjusting in her seat, cracking knuckles. Something was making her nervous. It could be whatever she had to say to Lily, but why would that be getting worse when there was no indication that Lily was any closer to arriving?

Cool air blew in from the window and traced its fingers over Zoe's exposed skin. She leaned into Elena's space so that her breath would reach her ear and her soft chest would impress onto Elena's arm. "If it's gonna be a while, I know a way to kill the time."

Elena jumped off the couch. "What the fuck is wrong with you?"

"Nothing, darling. That's the appeal."

"I—why? Are you just trying to fuck me so that Lily can walk in on us?"

"Of course not. I'm trying to fuck you because your shoulders look powerful in that little T-shirt."

In her anger, Elena flexed her muscles more and Zoe wanted to feel those muscles on her body. If that erotic dynamism was no longer an option, violence would do. "Lily doesn't live here anymore. By the way."

"You're sick."

"Oh, cure me." Zoe shrugged her shoulders and the bathrobe's sleeves glided obediently down her arms. "Lay those healing hands on me." She squeezed her breasts together and slid one hand up to her throat. Abundance was on offer for Elena; all she had to do was pick something and do it to Zoe.

"Is this what it was like for Lily? No wonder she left." Elena picked up her bag and made for the door, but Zoe caught hold of her hand and spun her momentum back until their bodies were pressed against each other.

"Lily never got an offer like this." Zoe guided Elena's hand up her body, limp fingers bumping over ribs and dragging across the expanse of her breast, jumping the collarbone, until they were touching Zoe's cheek and the thumb rested on Zoe's pink lower lip, hot breath inviting it into the mouth. "Take it."

Elena's thumb moved, first a flinch into Zoe's mouth, where her tongue awaited to drag Elena the rest of the way into lust, but then out, onto her cheek. A sudden sting, as Elena dragged her jagged nail against Zoe's cheek.

Zoe screamed. Her face. Her perfect face, marred by a scratch. She swiped her more-formidable nails toward Elena, but those powerful shoulders pushed her off and in a moment, Elena was at the door. "You don't deserve any of this," Elena said, rolling her eyes around at the house, at Zoe's career and fame and beauty. "But you deserved that."

The door slammed and rattled her. Zoe sat on the floor, mesmerized by the twinge of pain on her cheek. Every time her heart beat, the new flaw on her face pulsed.

# LILY

A massive spiral staircase ordered Dicks's house. Thick iron railings swirled up into a point that shrunk past the horizon point above Lily. Sound from rooms above echoed down; cries of joy and anguish and arguments and passive aggression toward no one in particular about how nice it would be if someone vacuumed, fluttered to the foyer. A joyous and brutal cacophony. Down the middle, three streams of water poured freely into a fountain around three statues at the center. Each of them wore a hood, and each of them had one visible eye painted and polished, shining like it was real enough to look around the room. They all reached one hand behind their backs, clasped in a tangle of fingers, while their other hands reached up so that the tips of their index fingers scattered the graceful streams of water into a clumsy spray.

"Sorry about the noise," Dicks said, in the perfunctory way one apologizes for a mess they have no intention of cleaning up. "Sometimes the house gets this way." They clanged up the steps. Some of the rooms had a window peering out. On one of the sills, a lush garden grew despite the lack of sunlight. On another was a cardboard sign with "NO" written on it in Sharpie. Unclear if she was the one being forbidden, Lily hopped up a couple steps to get away from it. On the climb up, Lily saw ten different roommates saunter down or jog up past her laborious ascent, burdened by her duffel bag. Roxy's nails tapped against the iron as she descended, before poking her head through the bars overlooking the foyer to bark. At someone new? Someone familiar? Another dog blew past her, with a fluffy white neck and heavy steps that seemed like they were finding the stairs only by accident.

"That's Tedward. He's an idiot," Dicks said. "But you'll love him after a couple weeks."

"Not before."

"No, it takes a while."

Below, Tedward jumped up into a window and the NO sign clattered to the ground. He scooted forward until his back legs hung useless and none of his wiggles carried him any further forward, but his tail kept wagging. Roxy ran down to join Tedward and barked at his butt. Maybe she was trying to help.

Eventually their breath got ragged enough that they had to take a break. While Lily gazed up the steps above, seemingly no fewer in number, Dicks laughed. "Guess who has to live at the top?"

"How do you climb all these stairs?"

Dicks rolled up their diaphanous pink pants to reveal thighs that looked like they were as hard as the iron they sat on. To demonstrate, Dicks jammed a fist against them to a resounding thud. "Sometimes the house comes up with little problems for me. But she hasn't beaten me once."

After another half hour of climbing and another half dozen new roommates to greet on the way, they arrived at Lily's room. "Remember, stay as long as you feel welcome here."

"How long do you think that'll be?"

"You'll know if you have to leave." Dicks opened the door, which revealed a blank-walled room the size of a walk-in closet. It had no windows and no features except for a bare lightbulb with a chain dangling from it. When Lily pulled it, the light came out gray.

"Can I get another room?"

"No, this one's yours. If you pick another one, it'll just look like this."

"Am I... already unwelcome?" The prospect of moving, now to somewhere completely unknown with no clear way to even find a place, made Lily want to throw up.

"If there's any question, you're good. When it happens, you'll know." Dicks dropped her duffel bag into the room. "No one's ever asked me if I think it's time to leave. Tough break, though. She's being kind of a bitch right now."

"I guess it's not so bad." With the bag inside, there was only room for Lily to lie down on her back on the floor, arms directly at her sides. No living was possible in this room, but before long, she'd make friends with her roommates and get to spend time in their space. Plus the staircase and its expanse could be a good place to sit throughout the day and greet people as they journeyed up and down. After the complications everywhere she'd lived over the last year, something this spartan didn't sound so terrible.

"Settle in as long as you want. There's a movie night in... one of these rooms. Unbelievable, it's this bitch. One second." Dicks peeled away and followed a girl in skin-tight plaid pants and a flowy white dress shirt up the stairs. They said, "I know you're the one who's leaving half-full yogurt cups all over the steps. When we were on one floor all day it was annoying. I don't know why you can't finish a yogurt. Buy smaller cups. I don't care."

They were far enough away and the girl's voice was soft enough—if she spoke at all—that Lily couldn't hear her, but her hands gestured wildly in defense against the accusation.

"It's a hazard," Dicks said. And then they were beyond her, caught up in the funnel of indistinguishable noise.

Rather than lay down in her spot, Lily leaned against the wall. Bland as they were, the gray walls buzzed when she looked at them long enough. They were smooth to the touch, but warmer than she expected the walls to be. Warm like laundry just out of the dryer, though hard and smooth like standard drywall. She closed the door so that it was pitch black, and then turned the light on again. Before, the gray muddied the light coming from outside. But now it brought the objects in the room to life beneath an impressionistic fog. Her fingers smeared as she moved them. Her bag looked like layer over layer of the same transparent gray had been used to build up a three-dimensional image. How were there so many values beneath this one lightbulb?

Dicks's voice snaked into the room from up the stairs. "Everyone loves those fish. They're beauties. I'm not disputing that. But you gotta keep them in a conventional aquarium. No more surprises." A knock signaled they were about to enter. Some muttering came from their interlocutor.

"I get it. But you're their caretaker. You have to put your foot down." The conversation ended, and Dicks knocked again. When Lily opened the door, they were staring down the staircase, mouth agape. Whatever they had to say to her had been interrupted by a torrent of sand flowing out of one of the rooms below her. Individual grains bounced and caught the light, some of them sparkling. Several residents waited at the bottom of the staircase, just outside of the growing dune in the entryway. One forged upward step after step against the powerful flow, but it couldn't bend him even an inch backward.

What would it be like to be so formidable? Lily tried to picture herself in that situation: she fell to her knees, spun down the stairs, tumbled off the railing, collapsed beneath the sand, breathed wrong and let it fill up her lungs. As the resident emerged from the sand and continued up the stairs, Lily stepped out of her room. His eyes were just like the rest of him, hard and unyielding. Lily's attempt to say hello died in her throat and soon he was two steps above her and for all she knew, she'd never see him again. So she grabbed a handful of his shirt, immediately blushing with embarrassment. He continued going up until the red and tan plaid held taut. The resident leaned forward as if to confirm to himself that he could easily overcome her hold, then turned toward her. He held his face in perfect neutrality. Not the coldness of hostile indifference, but truly unbothered. He didn't care that she had attempted to arrest his journey up. He could continue at any time, and while he wasn't excited to speak to her, his eyes didn't betray any resentment either.

"How did you walk through that sand?"

"I had to, or it wouldn't get done."

Lily let the fabric brush past her fingers, and the resident continued his climb.

"Who was that?" Lily said.

"A guy who's donated his share to the house fund every month without fail for ten years. Sometimes I think the house will be done with me before him." Dicks headed down toward the sand room. Lily was tempted to follow, but once they started battering the sand with their fists and yelling at it, she decided she didn't have the stomach. Instead, she returned to the spot beneath the gray light, and lay down on the floor. It was hard and her shoulders hurt, but she had nothing else to do. So she got used to it, looked up into the light, and thought in many shades of gray.

# ZOE

Zoe ignored ten calls from Sage, five from the producer, and two from Nate. Sure, it was urgent. What wasn't? But Zoe needed to brush her hair. The humidity in Pittsburgh was worse than normal, and every bit of unruly frizz was a direct affront to her. Urgency was for people whose livelihood didn't rely on looking pretty. But when someone came knocking on her door, then yelling and throwing pebbles at her window, she considered that there might be an emergency. Before she could finish brushing and head down, the bedroom window opened and Nate tumbled through to the floor in a single motion. "I learned that in gymnastics class."

"You and the ten-year-old girls?"

"It's not a tae kwon do situation, Ms. Berger. Those kids have every advantage. Have you heard about Tevin?"

"Oh, did he land a Wes Anderson role or something? I'm not in the mood to hear it."

"He killed someone."

Zoe set down the brush, parallel to her comb and straightening iron, and turned off the lights that circled her mirror. "In a good way or a bad way?" When Nate didn't respond, she found his reflection. The answer lay etched in his bemused frown. "Did he kill some school shooter or something? What was it?"

"He killed a ten-year-old boy."

"Shit."

"Beat him to death in a public park. There are so many videos of it. He said he did it in the name of the Clenched Fist of God."

"Oh, that bitch." Zoe looked back in the mirror. Anger lined her mouth and there were no lights on to brush the lines under the rug. A few deep breaths could usually help her dispel emotion from her face when she didn't need it. A blank expression ages you slower. "They're shelving *Somnolences*, aren't they?"

"There's some concern. The scene where you ask him to punch you in the face..."

She threw the brush at Nate. Then the comb. Then the straightening iron. Everything within grasp, until the vanity was bare and the floor was cluttered. Nate was covered in red marks from impact, black from eyeliner that scraped across his face, and from where a few tears had carried the eyeliner down with them. "You're the one who didn't stop them from shelving it. I have a contract. I have rights. They're supposed to release it," Zoe said.

"I'm sorry."

"You're sorry. You're sorry. Sorry doesn't save my career. You're useless." She left the room, with Nate still on his knees, his spine curled up in weakness. The Clenched Fist of God was Steph's bullshit. Did she ensnare Tevin to ruin Zoe's career? Was she getting revenge for Lily? Was it at Lily's request?

When a large hairy man in a harness cracked open Steph's front door after Zoe's insistent pounding, he tried to whisper something to get her to go away. "This is a bad time" or "She's not in" or any other light deflection that would send Zoe's fury away from their doorstep. But she lowered her shoulder into the door and the knob caught him right in the stomach and he doubled over.

The low light and mist in the living room were tools of a person unconvinced in her ability to summon a mystique around herself. Like every other cult leader, half-charismatic and reliant on a handful of parlor tricks to mask her unfitness to lead anyone anywhere. Actual leadership requires showing everyone the light, cutting through the illusions and serving up only the essential truths of the world.

Steph's unsteadiness was evident in her hurried voice as she rushed out to confront Zoe. "Get out. I'm not talking with you today." An assortment of appalling men in all-white clothing crowded behind her. She was supposed to be their messiah, touched by god and therefore god-in-part, and they wouldn't even get out front to defend her. Good.

Rather than let her speak, try any of her cult tricks that had gotten her the adoration of a scattered collection of desperate half-wits, Zoe grabbed two fistfuls of her diaphanous top and shoved Steph into the wall. "You're going to pay." But one second, and all of the men had grabbed her by the waist, the shoulders, the neck. "Let me go if you don't want another fucking news story," Zoe growled. They did.

"Don't let her just attack me," Steph said. But they paused, and Zoe spun out of their reach and grabbed a handful of Steph's hair.

"You fucked everything up for me." She rammed Steph's face into the wall. Zoe's shoulder flexed and she felt the line of tension connecting wood and bone and brain. No one would miss a cult leader; no police would believe anything the cultists said. She could make Steph repay the debt she'd incurred to the world by obstructing Zoe's brilliance. But again, the cultists snatched her away. This time they didn't let go, despite Zoe's threats to go public and call the police. No matter how weak-willed they were, eight hands could subdue Zoe. They held every part of her body still, as the twink sub picked Steph up off her feet. She gathered some of the blood trickling down her forehead on her fingertips and presented it to the twink sub, who sucked it off her fingers.

"Who wants the blood of divinity?" Steph said, smearing more on her hand and across her forehead and down her cheek. The cultists became puppies suckling at their mother, though rapture didn't loosen their grip. By the time they got their fill, Steph's face and neck sparkled, clean with saliva. Only one little globule of blood remained on her fingertip, just outside Zoe's mouth.

"Don't you want to know what salvation tastes like?"

"Fuck off. You might have AIDS." The cultists' grip tightened and some of them cleared their throats. "I can say that. I was a gay man."

"I'm being generous. Most people would beg to know what a goddess tastes like."

"I'm sure I can ask Lily. Or maybe half the other t-girls in town." The hand that didn't offer the blood slapped Zoe. A hot sting and her vision sparkled. The droplet of blood wavered with each of Zoe's heavy breaths. Out, and it nearly spilled down Steph's finger. In, and its surface tension almost broke and splattered to the ground. But neither happened and this dance continued as her finger got closer and closer.

"Open her mouth."

The cultists grabbed Zoe's jaw and wrenched it open. For a moment, Zoe let herself believe it might really be special blood. But as she licked it off Steph's finger, it just tasted like normal blood. She spit it back in Steph's face, and in return, Steph grabbed her cheeks and squeezed them together in a ridiculous blowfish expression.

"Today, you're lucky. I have to do what my people need, not what I want. But if you try to start any more shit, I'm telling everyone that you were the one who got Tevin involved with me, that you were my number two, and that the murder was your idea. A plan to get Tevin higher up in the ranks. All of them will back me up. Lily will too. Lower her to her knees, face to the ground."

Zoe wanted her back to be unyielding—to become a steel rod that all of their might couldn't bend. But after a second of resistance, they had her on the floor. "If you kiss my feet, you can leave unharmed."

Zoe spat right on Steph's big toe. The brutality of

the kick that followed rattled Zoe's teeth, and the shock made her wail. Weak. So weak. So helpless. All Steph had to do was command a room full of losers, and she could have anything she wanted. If the blood had tasted divine, would Zoe have despaired so much over their relative positions?

Steph crouched, making no effort to close her skirt and conceal her pussy from Zoe. She whispered in Zoe's ear, her hot breath like poison gas, "I didn't tell Tevin to do anything. But I don't hate that it ruined your movie. Come back, and you'll see what else I can get them to do."

With that, they tossed her out of the apartment. Zoe's cashmere joggers tore on a nail sticking out of the doorframe. Blood trickled from a small cut on her skin. It tasted just like Steph's blood. If only it was better. If only it was worse.

# LILY

During her first week in the house, nothing about Lily's room changed, but the rest of the house offered plenty to explore. An hour before she and some of the other roommates planned to watch a movie in the living room near the bottom of the stairs, she took a slow walk up to see what she found. Even if her own room was boring, the rest of the house certainly wasn't.

For the first ten minutes, all she found was closed doors, blank walls, and portraits of the same woman, repeated over and over. Maybe this was the first owner, or steward or whatever Dicks was, of the house. Her gentle smile, warm gaze, and worry lines on her forehead made her look maternal. It was so easy to picture her living in this house, raising a family with her husband. Then maybe her husband left, off to chase some flashing thread of excitement, and it was her and her two teenagers. Then the house transformed, creating a smaller space for them to huddle closer together. Or maybe the mother wished it had, when instead it stayed the same. Three bedrooms, a living room, the father's old office, a kitchen, and two bathrooms where only echoes lived.

All the worse when the older kid went off to college. No, when the younger one ran away. Then it was just the two and every day the mother woke up, the house felt larger still, and no matter how much she had wished for it to just stay the same size by getting smaller, it had ballooned. When the older one had finally left, it was just the mother and the house. Unused rooms confronted her at every turn, and years went by without her opening some doors. When she died sitting in the living room, her consciousness slipped through the cracks in the ceiling paint and grew like vines around the wooden studs.

She would let no one repeat her tragedy, and now that she was the house, everyone would find what they needed from her. The portraits were there to tell everyone that she was here, that they were constantly held within a mother's embrace.

A nice story to tell about the house, even if it wasn't true. When Lily asked one of her roommates who was heading down the stairs, they said, "I don't know, I think Dicks picked up all of these portraits in bulk at a thrift store and thought it'd be funny."

"Really?"

"Not sure. It is kinda funny, though."

After another fifteen minutes of walking upstairs, Lily's legs ached. She found an open door and wandered in. Though it was pitch black inside, ever since the staircase had appeared, the roommates had instituted a rest rule: if someone was heading up the stairs and your door was open, you had no choice but to let them take a break in your room. Offering a drink was encouraged, but not obligatory. So Lily sat in the middle of the room. The cool darkness sapped heat from her sweaty skin. Something rustled in the corner.

"Hello? Is anyone there?" Lily asked. Little skitters and scrapes sounded all around her, like someone's pet mice were running laps. "Hello?"

The noises stopped and someone exhaled for a full minute. Their breath warmed the air and Lily began to sweat again. A voice said, "I'm here. Oh, I've been here."

"Who are you? It's me, Lily."

"We haven't met. I don't go out and meet. Unless you've been in here before? My memory isn't what it was when it was my memory. I'm... hm. Let's call me Nought. That has a feeling to it, doesn't it?"

"I guess. I don't feel anything." Not entirely true. The hairs on the back of Lily's neck stood up, but she couldn't tell whether her body was telling her to be afraid—if her mind was telling her body, if both were screaming at both, or if there was a soul communicating simultaneously to mind and body because only it knew true fear.

"That's good, that's good. It means you're not me. That's preferable. A waste of a conversation, introducing yourself to yourself. Let me tell you. May I tell you?"

"Sure." Through the open door, she could see a couple people passing by on the staircase. Light still touched her shoulder and neck. If she didn't go in any further, she'd be safe. Even though shitty people ended up in the house sometimes, Dicks wouldn't let anything monstrous stay. Unless Dicks didn't know this person—person?—was there. Could a darkness—which, in times of smaller house layouts, hid in a just-thicker shadow between the fridge and counters and thrived in the line where the floor just barely didn't meet the bottom of the baseboard—have escaped Dicks's notice?

"Every time I find myself, I have to tell myself, 'myself.' And then I get it. But it's tiring. Too tiring. I've been here so long, only she will have me."

" 'She'?"

"Our lady of the house, the house. She always keeps a place for me in her heart, heartless though she is. Heart-disheartened. Heartful in absentia." The voice coalesced in the furthest corner of the room and its whisper solidified into a smooth baritone.

"Do you know how the house got this way? Does she speak to you?" What would Lily say if she could query the house? She could ask how it came to be this way, what it thought of her, or even why Dicks, of all people, was in charge of it. To the degree that anyone could be in charge of a house that reconfigured at a moment's notice.

"No, no speech. She is, but she isn't. We are housed, but she is housed. No more me than you, you to her, me to you, me to me. No, I know me quite well." External light pushed further into the room from the doorway, and a pinprick of light shone on the wall opposite the beginnings of a window. "Ah, she's chosen something new for me. But for you, she wouldn't have. Excitement. Exciting times."

The window grew larger and the darkness wrapped up into a shroud in the corner, hanging on top of a body sitting on the chair. Beneath, large white eyes and bright white teeth moved.

"How long have you been here?" Lily asked.

"Clarity. Ahhhh, ow. Her kind razor. Years. A life spent years in prologue, not as many yet postlogue." The figure removed the shroud and folded it into a neat triangle, as Lily had once seen some ROTC kids at her high school fold a flag. The figure's smile glittered in the light and their curly hair spilled down past their shoulders. Lily couldn't pin a gender onto them at first sight, couldn't place the voice, which dipped deep into bass at times, but carried a consistent lightness as it hopped weightless from word to word. Their collared shirt, decorated with black snaps and some lace frills, didn't end at their waist but spilled to the floor in a pile of extraneous collars and sleeves all tangled together.

"Who are you?" Lily asked.

The figure smiled and gestured to their face. "I'm before you. Answered when asked."

Lily had so many questions for them, but recognized that it would take the rest of her remaining half hour to get downstairs in time to see the start of the movie. "Do you know how the house got this way? Like, how it transforms?"

"Snail-shelled dreams expand outways. Ambition is best eaten one bite at once, then once, and once, and once, and once more. With a full stomach, her jaws can hold the sky." The shroud foamed in their hands and dripped down their legs, staining the shirt darker and darker black by the second. "No again but repeated pleasure." They reached out their hand and Lily shook it. It crinkled like tissue paper. "Ah, impractice. Goodbye." The shroud curled around their own face like a flower closing at night and the window shrank again to a sliver of light, focused on the impressionist smear of their grin beneath the fabric.

"Bye. Thank you, I think."

The shrouded figure bowed long past the limit of a human waist or back and, when the top of their head touched the ground, a puff of darkness stole all the light from the room. When Lily exited, it looked just the way it had when she had arrived: pitch black just beyond the door frame.

Her journey downstairs was easier, though her ankles still complained. After about ten minutes, she saw Dicks jogging up the stairs. No way could they keep up that pace the entire time, though their sweat-soaked muscles glistened like polished stone beneath their shorts and tank top. Before they could blow past in a salty blur, Lily flagged them down. The dedicated host, always willing to interrupt even their workout routine for someone living at the house. Though they were sometimes pissy, Lily wondered where the endless reserve of patience they kept while in the house went whenever they left, when their fuse shortened to nothing. "Hey, Dicks, you coming to the movie?"

"I'm gonna be late. Gotta get back to my room for something. Still can't believe she'd fuck with me like this."

"Does she do that a lot?"

"Sort of. She's probably just having some fun." They slapped the wall playfully like it was a dog's belly. "Whatever it is, it's a way she shows that she wants me here, wants me to keep doing what I'm doing. So I'll do it."

"Do you know how the house got like this?"

"Not really. When I bought it, it was a mess inside. Just studs and corroded pipes. Cost me nothing. I wanted a fixer-upper, you know how it goes. I bought a shitty-looking house because I craved one. She stayed that way all while I did the slow work of trying to get it half-livable. Then, once I had it just decent enough, I invited some people over who needed a place to crash. I think it was when I cooked a meal for them on the hot plate. That's what did it. The next day, she'd made a shitload of moves. I thought I'd blacked out and broken into someone else's house. But no, she'd totally renovated herself. Now she does it from time to time to accommodate how many people I invite to stay here. She gets bigger, I invite more; she gets bigger, and so on. We're in a lovely little dance together." Dicks let their hand fall in a trickling caress along a picture frame. "Anyway I gotta run. See you downstairs?"

"Yeah, see you. Thanks. For everything."

Dicks nodded and resumed their jog, disappearing around the curving stairs so that the only sign of them was the clomp of their sneakers on the steps above. The house remained a mystery, though it pleased Lily to hear that it had some kind of volition. For the rest of the way down, she imagined what kind of voice it might have, if it could talk. A warm voice, full of love, but raspy as if from years of smoking. Even in her wildest dreams, the house's embodiment could only ever be half-achieved because a human body, a human voice, could not contain all she saw around her. Whatever the house was, it was more than her, more than any one of them. A grander being in scope and purpose.

Lily passed by a door with a window next to it: uncanniness held her foot in place and turned her gaze toward it. That was her door. She hadn't recognized it with the new window. Inside, the floor had sprouted a few gentle curves. A few shelves and nooks were on the walls, and when Lily turned the light on, it shimmered blue and made her feel like she was in an aquarium. Sitting on the curve on the floor forced her into a deep squat, and then when she pushed her legs out straight, they felt some strain too. But when she lay on her side, heaven clicked into place. The curve perfectly mirrored her waist and hip, and the floor went from hardwood to surfacelessness; Lily felt like she no longer had a body and sighed into the comfort of the perfect support which relieved her muscles of their endless duty. A few seconds later, as sleep wrapped its arms around her and carried her deep into its chest, she remembered the movie and jumped up. The sudden ache of physics confirmed how effective the little curves were. Lily was excited to go to sleep that night and see how they felt after eight hours. But she wanted to make friends with her roommates, and the movie night had been arranged in part so she could hang out with people. So she resumed her lifelong war with gravity and descended the stairs.

Twenty people were already piled into the living room. Two couches hosted ten of them, some slouching with their legs extended along a retractable leg-rest, others curled up into compact swirls along the arm. One in the lap of another and both of them looking pleased with themselves, and several on the floor, using the couch as a backrest. More still cuddled together in affections equal parts mysterious and obvious to Lily. She'd come to know them all in time. Faces she recognized smiled, and hands she didn't know waved and offered her a reserved spot in the middle of the red leather couch, next to the two connected at the lap.

Pleasant small talk was the order of the moment, since Lily didn't know anyone in the room well enough to bridge the gap. But they were all friends of Dicks, or friends of friends of Dicks, and were all united in the confidence that they belonged, and presumably had all been told the same as her: that the house wanted them there.

Dicks was panting when they got into the room with a DVD case slipped beneath their armpit. The person on top of the lap next to Lily said, "Dicks! Dude! You're gonna stink up the movie." They waved off the jeer and approached the TV.

"In honor of our new roommate, Lily, we are going to be watching a classic film by Rainer Werner Fassbinder: *Querelle*."

A couple people groaned. One of them, who was wearing a denim vest with no shirt underneath, exposing a thick patch of chest hair above a couple of small, perky breasts, said, "Is this that French shit again?"

"One, it's in English."

"French people know English, Dicks!"

Dicks laughed. The version of them outside the house would have whirled into a rage by now, but here they just smiled and took the ribbing with serenity. "You know what, I was going to let it be a surprise, but you win: it's about boys fucking each other." Over half the room clapped when they announced it. "That's right, we all love gay boys who have gay sex, don't we?"

Dicks slipped the DVD into the player and sat down by Lily's feet. "That sound good to you?"

"I'm more of a horror girl, but I'm very supportive of the boys." The movie was strange and felt kind of dreamlike by virtue of every bit of dialogue being just too straightforward, too laden with meaning. During the movie, Tedward climbed onto her lap and occasionally blocked the screen with his big head and dumb smile, his tail whacking the head of someone on the ground as it wagged. Roxy also wandered in, but never settled in one place. Instead, she wandered from person to person, getting just enough attention and scratches before moving on to the next one.

Lily enjoyed herself, and after hours of getting to know too many people to remember, she trudged upstairs half-full of liquor. Having decided to count how many rooms preceded hers and immediately losing track of the count, she found herself assigning random numbers to each door she passed: Room 7 was closed, but the sound of crickets escaped. Room 399999 had no door on the outside, but a set of three doors internally that Lily had no desire to explore. Room 123 looked exactly like her room, except there were multicolored snakes writhing along the walls and floor. Room 31 had a chair in the middle and a single lightbulb above it and something about it told her it was the least comfortable chair in the world and she wanted to know what perfect discomfort felt like, but as she took another step up, she realized that room 123 was obviously hers and just had snakes in it all of a sudden.

When she stepped in, the floors and walls looked still. No snakes. Maybe they were a drunken illusion. She would stand in the doorway until she got sober. Or she would sit in the doorway until she got sober. Or she would lie in a heap on the ground until she got sober. Or, maybe, she would climb into that nice little curve and drift off to sleep and when she woke up, sober, she could worry about any snake problem if one existed.

She crawled into the room and the snakes surged from the floor and walls, surrounding her, squeezing her. But not too tight. No biting. A gentle hug from snakes the color of the sky, of raspberries, of pistachio ice cream. They lifted her into the air, and even though she was at their mercy, she felt safe. While she couldn't tell them what to do, she sensed that they wouldn't do anything that she didn't want them to, and when she yawned, when the liquor started to drag her consciousness down into its depths, the snakes carried her over to the curve and lowered her onto it. The last few snakes wriggled free and her body fit into its perfect groove. In perfect comfort, in her perfect room, after hours of meeting people who seemed excited to know her, Lily went to sleep in less than a minute.

# ZOE

No matter how many people suggested to Nate that he use a phone or a tablet to take notes, he stuck with his paper notepad. Between that, his loom, and the videos of Eastern European women singing harmonies in the mountains, Zoe sometimes worried that he might harbor secret, horrifying politics, but those never came up. Whenever he flipped a page over, he licked his fingers beforehand to ensure a secure enough grip to change pages with a flourish. Most of the time, Zoe enjoyed this little show he put on, whether consciously or not, but that evening, she could hear the wetness in his fingers and voice, as though the saliva on his fingers soaked onto the words on the page and Nate was pronouncing the words in their dampened form.

"Given the ongoing controversy with the Clenched Fist of God cult, with the leader and other cultists missing, and with Tevin publicly affirming that he stands by his murder as an act of divine justice, the chance that the movie comes out is pretty low."

"What, like this year?"

"Ever. The studio is concerned about the public relations hit of profiting off of a movie with a murderer in a starring role."

"Well, what about me? That's one murderer, one not murderer. Give me top billing and then I'm the star."

"I'll propose that to the studio, but they're set on holding the movie off. At least for the foreseeable future. Unfortunately since this was a smaller film, there's not much public demand that they release it. The hope was that some minor award buzz would elevate it, but—"

"Yeah, yeah. But he's a murderer and no one's nominating. I get it. What do my offers look like?" The greatest work of her career yet, held under lock and key forever. Tevin may have claimed divine justice, but how could this be anything but punishment for Zoe? She wanted Nate to offer to break into the studio's offices, hack their computers, do anything to right this wrong and carry her brilliance to the world like Prometheus had with his fire, even if only in clandestine snippets passed from hand to hand online, but the studio had said no and he'd backed down without a fight.

"A web series about a trans girl who stumbles onto a murder the first day out at work, gets framed, and has to continue to pass in order to avoid arrest."

"She's just come out? Get a girl with a brow ridge or something. I'm not taking that brick make-work."

"A cable TV show. You're a minor character. A cis woman who can't tell that her boyfriend has become a vampire lawyer."

"She doesn't know he's become a vampire? I can maybe work with that. Like one, two scenes an episode?"

"Your character also wouldn't know that he's become a lawyer. It seems that he sells out and gives up his art because he needs the money to afford black market blood." How Nate received these offers without laughing in anyone's face was beyond Zoe, and it worried her. She wanted an agent that thought of her highly enough that the notion of her taking a role in such a ridiculous TV show would strike him as so absurd, he'd have to laugh just to resolve the unthinkable. But it didn't seem to bother him.

"Pass."

"It's a silly show, Ms. Berger, but it's a good part. It's another chance to get a role outside the transgender silo."

"I was just in a movie, Nate. I got my launching pad and it was stolen from me. But I'm not going to pretend that I'm less of a commodity now than I was two years ago."

"Understood, Ms. Berger." When Zoe went fishing for sympathy and compliments, she normally caught something, but his face stayed impassive.

"What's left? What movie offers do I have? I don't even need a name like Sage, just... something where I can stretch my wings. At least until *Somnolences* comes out."

Nate lowered his notepad and stared into Zoe's eyes. With pity. He, the worm who sold his loyalty for scraps, pitied Zoe. He, the man whose entire life was lubrication for someone else's dream, who went home and plucked away at his loom and pecked his husband goodnight after achieving nothing; he, who would never know how the soft caress of stardom singed the skin as it warmed the soul, thought she deserved pity. And he had the cowardice to hide it, too. A challenge would lead to a simple denial; then it would be Zoe who'd gone off the deep end, who had been cruel and unfair to her employee. So no, she wouldn't scream at him. But she stared into his eyes with defiance. He was weak. She was strong. He was irrelevant. She was important. He was a functionary. She was a queen.

"Any other offers?"

"One. A *Drama Dolls* sequel."

Zoe leaped up from the couch. A strange ferocity coursed through her legs as she paced around the room. Reprising her role on *Drama Dolls* wasn't the worst move. It had gained an even bigger following since it had ended, and her character was the most popular. But the showrunner, the other girls, had been so cruel to her. Jealous of her talent, they had wanted to either claw her down into the chasm with them, or else climb up to her ever-ascending summit. No, going back there now would be the worst of both worlds: she'd gotten her part in the movie, which they would all resent her for, but it hadn't come out, so she had none of the prestige to fight that resentment with. They'd tear her apart; make her character do awful, humiliating things in the name of comedy. And they might succeed. If they tarnished the audience's love for her character, she'd be substantially worse off than she was now.

"Too risky. I don't trust them."

"Ms. Berger, I strongly recommend you accept one of these offers. Your market is cooling every day. Without *Somnolences*, you need to get your name out there immediately."

"My name, Nate, is carved into the mind of everyone who's ever seen me. They won't forget. No one has ever forgotten me once they've gotten a glimpse."

"Ms. Berger."

"I see what's happening. I see it. You're trying to sabotage me. Get me onto *Drama Dolls*; let them destroy my career, and hop off the sinking ship to the next girl dumb enough to let you attach your little lamprey-mouth to her."

Nate's hand covered his lips in an instant. She went on.

"I won't let you do it. I bet I have tons of movie offers. And you won't tell me because you want me to fail. You only told me about these three offers to push me back to *Drama Dolls*. How much are they paying you? I won't go back. My career only goes upward. Forward."

More pity in his eyes. Nate sat on the couch and reached out a hand, beckoning Zoe to sit next to him. She slapped it away. "No. Tell me, what were my other offers?"

"There weren't any."

"Liar."

"There weren't."

If there weren't, then Sage must have broken their promise. Even without the movie coming out, there should have been buzz about how good Zoe's performance was. Everyone on set had seen it. There had been award rumors. None had mentioned her name, but once she broke out upon the movie's release, they would have. Sage was a worm, no surprise there. Still. It didn't make sense.

"You failed me. I should have offers, directors begging me to audition."

"I'm doing my best, Ms. Berger. This is an unfortunate situation, and we—"

"No. No more 'we.' If you were any good, you'd have raised my profile so hard that even if *Somnolences* went to shit, I'd be fine. But you didn't do that. You're fired."

The color drained out of Nate's face. The shadow of his dark facial hair that always lurked beneath the skin was more visible for his sudden paleness. But a manager couldn't die of heartbreak, and he stumbled from her home, unable to even beg for forgiveness like he should have. Unencumbered by her saboteur, whether he'd done it in malice or incompetence, Zoe contemplated her next step. She'd get some auditions and find a movie to be in. All she needed was to offer herself to stardom's loving grasp once again, and it would embrace her.

Two weeks later, she heard they were re-shooting *Somnolences*. Both leading roles had been re-cast. Zoe deserved that role. She had deserved a phone call. She deserved better than an article with Sage's placid smile and the new actress who wasn't even as pretty as her and no pictures of Zoe at all. Halfway through plotting how to ruin their lives, well past the point of figuring out exactly how to poison their pets, Zoe took a breath. There was a better way. Instead of dragging them down into an abyss they'd never bothered to see glimmering in all its darkness right beneath their feet, she would rise above them. She'd rise above everyone.

# LILY

All week, Lily had been afraid to go looking for the dark room again. Yes, the presence inside had been friendly, if strange. Yes, the house seemed to regard it kindly. Yes, she was terrified. Sometimes, when she wanted to sit with that terror, she lay down on the floor. Her quickening heartbeat turned the floor black, and the snakes emerged to wriggle all over her, embrace her. But with every touch, the snakes oozed benevolence. Lily couldn't make herself fear them for even a moment, and that inaccessible fear took the edge off the bigger one. One morning, she woke up and, rather than fearing the dark entity, just felt like she wanted to talk to them again. Some wisdom lay within it, and she wanted to know what it thought about her life.

Lily climbed the staircase once again, but she got all the way to Dicks's room at the top without seeing that pitch black doorway. Strange. She thought she'd been watchful, looking every doorway up and down before passing by, but she must have missed it. Or else the house had closed it off. Rather than make the journey all the way back down, checking door-by-door, she trusted that she wouldn't have stared at the exact doorway she was looking for and decided that wasn't it. First she peeked into Calamity's room and waved hello, receiving a wave in return and nothing more. She knocked an improvised rhythm into Dicks's door, something in 3/4. Nothing fancy, but it was peppy enough to get them moving.

When Dicks opened the door, they were bopping their head a little bit. Her knocking had gotten them into a pleasant mood. "What's up, Lil?"

"Not much. Thought I'd see what you're up to." She peered into Dicks's room. The pegboard wall with hooks jammed into it, which together displayed Dicks's multi-colored array of sex toys for every possible combination of genitals, was directly opposite the doorway. Each wall was painted a different color—red, dark blue, brown—and after Lily blinked, she was pretty sure that which wall was which color changed. A little fun, but not as extravagant a room as Lily had expected Dicks to have, given how long they'd lived in the house and how hard they'd worked to make it comfortable for everyone.

Dicks said, "Not much going on. You can come in if you want, but my room is a little disorienting."

"Please. I've been all over this place. Your room looks more normal than anything else I've seen so far."

As soon as Lily set foot inside, the walls multiplied. Each of the four walls became an infinitude, every color imaginable. She took another step toward the center of the room and her footstep tapped against the tile and rustled the grass and sunk into the sand and bounced her into the air with its taut-wire elasticity. When she closed her hands, they stayed open. Her nails were long acrylics, short and buffed, chewed down to the quick, no longer there because her fingers were gone and nubs were in its place, gone because her hands too were gone, curled into spirals because they'd never been cut. Where was she? What was happening?

She flinched when Dicks put their hand on her shoulder. It was the only thing in her vision which didn't vibrate with multiplicity, and the rest of Dicks evinced the same solidity. They were a lighthouse amid these sudden, ever-crashing waves.

"What is this?"

"It's my room. It's all of my possible rooms."

"What's happening to me?"

"Nothing. You're you." They guided her over to a mirror, but she shut her eyes before her face slid into the frame. There were no possibilities for the inside of her eyelids but dark. In all her lives, all her selves, the wandering fuzz of sightless eyes was a constant, even as her brain interpreted patterns into the nothingness.

"Open your eyes when you're ready."

"Will it be normal?"

"No, it'll be terrifying."

All her possible elbows tried to jab Dicks in the side a bit. Most connected, but a few missed. She took a deep breath. Her lungs felt the way they always did. So did her ribs, her skin: all of her body tingled and ached where it always did. No matter what she saw, she felt herself and she was whole.

When she opened her eyes, she saw her face, and another of her faces, and another and another. Countless hairstyles, some injuries; only one with facial hair, also, with a dead look in her eyes. The eyes were where it changed the most. Some of them radiated joy, while others sagged under the weight of fatigue. Some of them had huge fake tits, which made her laugh and also made her want them, just a little. The few that had the courage to try bangs made her contemplate for a moment, but none of them looked happier than the current her. Maybe their bangs were a result of some tragedy; emotional crisis and a rash decision to cut one's hair into bangs had long since entwined their fingers and pressed their warm palms together in bliss.

One of her selves had a wide smile, but the way it strained at the edges reminded Lily of fabric stretched too taut. Like the person under the shroud. "What version of me is this? How did she get here?"

"I don't know," Dicks said. They looked into the mirror, and Lily saw the subtle hints of possible changes. A septum piercing instead of a nostril ring. Sparse facial hair dyed pink and hair kept black, rather than the reverse. A tattoo of a hand grasping their throat. "These are the ways the house thinks you could've ended up."

"Is it right?"

Dicks shrugged. "It's a house. I don't know what it could know that you don't."

One particular self solidified among the crowd, and Lily's focus brought it further forward. Her cheeks breached the choppy water of the rest of the faces. Her eyes shone as if they'd been polished. Her hair looked exactly like Lily's did. So did her skin, her smile, her clothes, her body. It was a perfect reflection in every way but one: her eyes radiated a warm peace which Lily could feel slowing her heartbeat, soothing her worries. If they weren't different, if the house didn't think the two of them were different, then why was that version of her like this? Gently, so as not to spook Dicks, she unhooked the mirror from the wall and held it to her forehead, eye to eye with this reflection which led her to calm, which worried her so much.

Lily got no closer to an answer about how the two of them were different, how Lily could get to that person from where she was, no matter how long she stared. The closest possible inspection revealed that the two were, truly, identical except for the peace in her eyes. So she hooked the mirror back onto the wall. "Sorry about that. I didn't expect to see that."

"You know how many mirrors I've had to replace in here?"

Lily laughed and moved toward the door, but with her hand on the doorknob, she remembered why she'd come. "Oh, before I go: do you know what the deal with the dark figure that lives in the pitch black room is? I found them once before, but they're gone now."

"Oh, that guy. Talks weird? Does the whole total darkness bit? He's my cousin. The house likes him, so it helps him keep up this whole mystique. He just wants people to think he's important. Ignore him."

Instead of leaving, Lily sat down amongst the multiplicity and played Mario Kart with Dicks for an hour. Despite the distraction of her multiplied hands, Lily easily won. On her way down, just a few steps above her room, she saw the doorway she'd been looking for the whole time. When she called into it, telling Dicks's cousin he couldn't fool her again, the room didn't respond other than to growl at some frequency below what she could hear, so that she could only feel it vibrating through her bones. Even though she knew it was just Dicks's cousin bluffing once again, she ran into her room and huddled in the corner. The snakes wriggled from the floorboards white as snow and wrapped around her. In their warmth, her breathing leveled. What peace she could find, for now, was there in that room, shaped to her needs.

# ZOE

As Zoe looked up at the massive staircase, she wished she hadn't worn heels. But then, if she was going to meet a goddess, she wanted to be able to look her in the eye. A few random queers were gathered in the foyer. The bowl-cut and mullet crowd, who had decided that beauty, too, was heteronormative and had stumbled onto a contrarian ugliness that demeaned themselves and the entire liberation project. Trying to carve out a place in the world and abandoning the beautiful as a tactic was guaranteeing that everyone one day would wake up in a desert and wonder what they'd lost while they were sleeping. Not Zoe.

The tension between their looks bred immediate suspicion. One of them, with curly brown hair that spilled all over their head without any care or curation, sauntered over. A faux-casual non-hierarchical gatekeeper. Nothing was forbidden and everything was monitored.

"Hey friend, who are you visiting?"

It would be unwise to say Calamity. Why would a girl that none of them could clock visit Calamity? The idea of telling them that she, of all people, needed a boon from Calamity made Zoe's skin crawl. But it would be bad if they got suspicious and followed her up.

"I'm visiting Lily."

"Oh! You must be Zoe. From, uh, *Drama Dolls*, right?"

"That's me."

The curly one's friend sauntered up. Cowboy boots, a wrestling T-shirt, and snakebite piercings. Kind of hot, in a ridiculous way. Zoe could imagine fucking them, if she could also make fun of them the entire time. Their costumes betrayed insecurity. A well-placed word, a judgmental look, and they'd crumble to pieces. But she didn't need to do that. Not to them. Cowboy Boots said, "I heard you were doing some fucked up stuff."

"That's the community we're in, isn't it? Everyone's traumatizing everyone. I'm here to work some things out. Both Lily and I will be happier for it."

The third one, denim shorts and denim vest, just so happened to sit on the staircase and kick their feet up onto the railing, blocking it. Dicks had a suitably low-rent idea of a security crew.

"Look, I get that you're all looking out for Lily. But I'm a famous actress. If I show up and cause problems, that's hurting me more than anyone. You know?"

The denim one scoffed. "Famous? I've never heard of you."

"Whatever." She beamed positivity at the curly one. All at once, Zoe became the dedicated, caring friend. The beacon of kindness. "I appreciate what the three of you are doing. It makes me feel better to know that Lily has been safe here with friends like you to look after her. But I want to bring her back to her life."

With a sigh, the denim one removed their feet from the railing, and the other two stepped aside. Her path was clear.

"Thank you. I'll be thinking kindly of you."

Zoe assumed that Calamity's doorway would be the same as it was last time, but she stopped and looked in every door or window she passed, just in case. Pitch black, full of multi-colored glass, full of multi-colored grass, vibrating a little bit, and so on. All of them were ridiculous ways to live, but that's why people moved into this awful house. Then she peeked through a window and saw a warm, orange glow from the ceiling. Soft curves lined the floor and walls, and a body was nestled into one of them, napping. Lily. What a surprise: she moved in somewhere and it immediately conformed to her needs. It would be so easy to punch through the window; disrupt her sleep; remind her that she didn't deserve to think she was better than anyone.

But Zoe wasn't there for Lily, and soon the tension between them would be resolved. Once Calamity elevated Zoe to the true top of the pecking order, there'd be no need to compete anymore. Still, she felt the pull of years spent revolving around each other—memories of their fights, of painting each other's nails on the couch, of holding back Lily's hair while she puked—and wondered what Lily would look like when their eyes met. Would the gravity of those years make her drift toward pleasure, before anger remembered and asserted itself?

Zoe knocked a hand against the window. Lily shifted a little, but her head nuzzled the delicate groove that held it and she became still again. Instead of pressing the issue, Zoe returned her focus to the staircase. Step after step drained the energy from her legs, and none of the rooms she passed were Calamity's. So much stairway awaited her. Too much. When she took a seat and rested for a while, she thought she could hear the crunching noise of pills. Maybe she was close. But the sound got nearer and nearer and transformed from that wishful crunch to the clang of footsteps down the stairs.

"What are you doing here?"

Dicks towered over her, only because she was sitting and they were two steps above. All the authority they could summon: the result of a couple steps. She'd see to that. Creaky knees and tight hamstrings extracted a cost, but soon she was upright and towering over Dicks. Disdain beamed into them, right from her eyes.

"I'm going upstairs."

"What are you doing on the stairs? Near the stairs? In the door?"

"I've got an appointment with Calamity."

"Bullshit. I gave Lily my word she'd be safe here. Get out." They pointed down the steps. "Before I kick you out."

Zoe pushed them, hand right in the center of their chest. They tripped backwards and hit their head against the railing and crumpled against the stairs. As they tried to get up, Zoe forced them back down with the point of her heel planted in their back. If it were sharper, she could have pierced right through to their heart. Instead, it kept them in place. "I'm not going anywhere, and you're not making me. Doesn't this house shapeshift? Why doesn't it just become a shape that doesn't include me in it? Unless it wants me here."

"Get off me." Dicks squirmed, but another jab from the heel made them as still as a butterfly on display.

"I'm going up the stairs. If you try to follow me, you're going down them." Zoe removed her foot and returned to her ascent. Behind her, the rustle of motion.

"Fuck you, Zoe. You can't do this kind of—"

Another push, just as hard. All that changed was the direction. This time there was no railing, and Dicks hung in the air for a split-second before they collided with the stairs and continued to roll down, step after step battering their face, their arms, their legs. Zoe didn't know when they'd stop rolling and she didn't particularly care. Her meeting with Calamity was almost upon her. That was the only thing that mattered.

Sweating, breath far out of control, she came upon the doorway. Simple, varnished oak that led into a room with lavender walls, dusted in blue. As ever, Calamity ate her fill, and didn't pause when she made eye contact with Zoe. A polite smile paired with the inquisitive lilt in her eyelids. But instead of answering, Zoe stalked around the table.

"You know what I want. You know who I am, don't you?"

Calamity shrugged. Pills slipped from her hands. Zoe couldn't tear her eyes away from the curls and waves in her hair, the way the warm light shone off of her perfect, dewy skin. No sign of makeup, and no chance any makeup artist on Earth could make Zoe look like her. Her smile made Zoe want to sit down and bask in its warmth. And it made her want to die.

"Make me like you."

Calamity slammed some pills and, with a briefly empty hand, gestured at the pile. Couldn't she talk? Every doll in the city made pilgrimages to this table to see a girl who couldn't even talk? Pointless. A fantasy, like rubbing a statue's crotch for good luck. "Fine, if you're magic or whatever. Don't I get a favor or something? Where is it? Make me the prettiest girl in the world. Without equal."

Calamity waved her off. She was acting like she was bored with Zoe. A superstar, well known in her hometown, was visiting the dusty table that she never, ever left and she was bored. As if she had the right. Some random pretty girl who never said anything, who some other trans girls had created a mystique around because they were so desperate for meaning that they'd go occultly digging in barren soil looking for anything, found Zoe a distraction from her busy pill-eating schedule.

"You freak." Zoe shoved Calamity away from the table, but she spun around and returned to her spot. Again, Zoe muscled her away. Angry as Calamity appeared to be, she didn't do anything but move back to the table.

"Make people look at me the way they look at you," Zoe said as she drove Calamity back into the wall, pinning her shoulders against the wall with her forearm. Heavy breaths mingled. Calamity's smelled of subtle mint and Zoe's tasted like spite. She squirmed and tried to break Zoe's grasp. For a goddess, she was weak. Maybe Zoe was already better than her.

But when Calamity broke eye contact with the pills and directed a pleading gaze at Zoe, she felt the compelling force of beauty. Everything in her wanted to give Calamity anything she could. Freedom, a car, a house, the moon, every fish in every sea, and every diamond buried in the dark and waiting to glitter in the sunlight. Never in her life had Zoe compelled someone like that. But after a half-second flinch, Zoe pressed herself even tighter against Calamity. Her body felt like a down pillow against Zoe's hard ribs. She looked, she felt, she smelled perfect, and only a real goddess could be perfect. The impulse to give her everything had been so strong, but a stronger impulse still seized Zoe. Down the stairs was only misery and failure. Possession, consumption, replacement, desire after desire swirled in Zoe as she wrenched Calamity's head to the side and opened her mouth on the perfect tan skin right where the neck met the shoulder.

And bit down as hard as she could. The goddess tasted like salt, and mint, and air.

# LILY

Lily awoke groggy from her nap to a clamor. None of the words she heard outside her window registered their meanings until she woke all the way up en route to the door. Her little paradise kept her safe from worries finding her until she was ready to seek them out. Air sparkled as she breathed in and opened the door. Outside her cozy room, blood and panic. It would be so easy to retreat back in, lie down again. But she closed the door behind her, and her eyes followed the little spatter marks of blood down the stairs. Roommates were huddling around Dicks. They were injured.

"What happened?"

One of the roommates split off, while others wrapped bandages around the splints connected to their arms. "We don't know. It looks like they fell really bad. A few broken bones."

"It seems like it happened right after Zoe went up," Amaranth said. The housemate with the extra curly hair, who lived in the room that had deep, pitch-black grooves dug into the floor. "Maybe ask her if she saw anything?"

"Zoe?" Lily spun around. If she was hiding somewhere in the crowd, Lily needed to find her. Why would Zoe be here? Dicks muttered something, but the sound was too fragile and broke apart as soon as it passed their lips.

"She said she was here to see you. To patch things up."

"And you believed her?"

Lily ran up the stairs. Where was Zoe? Where was she, where was she, where was she? Running up the stairs, peeking into every room she passed, Lily hoped she would find Zoe, hands clean of violence and innocent at first sight. But all she saw was empty room after empty room. Lily ran higher and higher, breath stinging her lungs more and more and more. Zoe had done it. Dicks would never fall. The house wouldn't have done that to them. Even if its disposal methods were so callous, the two existed in such perfect symbiosis. She stopped and caught her breath in blades of air cutting between her thin lips. The wall felt warm against her touch. Was the house suffering? Did it worry that it would no longer have Dicks?

Maybe it had captured Zoe in one of these rooms already. Since Lily had moved in, changes were often glacial, but nothing said that it was the only way it worked. The staircase and the orientation of rooms around it must have appeared all at once. Did the walls rumble and debris fall as it shifted? Or could it be an instant, a blink and everything was different? Once Dicks recovered, Lily would ask them.

Her hopes that the house might intervene dwindled as the climb continued. If it was going to act, it would have done so before she got that far. At the very top, just below Dicks's room, was Calamity's. What could Zoe want with her? Being in the same room would be agony. Inferiority had always pierced Zoe's skin the most cleanly, buried itself in her the deepest. Could she have come in search of pain? Before all this mess, Lily had understood Zoe better than anyone in the world. This was another reminder that this wasn't true anymore. She walked into Calamity's room.

The first thing Lily noticed was the walls. They were dull and gray instead of lavender. They used to glow with warmth; now, they looked like they might crumble with a touch. Calamity's pills were strewn all over the floor. She wasn't at her spot. She wouldn't have left without her pills. Gnawing sounds drew Lily's head further into the room. Estradiol half-dissolved in a pool of blood, a half-blue sludge. Two legs with soft thighs curving down into muscular calves splayed on the floor. Blocking the rest of the body, a back with a long blonde ponytail dangling down it. The blood pooled beneath the two of them, and only the blonde moved.

It couldn't be. Even she wouldn't go this far. The figure in front of Calamity's body leaned forward, revealing a red tangle of muscle, blood, and bone surrounding Calamity's open chest, and ripped another streak of flesh from it. On the upswing, bloody meat hung in her maw, and Zoe's face was finally visible.

"Hey, Lil. Wanna help me eat a goddess?"

The room would be safe. Lily could turn and run and hide in her room amid the snakes until the house changed and everything was fine. But instead, the smell drew Lily further in. The iron smell of blood cut through sweet estrogen haze. Calamity's mouth was open, a few half chewed tablets in her mouth and several more still clenched in her hand. To the end, she wouldn't stop. Maybe she thought the pills would save her, that there was still a plane of femininity to reach beyond which no harm could befall her. But blood poured from her torn-up body and smeared over Zoe, who went back for another bite.

"You wouldn't believe the flavor. It's awful. If any of us were going to be sugar, spice, the rest, it'd be her, right? Ugh." Zoe dabbed her lips with a napkin, which did nothing to ameliorate the mess. "What're you looking so scared for?"

Lily took a step back, afraid to fall, afraid to lose her footing and surrender the half-second of distance she might need.

"I'm not going to eat you. I'm not a cannibal. This is like... what if a mouse ate a cat? That's not right. I'm a little delirious. Blood goes right to the head. Woo!" Another bite. The meat squelched as Zoe's mouth squeezed a waterfall of blood out of it. Her jaw worked at the meat, but her eyes stayed open in an unfocused stare.

"Calamity, wake up." Lily said, sacrificing that distance after all to see if Calamity would stir at all at her name. She shook her shoulder. A goddess doesn't need her blood and her muscles, right? They're just for show. She should be fine.

"She's done. Didn't even fight back. I thought when I went for her neck I'd get sissified or something for sure."

"Calamity!"

"You should be happy. This solves everything between us, you know. Our problem was that we were equals. But now, with this, I'll be on another level entirely. The most girl. In the entire world." Zoe plunged her hands into Calamity's ruined chest, between the scratched and cut remains of two soft breasts. No blink, flinch, nothing. Every time Lily hoped Calamity might spark back to life, she seemed to become even deader. Her eyes tumbled and her tongue lolled as Zoe moved her body around. Her limbs stiffened, pointing straight up. Flies buzzed around her as her flesh decayed much too soon. But the heart which Zoe plucked from her chest still beat, even separated from the rest of the body. Until Zoe bit into it. Tears spilled from Calamity's wounds and flowed out of Zoe's mouth. "Bleh. Salty. Wish I was still on spiro for this one."

"Put that down."

"It's not going to start beating again if I shove it back in there. The milk's spilled, babe." Zoe took another bite. "Oh, that is a rich flavor. I'd give you a taste, but I don't want you to have it. You know how it is."

Lily pulled at Zoe's arm, but she didn't move. Yanking on her clothes, her hair, nothing. Zoe kept eating and eating. "Wow, this is a serious meal. You know how little I usually eat?"

"You..."

"That's the acting game, though. I knew the rules going in. Besides, I'm sure this meal will all go right to my hips." Zoe laughed, and Lily started sobbing. If only it was a nightmare, if only the last year had been a nightmare. But this was real, this was the real Zoe. Nothing meant anything to her, not even Lily. Especially not Lily. She never had. Lily staggered out the door and vomited, and it took the exact shape it had that afternoon at the point, when she and Zoe had separated forever. Behind her, Zoe kept chewing, steadily consuming more and more of Calamity and wouldn't stop until there were only bones left. But Lily didn't look back at her. She could only go forward, go down the stairs.

# ZOE

Once again, Lily couldn't bear to see how the sausage gets made. Maybe one day, she'd grow up; but that was her problem. Zoe didn't have to care anymore. With her stomach fuller than it had ever been, she leaned against the wall. Her meal radiated warmth in her stomach. Calamity's bones were all cracked open and discarded, her flesh and guts all consumed, even her beautiful skin had gone down Zoe's hungry throat. In the middle of eating her, Zoe had worried that she might have overreacted. But they don't teach etiquette classes for how to deal with a goddess, and eating one was de rigueur, as far as Zoe could tell. Her stomach pulsed, and she felt the warmth spread to her bones. This was it. Not only had she removed the only girl in the world prettier than her, but Calamity's glamour had begun to flow through her veins, elevating her still. Her hair shed its blonde dye, curling and waving into a new gold that sparkled with so much depth that Zoe could get lost staring at it for hours. Little blemishes along her arms, the zit on her chin that she'd covered up with concealer, vanished. So, too, did her makeup. The highlighter and carefully applied eyeshadow to shape her face and make her eyes look bigger were no longer necessary. Beauty was no longer a thing she did; it was what she was.

She stood, despite her still-dense stomach weighing her down. Digestion would take care of it. Calamity's bones, less the marrow Zoe had eaten, began to crumble into blue dust. Within a minute, what little remained of Calamity was either scooped up by the air or smeared onto the floor. Zoe hoped that she hadn't been too scared when Zoe had bit her. It was tempting to think that a goddess saw the world with perfect equanimity, but facing the end of one's divinity was probably frightening. Zoe whispered, "Thank you for your sacrifice. I'm sorry if I hurt you." She also wished that Lily hadn't seen her messy becoming. The two of them had been through so much over the last year, and now it was over. It would be nice to reach a place of understanding and compassion, to have a conversation about how things went wrong and hurt, and to wish each other the best. Maybe in the future. Wounds were still fresh, feelings still hurt.

Until then, the best thing she could do was walk out of the room and begin this new chapter of her life. When she tried to leave, her heavy stomach staggered Zoe and sent her leaning on the table for support. A few minutes' rest wouldn't matter. Though everyone outside might be angry if they realized she'd pushed Dicks down the stairs, they'd understand when they looked into her deep green eyes and saw how sincerely sorry she was to have done it. And she was. She was. It looked like they'd gotten injured, and she wished that, in the moment, she'd seen any of the other ways to resolve the problem. Once they saw her, the new her, whose soft flesh sang of the great potential for life and creation, they wouldn't do anything to inhibit her return to the screen. The people who lived in the house recognized the importance of the beauty of art.

As her stomach settled, she looked down at the table. While Calamity had been a large meal, it felt somewhat incomplete. A little dessert would do the trick. Though it would have been better if Calamity had kept some chocolate around, or maybe a freezer with a little ice cream, the only flavor at hand was that mound of pills. A bit silly, especially since Zoe did injections, but it would taste exquisite and giving Calamity's body one last snack right before it dissolved completely into Zoe felt like a kindness. So she took five or ten into her hand and rattled them around, laughing at herself a bit. Down the hatch. The pills were more delicious than any cake or cookie, more satisfying than any dinner cooked with love. When they hit her stomach, they felt like fireworks rushing through her body, and she wanted nothing more than for the show to go on. So fine, another handful or two. These were even better. Waves of pleasure washed over Zoe's thoughts, pure ecstasy beyond the filter of rational thought flooding her consciousness.

Once she left, she'd schedule more auditions. Another handful of pills. They'd take one look at her and know that having a lead actress imbued with the power of a goddess would make their movies into hits. She'd have her pick of projects. Two more handfuls. Every crunch in her mouth felt like an orgasm. Would she prioritize artistic movies likely to win awards, or blockbusters that would make her a more widely known name? Different kinds of fame and prestige carried different benefits, after all. Another full mouth; her perfect jaw worked ceaselessly. She could get into modeling too. Be beautiful, get some pictures taken wearing fancy clothes, easy. Her beauty required no more maintenance, so she could easily do it on the side. She'd just have to show up. Everything in the world was attainable to her once she left the room, which she would do after just one or two or three more handfuls of estrogen.

# LILY

Lily couldn't stay in Dicks's house without them there, knowing Zoe was lurking somewhere above. With everyone scrambling around in panic, no one bothered to ask if she had found Zoe. She didn't know if she had, anyway. The smile was the same, but the eyes were different. So she walked down the steps in a daze, and everyone who ran up or down the stairs past her was a blur on the way to some task, some way to help, some responsibility of Dicks's that needed to be kept up until the house's steward returned. The door to her safe little cove dangled open. Its comforts beckoned her, but when she thought of herself inside, she saw Zoe's face again. The endless chewing and tearing. Then her own time here, endless sleep and dreaming. As she turned away, the sound of a ringing bell came from just beyond the door. The comfortable waves of the floor faded into a flat beige; the lights and colors along the wall wafted off like clouds of colored chalk, and soon it was just the way it had been when she'd arrived.

Dicks was right: Lily knew it was time to leave. All of her possessions sat in a pile in the middle of the room, expelled from closets and drawers which no longer existed. Packing them into her duffel bag was short work. After months of traveling light, she had the process down to a science. The little waterfalls gleamed at Lily as she left. They looked like tears instead of regular water, but Lily didn't want to reach out for a taste. With one last look from the doorway, she surveyed the house. It looked the same as when she'd arrived, but every crevice was burdened by mourning. Was it aware enough to fear for Dicks? Would it miss Lily? All she could do was brush her hand against the doorframe, give Roxy a scratch under the chin to say goodbye, and hope to communicate some of the warmth of her affection for this house that had finally given her a little room of her own and nurtured her the best it could. But it had so many responsibilities to so many people, and Lily wasn't one of them anymore.

With Zoe occupied—certainly, she'd be detained in some capacity by everyone else there once they realized what she'd done to Calamity—Lily was going home. At the very least, Zoe couldn't stop her from entering while she was busy eating. Every step lent more energy to the next one, and by the time Lily turned the corner and saw the house with its neat red bricks and overgrown hedge along the fence, she was sprinting. The doors were locked, the keys still changed. But had Zoe really been thorough, or was she just focused on making a spiteful point to Lily? Lily circled the house. The window outside the back door was locked. Zoe always got wrapped up in the excitement of her emotional victories. She would have imagined the moment when Lily tried the door and felt the arrested jiggle as the key failed to turn the lock. All of Lily's future fear and anger and resentment and hopelessness would have satiated Zoe better than food ever could. Lily dumped her bag on the dirt and stepped onto a lawn chair. What Zoe would have failed to consider, in all her glee, was that Lily might try every window. Even the ones that seemed a bit out of reach. The kitchen window's lock, never reliable, failed and Lily cracked the window open. They had never opened this one, and Lily remembered why now. It stuck in its grooves as her shoulders burned, but inch by inch it ascended until there was nothing but open space between Lily and home.

She hoisted herself through and tumbled over the kitchen counter. Takeout boxes crumpled beneath her, and she kicked stacked boxes of tea onto the floor. The kitchen was a mess. After all that had happened, the stack of dishes in the sink looked exactly the same as it always did. The trash was just full enough that maybe one more thing could fit in there. Lily sunk to the floor and her legs splayed out over the cold tile. None of the walls looked like she remembered. Zoe had installed mirrors all over the walls and ceiling so that the mess reflected until it became infinite, uncleanable in its enormity. Fine.

Back then, a couple days after Lily and Zoe had moved in, they'd gone out and bought the kitchen table that now sat covered in unopened mail and empty shopping bags. It was so much bigger than they'd thought it would be and hadn't fit in their friend's van, so they'd had to rope it to the top. On the drive home, wind had gusted through the open windows as they each kept one hand on it to keep the dark wood from falling and being pummeled into splinters on the highway. With messy hair and laughter escaping with every breath out, they'd wedged the enormous table in through the single doorway, until their combined effort had brought it to the kitchen. Afterwards they'd split a pizza and ate it at the table, laughing about each other's reactions when they saw how big it was. Lily had wanted that meal to last forever.

But now she was alone. She opened the back door and retrieved her duffel bag. In the little patch of grass surrounding the firepit, clover popped up amongst the weeds. She'd have to pull some of them, but as she knelt down and picked a little three-leaf clover, Lily decided she wanted them to stay. Maybe they'd take over the grass and become a cultivated garden that occasionally yielded good fortune.

In the living room, the blanket that used to cover the light sat amongst the shards of glass scattered around the floor. When Lily looked up at the spotlight, it shuddered and, after a few clicks of misfired activation, pointed directly at her. But the bulb was a broken stem, and so no light greeted her. It'd be easy enough to sweep up.

Lily didn't know if she should. When she opened her room, the lights were out, just like last time. Part of her worried that flipping on the switch would take her back to that night, that argument. Zoe's nails scratching her arm. Instead, track lighting along the floor turned on, and colored bulbs illuminated different sections of wall. Every inch was covered by collages of Zoe. Not even an inch of negative space interrupted the flow of her face into her hair into her hip into her face. Hundreds of her eyes stared at Lily. They challenged her to face their wrath, to endure the hatred etched into every black pixel in their pupils, or else to run and go back to Dicks's or somewhere in another city where those eyes could never conquer her again. But they weakened as she tore one picture down. Only a few little loops of tape held it to the wall. Then another, and another, each rip of paper diminishing Zoe's stare until only two remained: an enormous face, and a full body nestled next to it. The face had to go first, even though it extended to the top of her reach. When she ripped it from the wall, Lily found it was hiding a picture of herself and Zoe, arm-in-arm.

Lily felt behind the picture of the two of them. She passed her hand between the paper and the tape, the tape and the wall, destroying whichever bond was weakest, until it fell to the floor. After she rolled it up, it felt so tight that she took a few swings with it like a bat. It could break a window, if she put her mind to it. But she set it down on the pile of shredded Zoes, and carried the pile out to the fire pit out back.

She set the paper on one lawn chair and pointed another towards the pit, then lit a cigarette. Smoke raced back toward her hair, desperate to cling to the closest object and encode its scent forever. Picture after picture burned in that pit. The tight-rolled cylinder went slower—for a moment, like a log; but it was only paper and the fire ate it quickly. As the sun set and the sky darkened into light-polluted orange-gray, the fire burned brighter. At first, Lily fed each scrap carefully, somberly, but halfway through the pile she laughed as each one vanished into smoke, and by the time she reached the last piece she was dancing while she fed them in. With nothing left to consume, the fire dwindled and dull ash took its place. A while later, once it had had time to cool, Lily dug her hands into the ash and lifted up two scoops. Bits flaked off and disappeared in the breeze. She carried those handfuls through the house and up the stairs, knowing full well that she'd have numerous smudges to clean up later. She faced Zoe's mirror, the vain portal which had ruled her life. Smeared the ash over its surface, working out clumps and pushing it around until the mirror couldn't reflect anything. A gray oval, surrounded by lights.

There was no chance Lily would sleep in that room, so she dragged Zoe's mattress into the middle of her own room, now empty and undecorated. The bare walls challenged her, demanded that she see their emptiness. She recognized it. But she turned off the lights and resolved to face them another day. For now, the most important thing was getting a good night's sleep in her room.

# ZOE

Pills. Pills. Pills pills pills. Her hunger wrapped its greedy tendrils around her arms, wound down her legs and rooted into the ground to still her feet. Opened and closed her jaw. Only her eyes felt like they were hers alone. Not that she wanted to look at anything but the pills. No visitors had come to see her over the last week. Any residual anger would subside with time. Queer communities loved to make villains of their heroes, but memories were short, and soon a new group of young girls desperate for a piece of her beauty would make the same pilgrimages that Calamity had used to receive. The long and winding road of supplicants pleased Zoe despite its briefly hypothetical state. If something was bound to happen, it made no sense to wait to enjoy it. One day, she too would have her fill and walk away from the table, and go out into the world. Men would dissolve into paper, women scorch into envy, non-binary people would do whatever it is they do, and the world's orbit would shred into ribbons of earth and water and pure heat spinning around her perfect stride. Everything she'd ever wanted, everything she'd never dared to want, was so inevitable that it might as well have already happened.

Maybe it had. Those could easily be memories which flitted through her mind like fickle sparrows. Though her hunger took all her focus, the pills and their promise solicited a demand from depths within her that she had never known. Begging for more and more and more until she was complete. Until she'd consumed the totality of femininity and left not a single bite for anyone else, becoming not just the perfect woman, but the ultimate woman. No matter what a baby was born as, they could come and ask for a shred of her womanhood to wear like a rag for their pitifully short lives, and she would grant it. Magnanimous and eternal. Maybe all of that, enough to completely overwhelm lesser minds, had distracted her from walking around in the world. Maybe she was doing it right then. No, still at the table. She resolved to look at what she was seeing more often.

When she had killed Calamity, Zoe hadn't really seen this coming. Her only plan had been to get rid of the prettiest girl in the world. Eating her was just a whim that had come out of nowhere, and picking up Calamity's hunger—just for a while, not forever—was a surprise. Not that she minded. Yes, the hunger was intense, but satisfying it was sublime. No wonder Calamity had turned down every date. Sex couldn't compare.

As time passed, she saw people wander by. Adam came looking, stared at her through the doorway, but didn't come in. Why not? He wouldn't be up there to go to Dicks's bedroom. The two of them weren't friends like that. Plus, something had happened to Dicks recently. Zoe tried to concentrate, but couldn't summon a mental image. She just had a bad feeling about them. A memory of a memory, a plain white placard with simple black lettering which read, "THIS IS A MEMORY OF ANGUISH." If it was important, it'd come back to her eventually.

After a few weeks (months?), Nate walked into the room. Why Adam couldn't find the courage to face her, but Nate could, mystified Zoe. Nate said something to her, but Zoe was distracted and didn't want to stop eating to reply, so she just waved her hand in a circle, gesturing to Nate that he should keep talking.

He said, "Ms. Berger. Zoe. A lot of things have gone wrong, but you need to leave this place. You've got a movie offer. The creator of *Drama Dolls* is directing a SOPHIE biopic, and wants you to star."

The role of a lifetime. Zoe stepped away from the

table. She'd probably left before, right? Zoe remembered remembering that she'd left before. But she was so hungry. One more bite. As she hoisted another mound of pills to her mouth, her arm felt heavy. Nate held her back, his wet eyes pleading with her to stop. Another display of devotion. Of tender love, unlike any man she'd ever known. And she'd found him here. That explained everything. She shoved the pills into his mouth. He coughed and scattered them everywhere. She yanked the back of his hair and shoved him face-first into the pile. For a minute, everything was still. The hunger gnawed at Zoe, but she needed to see this through. If he was suffocating, he'd struggle, right?

The pile quivered. He was chewing. She let go and returned to her own consumption. Together, they ate pill after pill, though Nate didn't do it with quite her voracity. He snacked on one pill at a time, every now and then, but Zoe couldn't keep track because tearing her eyes away from her meal became harder and harder. The last thing she saw was wooden bars growing in a crisscross from the walls, barring the door. That was fine. She didn't have any plans to leave.

# LILY

Everything beeped in the hospital. The automatic door when she entered, the machines interlocked by countless wires in the hallways and private rooms, the buttons in the elevator, the nurse when she directed Lily to Dicks's room, Lily's memory when she tried to recall the name the nurse referred to them by, the floor with every step she took, louder and louder the closer she got to Dicks's room, until it felt so urgent that she had to get there right away. The beeping might be telling her that Dicks was in trouble, but the cacophony of running was too much to consider so she weaved through the patients beeping along with their IVs or in wheelchairs, and when she turned into Dicks's room, the beeping stopped. Except for a little machine hooked up to their arm that sounded a friendly one every few minutes. They smiled and waved an arm in a wrist brace, and Elena turned her attention from Dicks to Lily.

"Hi," she said.

"Hey."

Wind rustled the curtain separating Dicks's bed from their roommate's. Foam wrapped the old man's arm, and twenty long needles poked out of it. The man rolled his eyes upon seeing Lily. "Oh god, another one."

Dicks lurched up in bed and winced. "One more word, fucker, and I'll break all my bones to break all your bones." The breeze weakened, and the curtain returned to pretending to be a wall. So Dicks yelled louder, "I will ride you to hell, you old bitch."

The old man didn't elect to continue the fight. Maybe with the curtain restored, his objection to Lily and Dicks and Elena entering his sightline had been resolved. Lily sat in the chair next to Elena. The space between the two of them prickled at her skin, but Elena leaned a little closer and laughed behind their hand and then Lily and Dicks joined her. Once Lily surfaced from the giggles, she asked, "Dicks, how are you feeling?"

"Terrible. God-awful. They tried to put me on opiates but I said fuck no. So all they've got for me is Tylenol and good vibes." They pointed their index finger up demonstratively, defiantly. "But I smuggled in my own bad vibes to counteract them. Because I'm smart."

"Did Zoe do this to you?"

Elena nodded, possibly to cut off the conversation at the pass. Maybe she'd heard it already.

"She did. I guess I shouldn't complain, with what happened to Calamity. I don't know, she got her revenge on Zoe."

"Revenge?"

"Yeah. Zoe's snacking at the table now. Her and her little guy. Though I guess he won't be for long. Calamity's probably on the damn astral plane or something."

Lily had wondered why Zoe hadn't come back. She'd expected a reversal of their last encounter at the house. Part of her had been dreading it, but the other part had been excited to show her strength, to repel Zoe's invasion. But she wasn't coming. There would be no grand confrontation at the house. "Wow. I was afraid she'd just keep eating people."

Elena said, "I don't know. When you eat a person, it's cannibalism. But is it cannibalism to eat a goddess?"

"They're not people," Dicks said. "Calamity was really nice, but she was not a person. Believe me. If you're an easily accessible god and someone comes by and eats you, that's the cost of doing business. And then if you curse that person to take your place at the table? Business."

"Well. I'm glad she didn't kill you, anyway."

"Me too. I couldn't have cursed her for shit. Not for

lack of trying. How's the house? Is your room stable? I know she gets a little wobbly when I'm not there sometimes."

"I moved out! The house shrunk my room back into a little box and told me it was time to go."

"Aw, I'm sorry. After you saw all that. She doesn't have a good sense of manners, you know how it is."

Elena rubbed Lily's shoulder. The tenderness vibrated through the muscle and bones and it felt like the knots and taut wire that had collected there over months went limp and soft. Lily leaned into the touch, and Elena didn't take her hand away. Elena said, "Aw, I'm sorry. It's been one place after the other for you." A pause. "Sorry. It's not right for me to say that."

"It's fine. I'm back home."

"Home? Wait, home?"

"Zoe's gone, so..." The sudden ferocity of Elena's hug rattled Lily's teeth. She smiled, and nestled herself into the soft spot between Elena's neck and shoulder while their powerful arms squeezed the breath out of Lily. Not that she needed it, compared to the vital warmth she absorbed from Elena, which she had been without for so many long months.

"I'm sorry about how everything went," Elena said, with a few tears in her eyes.

"Me too. It wasn't the best time for me."

"Me either," Dicks said. "I'm glad you're being gay and all, but can we focus on my suffering?"

Lily nodded, but it was a lie. While Dicks enumerated their many ailments, all surprisingly minor given their original injuries, Lily focused on the alignment of her hand and Elena's on the armchairs. Touching, but not entwined. When she moved her hand away, no magnetic pull brought it back, desperate to return to its mate. And when it went back, she felt no guilt or worry that she might have returned it too soon.

"Oh, while I'm here," Lily said, interrupting Dicks's complaints, which satisfied Dicks in a way that suggested they'd been waiting for someone to interrupt them. No doctors or nurses had wandered in since Lily got there. They were probably avoiding Dicks's bad attitude. "I'm thinking about throwing a housewarming party. Would you two come?"

Elena smiled. "Sure."

"If I can walk."

"Okay. Once I've got the house all decorated, especially if Zoe is gone for good..."

The words tasted sweet. That last terror, her looming specter, melted away. That house, her life, none of it would involve Zoe at all. It was hers. When visiting hours ended, she and Elena walked out together. A cold breeze tickled Lily's exposed shoulders. The two of them walked hand-in-hand for a while, until they reached the street where Lily had to turn off and walk home. It would be easy enough to keep going straight. They'd end up at Elena's house and Elena would invite her in and the two of them would end up in each other's arms and it would feel just like the beginning when she had moved in there and then the end would come too.

"I'm gonna go home. I've gotta go to work soon. See you soon?"

"Yeah, I'm free whenever."

"Cool." Lily kissed Elena on the cheek, smiled, and walked away. Somewhere down the road, after Elena was already small in the distance, she saw Lewis pop out of the bushes and walk with Elena, weaving between their legs in perfect rhythm with their steps. The leaves were blood red and all Lily could think about was how beautiful it was and how horrifying it had been when the same color had trickled past her feet. What a difference a little time made.

# CALAMITY

New bones, new flesh. Shaped, shaping. The brief thrill of formlessness gave way to confinement away from the sensate world before long. Every time her body died, Calamity was tempted to throw away the individual and scatter. If she chose, she could become the warmth on a trans girl's breath, the sharp angle of another's collarbones, the beautiful high pitch of another's voice. All would be elevated, but just a little, in ways which didn't stand out as much as questions of passing or fuckability. But embodiment was her calling. The glow beneath the skin doesn't matter if its possessor's concerns sit above. She was the standard, the measure of what could happen if everything went right, but more likely, every trans girl could look at her and wonder what pieces of Calamity would filter down. The hair, the eyes, the skin, the tits: as soon as someone stuck that little blue pill under her tongue—or stuck on a patch, pierced the skin with a syringe, and so on, Calamity didn't care much about form—she was promised a gift from Calamity. Her body would change. Her hair would grow. How well, and how much to each girl's liking, no one could say.

Once, in her room, a girl who had received the greatest bounty Calamity had ever offered had demanded more from her. No matter how Calamity insisted, the girl would not be satisfied and instead decided to contain the whole of Calamity within her. Except for the bones. She got what she wanted. Her beauty was Calamity's own and so was her hunger and as she ate more and more, more and more of Calamity became hers. Her hair thickened and darkened from blonde to dark brown, soft flesh grew in abundance over her skinny frame, her desperate eyes calmed and turned the shade of teal that matched her pills because her eyes hungered as much as her stomach.

When the girl's thoughts were finally quiet, Calamity awoke. Her mouth was full of pills already and she chewed. Every body was different. These teeth were sharper than her old ones, and the pills cracked much more easily but didn't grind to a powder quite the same way. When she grabbed the pills, her hands didn't take gentle scoops which let pills scatter where they might without concern for whether they'd ever find their way back to her fingertips, but instead took tight, greedy handfuls snatched out of the heart of the pile. Better posture, which was a bonus. The hunched posture over her pile always worried her. Visitors might interpret her as a desperate creature, but her new body's proud bearing toward the table allowed for no mistakes.

At her side, a crying girl with long black hair and a scraggly beard chewed along with her. The girl paused before each swallow to kindle the necessary will. Calamity reached out her hand, ready to gesture and intimate to this girl that she need not force herself to do anything, but a new capacity stirred inside her. "Who are you?"

"I'm Nate, Ms. Berger."

"That's not who I am."

"Oh." Nate looked her up and down. "I guess not."

"Why are you here?"

"You made me eat with you, and then..." Nate pointed to the doorway, barred by crisscrossed wooden beams.

"Strange." Calamity closed her eyes and tried to feel the house around her. Deep breaths matched the pulse of life beneath the walls. The house was angry at her, whoever preceded her, everyone around her. But the house recognized her breath, and the bars on the door cracked and splintered and crumbled further into sawdust and before long, a breeze took it up and it was as though the wood had never been there. "Stop if you don't want to do it. Leave if you want."

"Ms. Berger..."

"I'm not."

"Then who are you?"

"Calamity."

"That's a frightening answer."

"I suppose so. Go, leave."

Nate scratched her beard, felt her estrogen-softened body and gazed at the doorway. "Can you pay me to perform tasks for you? My husband isn't going to like me this way."

"I don't have any money."

"Do you have any food? Room and board might work for a bit."

"I don't eat." All the talking was encroaching on Calamity's pill time. "I can offer you nothing but company and my blessing, which you've already begun to receive. Take it or leave it." Her new tongue spoke callously. After decades of communicating only with graceful hands and winks, she finally had a hammer to deal with all these nails around her.

"Can I go get my loom?"

"I don't care."

Nate scurried out of the room. Calamity didn't know whether or not she'd return, but hoped she would. An interlocutor, after all this time, felt like a luxury, even if her lively new tongue still spent most of its time beneath pills. At the end of her first week back, Calamity started to worry that her supply might dwindle, that the young girls of all ages were wary after the bloodshed. But the hope for blessings retained its strength, while the memory of the violence quickly faded.

Before long, a line of girls extended down the stairs. Each came in, handed a pill to Nate while she worked at her loom, and then dumped the rest on Calamity's hoard. Calamity sensed the girl's disposition, a breeze which resonated with the swirling wind inside her, and if it flowed in the same direction, she would offer some boon. Calamity couldn't really choose what would happen, but it would be good. If the breeze felt hostile, Calamity would deny the girl anything. Each time, a voice in the back of her head told her to sabotage such a girl, curse her, before her ambition became too much and she came back here, hunting for Calamity. Each time, Calamity ignored the voice, but it would persist in her head forever, long past Nate's death, the deaths of all of the girls who came to see her over those years. Only she and that voice were forever.

# LILY

Sveta's last client for the day slithered out of the shop as soon as the street light the city had set up to manage the flow of strange distractions emerging from her door signaled for them to walk. Wordlessly, Sveta meandered over to Lily, and watched over her shoulder as she colored in a complicated back piece. Angel wings with detailed feathers over interlocking gears. The client had told her it was some kind of statement about deism, but she just thought he was a big dork. Nevertheless, dorks pay money. She'd learned that early on. Mickey Mouses, Marvel heroes, Doctor Who phone booths, and so on. Things that she would be horrified to find on her body, let alone actively seek out, but people who wanted them made up a significant portion of her income and always left happy. So she gave it her all as she colored in the rust scattered along the gears, tinged the feathers pink by the roots just like he wanted, and detailed the scraps at the bottom that suggested skin had been torn away, revealing the true nature of gears and wings beneath. When he left, she was a thousand dollars richer and he was so happy he nearly cried.

Before she was even done putting the money away, Sveta handed her the tattoo gun and the grapefruit. "Time to try."

The breathing exercises had become second nature. In, out, deep as it could go, slow as she could manage. Potential shapes vibrated within the grapefruit. Each begged to emerge up from possible through probable and erupt into existence. The tattoo gun turned on, and all other vibrations were subsumed into its buzz. It was the metronome, and everything around it was faithful to its rhythm. What within the grapefruit deserved to emerge? A human face? A baseball? Flower after blooming flower, with their stems tied in an elegant knot at the center?

Sveta massaged Lily's shoulder as she paused and thought. A tight knot in her neck that had been annoying her for ages came loose and tension dropped from her back. Lily didn't know what Sveta's hopes for her were. There was a path her life could take where she mastered this gun and the world became malleable to her touch, vulnerable at her discretion. Did Sveta want that for Lily?

Lily lowered the gun to the grapefruit. Just that morning, she'd been pacing around her home, trying to figure out how to decorate the kitchen. Now that the dishes were done and the stains mopped up, the most mess that she had allowed to gather there was a single takeout container sitting on the counter—to be taken out with the trash. Every other room had the art she wanted, the paint she wanted, but the kitchen eluded her. The blank walls depressed her worse for how stained they'd gotten over time. She painted little swatches of teal and red on them, to try and figure out what she'd like to do. Teal spoke to her, but red felt like more of an exciting kitchen color.

Everything Zoe did to the house had been undone, including the spotlight. During Lily's first few weeks in the house, it still flickered on from time to time despite being unplugged. Maybe it was a signal that Zoe was still conscious, that her lust for attention was being fulfilled. For the last few months it had sat on an end table next to the couch, very rarely shining its feeble warmth on Lily. Someday, if it ever stopped turning on, she'd throw it out. But until then, she liked to see it flicker.

While she reminisced, the grapefruit in her hand started to transform into a lightbulb, but she waved it away with a calming breath and it returned to its grapefruit shape. She turned the gun off and handed it back to Sveta, who said, "You're giving up? It was changing."

Lily dug her thumbs into the rind, tearing a hole in its toughness. Wet pulp and juice dribbled up from beneath her fingers. Little creeks flowed down her hands and dripped onto her pants, wetting little dots of her skin beneath the fabric. When she cracked it open, it burst into a ragged pile of grapefruit flesh, rather than individual slices. She dug her face into the rind and bit out a mouthful, then more, and more, and more. Grinning as sticky sweetness clung to her lips, Lily allowed the rind to drop, clean of every last bit of flesh.

# Acknowledgments

Thank you to Emma and Cara, whose support and love were greatly appreciated throughout the process of writing this book. To Leyla, with whom I talked about a great many things that were not this book. To Dakota, who provided a generous reading of this novel at a moment when my belief in it was wavering. To R.S., who created a writing community that helped me get through the dark days of writing the middle of this novel. To Rysz at tRaum Books for being the best editor I could have hoped for, and for wanting to see this book published as badly as I did. To Tai and Andrew, thank you for the help in how to present this novel to the world. To Trevor, thank you for letting me steal some of your essence for a character that ended up not being very much like you. To my friends in trans literature—I'm lucky enough to have too many to name individually—thank you for everything you've written.

# About the Author

Three years ago, June Martin declared herself the world's greatest writer and, since then, no one has challenged her for the title. From Oakland, she writes novels and short stories and draws comics that all take a step—sometimes gently, sometimes bounding—out of reality. Her short fiction has appeared in *X-R-A-Y, BULL*, and *New Session*. *LOVE/AGGRESSION* is her first novel.

# About the Press

tRaum Books is a tiny press dedicated to unconventional formats, with a focus on queer and trans narratives. You can visit us online at http://www.traumbooks.com

We would like to further thank:
Dermitzel
Brak
Jun Nozaki
Leon Sorensen
Clacks
Agnes Merey
Gele Croom
Philip O'Loughlin
Steven Askew
Tucker Lieberman
Lachelle Seville
Anna Otto

Your support is seen, felt, and appreciated.
Because of you, we can continue to put out the books
we believe in. If you'd like to support our press as well,
you can find us over at
https://www.patreon.com/tRaumbooks.